After that she saw him everywhere, or thought she did. It was always at a distance, in a crowd. He never tried to approach her. At night, he called. He might start early and call every hour, then skip two or three hours while she twisted and turned in bed waiting. Or he might not start till long after midnight. Varying the patterns, he kept her off balance.

She notified the telephone company. They offered to change her number. She said she'd already done that.

They suggested she contact the police.

She'd already done that.

On top of everything, her cat Theo had disappeared....

THE OTHER SIDE OF THE DOOR

Lillian O'Donnell

FAWCETT CREST ● NEW YORK

CHAPTER ONE

Alyssa Hanriot was shaking so hard she could barely manage to dial 911. Getting a busy signal, she hung up and tried again. Drenched in sweat, heart pounding, her breath came in short gasps as she waited counting the rings. Fifteen. Fifteen times, Alyssa Hanriot counted and nobody answered. *Pick it up, pick it up, please*, she pleaded inwardly.

"Police Department. Officer Bromberg."

At last. Thank God. By now Alyssa Hanriot's throat was so dry she had trouble getting the words out. "This is Alyssa Hanriot. I called a short time ago . . ."

"Yes, ma'am, and I told you a police car would be over as soon as possible."

At least she hadn't been forgotten, Alyssa thought and swallowed. "I know, but I'm all alone, you see. I've locked my door and turned out the lights in my office, but he's looking for me. I can hear his footsteps in the hall."

"You mean he's inside the building? You didn't say he was inside." Officer Bromberg was openly annoyed. "You said he was prowling outside."

"He was when I first called, but he got in somehow. I don't know how."

"All right." Ida Bromberg sighed lugubriously. "What's your name?"

"Alyssa Hanriot. I already told you."

"How do you spell that?"

"Oh, my God! Please . . ." Starting to protest, she decided it would be faster to go through the bureaucratic routine than to fight it. "A-l-y-s-s-a. H-a-n-r-i-o-t."

"Address?"

She'd already given that too. "I'm at the Senior Citizens' Center on Seagirt Boulevard in Far Rockaway at the intersection of Seagirt and—"

"I need a number."

"Yes. 1302-41 b."

The footsteps, measured, deliberate, drew near and stopped at her door. Holding the mouthpiece close, Alyssa repeated in a whisper, "1302-41 b." She knew that she was barely audible, but she couldn't risk speaking any louder. Gently, she replaced the receiver in its cradle.

It had been a slow night. Her Music Appreciation for Adults class had been the last one on the schedule, over at nine. However, she also served as substitute librarian and the library stayed open till ten. Nobody had been there, but conscientiously, Alyssa hadn't even considered locking up early. If someone should show, even in the last five minutes, she wouldn't have turned him away. Certainly not on this, her last night.

Neither pretty nor beautiful in the accepted sense, there was nevertheless something compelling about Alyssa Hanriot. She wore no makeup, dressed plainly, yet she was not easily passed over. A cursory glance pegged her as wholesome. A longer look revealed flawless skin with an exotic olive tinge, a brow high and clear, dark brown eyes exceptionally soft offering depths to be explored. Her hair, either a golden brown or a dark blonde depending on the lighting, was thick and lustrous. Usually she wore it neatly coiled at the nape of her neck. When she was going out on a date, as she'd planned to do this evening after work, she let it hang loose and it reached to the middle of her back. She presented a calm, serene self-possession. The turbulence lay buried deep. At twenty-six, Alyssa Hanriot was still searching for direction.

She had studied voice at Juilliard on a scholarship, but was honest enough to acknowledge she wasn't good enough for the concert stage and not suited vocally, nor for that matter temperamentally, for rock—hard or soft. She could teach, but the prospect of sitting at the piano all day accompanying a succession of pupils less talented than herself, wincing at uncertain pitch and undisciplined phrasing, was bleak. Instead, Alyssa chose a tour of duty with the Peace Corps as a bridge between failed dreams and an uncertain reality. After two years in the slums of Pulianthrope on the outskirts of Madras, India, a place without electricity, sanitation, or adequate water supply, where during the rainy season the entire area was under water and smelled of sewage, Alyssa felt that although she was performing unskilled labor, she was useful. She was even ready to sign on for a second tour, but her mother's illness brought her back home again. She arrived just in time to sit at her mother's bedside, hold her hand, and look into her eyes as she died. With her father dead several years, Alyssa was alone. She supported herself with odd jobs consisting mainly of the tedious singing lessons she had been so determined to avoid and the music appreciation classes she found she actually enjoyed. To these she added instruction in yoga and folk and ethnic dancing. In one day she might deal with kindergarten children, business men and women, or, as tonight, senior citizens.

Like a good salesman, Alyssa had built up her list of satisfied customers over the years. She had, she thought ruefully, a "small reputation." Having finally taken and passed the proper exams, she was now formally licensed by the state. She signed a contract with the Nassau Board of Education to conduct folk dancing sessions two days a week in certain of their grammar schools and high schools and two nights as part of their adult education program. She was excited. It meant money coming in regularly. Not much, but money she could depend on. It meant stability, an anchor. In order to accommodate the assignment, she had to give up the job here at the Senior Citizens' Center. At ten, she had locked up and gone to her fourth-floor office to clear out her desk. No more working in dilapidated, drafty buildings with cracked walls and roaches running boldly around the toilets and over wash stands, she thought. She wouldn't have to challenge rats amid festering garbage bags as she crossed the parking lot to her car. Across the county line less than half a mile away the schools and libraries and community centers were newly built, freshly painted, well heated. She wouldn't need to haul her antediluvian record player; each facility had its own turntables and sound system, the most modern and the best money could buy.

The new job meant she could move from the two cramped rooms on Cornaga Avenue in a so-called "garden complex," the garden consisting of a drought-parched square of lawn. Her new place was in a fine old building on a well-shaded, quiet street. The rooms were large, high-ceilinged, the kitchen completely remodeled and boasting all new appliances and cabinets. Alyssa had paused in her packing to look out the window past Seagirt Avenue and the boardwalk to the ocean, dark and silent. She'd felt a sense of loneliness and thought that in spite of the advantages, she would miss her old people. She had missed the Indians of Madras too at first. But she'd gotten over it.

It was mid-October, the seventeenth, and in this community close to the sea the seasons had notable impact. The children were the quickest to adjust and were already settled into the school routine and looking forward to Halloween. The oldsters were in a holding pattern between the warm sun and water of summer and the rigors of winter to come. Everybody else had returned to their regular hangouts. Mighty few took long walks along the shore. Alyssa would probably not have paid any attention to the solitary figure except that he wasn't wearing a coat or jacket—and was not hunched against what she knew must be a bitter offshore wind. It takes all kinds, she thought, and turned from the window, her ankle twisting in the unaccustomed high heels she'd put on for her date with Neil.

She was glad they'd decided to call the date for tonight off after all. Neil Jaros was leaving early Saturday on a business trip that would take him from Cleveland out to the Coast and had work to do in preparation. He'd been apologetic, but she hadn't minded. Neil was impatient, always looking at his watch, doling out the minutes even when there was no need for haste, no schedule to maintain. They'd been going together for over two years. It was taken for granted that they would marry—sometime, as soon as it was mutually convenient. Neither talked about it or mentioned a possible date. As Alyssa put away the stacks of sheet music, records, illustrations she'd accumulated during her work at the Center, it occurred to her that it was actually a relief not to have Neil at her shoulder urging her to hurry—without speaking a word.

It was when she'd started looking for cord to tie the carton that Alyssa became aware of the noise. Something slamming shut? A door or window? Couldn't be. She had closed everything. Made certain everything was secure.

She'd listened, every sense concentrated.

Something downstairs rattled, as if somebody had hold of a doorknob and was shaking the door. It was repeated three or four times then stopped. She breathed a sigh of relief. The sound had come from the back where her light couldn't be seen. Assuming the place was empty, somebody had tried to get in and failing, gone away. Relieved, she resumed her search for the twine she knew was squirreled away somewhere.

Now the building seemed to come alive around her. There were all sorts of creakings and settlings; normal in this kind of ramshackle structure. Then the rattling was repeated, louder and more determined. It was the wind, she told herself, but it wouldn't hurt to call 911. That was the first call.

Apparently, she hadn't sounded particularly frightened—and she hadn't been. Having made the complaint, Alyssa Hanriot found the twine and went on with her packing, all the while listening for the wail of the patrol car's siren. The precinct was only a few blocks away on Mott Avenue. She was finished and ready to leave, but she waited. Ten minutes. Fifteen. Somebody should have come by now. She checked from the window—no sign or sound of the police. No sign or sound of the prowler either. Whoever he was, he had either settled in for the night or was finally gone. Either way, he was no threat. Alyssa put on her coat, slung the strap of her handbag over her left shoulder, and picked up the two boxes by the string, one in each hand. At the door, she nudged the light switch down with an elbow and as the lights went out the phone rang.

She stood still, uncertain whether to go back or not. While she hesitated the phone continued to ring, a lonely, eerie pealing in the dark. She put the boxes down and without bothering to put the lights on again made her way to the desk.

"Hello?"

"I wouldn't try to leave if I were you."

"What? Who is this? What do you want? Who—"

He hung up.

Alyssa broke out in goose bumps. It took several moments before she could pull herself together and analyze the situation. To start with, the phone on her desk was an extension not accessible to the outside. All right, so he was inside—she had to clench her teeth to keep them from chattering—how had he known which extension to dial? The phone numbers didn't correspond to the room numbers. Once she had thought that dumb, now she appreciated the reason for it. So maybe he just punched up every button on the board downstairs till somebody answered. Why? Because he was no harmless vagrant looking for a flop for the night; he was a disturbed and violent man stalking a victim. The sudden whine of the elevator and hiss of the door opening on her floor put an end to speculation. She'd dialed 911 for the second time. Hunkering down behind her desk in the dark, she'd waited for the police operator to answer and listened for footsteps stopping at each door, coming inexorably closer.

"Police Department. Officer Bromberg."

The woman's voice was loud. It sounded as though it were coming over a loudspeaker. It must carry out into the hall. She whispered. "This is Alyssa Hanriot. I called a short time ago . . ."

Mechanically, she answered the dispatcher's questions while at the same time straining for any indication of his approach. Then he was there. His shadow fell across the frosted panel of her door and she remembered that it was closed but not locked. Quietly, hardly daring to breathe, Alyssa gave the operator her address and hung up. And waited. She waited for him to try the knob, turn it, come in.

But he didn't. After a few moments, he moved on.

Silent tears of tension relieved coursed down her cheeks, but she stayed where she was. She stayed squatting behind the desk for a long time till the pain in her calves and thighs made her get up. What should she do? Lock the door and wait for the police? Or get out now while she had the chance? Her instinct was to get out. She crept to the door and listened. Was he really gone? She inched it ajar, relying on inbred atavistic danger signals—increased body temperature, prickling of the nerves at the back of the neck, a sinking sensation in the pit of the stomach—to warn her. None of them manifested themselves, while the instinct to flee became overwhelming. After one more look up and down the hall, Alyssa made a dash for the elevator and got in. She punched the lobby button. The door shut.

Thank God.

The car started down. Then stopped. Between floors. According to the indicator light it had just passed Three. The damn thing was always going out, Alyssa thought; she should have known better than to use it when she was alone in the building. Only she wasn't alone. Should she ring the alarm bell? If she did, then he'd know where she was. What could he do to her? It might even scare him away. It would certainly attract the police when they finally showed up. Alyssa flipped the switch and the bell clanged loudly, persistently, irritatingly. Better irritated than scared to death, she thought.

Then the lights went out.

Darkness closed in instantly, but the clanging reverberated in her ears for several moments before silence too enveloped her.

A power failure? In the building, the neighborhood, the whole city? If that were so she'd have a long wait. Might as well try to get comfortable—sit on the floor, brace her back against a wall, but stay awake because when the police did come she'd have to yell and yell loud to let them know where she was. There was one consolation: If she couldn't get out, *he* couldn't get in. She was safe.

Alyssa had no idea how long she'd been sitting on the floor—her watch didn't have a radium dial. The darkness was unrelieved; she'd never experienced such an absolute absence of visibility. Yet, uncomfortable as it was, she was just beginning to doze off when, with a shudder, the elevator resumed its downward course. Still in the dark.

She could hardly believe it, but it was moving. Why didn't the lights come on? Never mind, the elevator was going down. She scrambled to her feet ready to get out as soon as it stopped and the door opened. The overhead indicator panel was dark, but mentally Alyssa counted out the floors. Well after she thought they should have reached the lobby, the car kept going. It seemed to be gathering speed. Falling? She braced herself for the crash. But the car stopped, smoothly, normally. The doors slid open on more darkness and silence.

A musty odor indicated she was in the basement. Alyssa had been down here before; she knew what it looked like in general. It was dirty, choked with dust, a firetrap. She was familiar with the layout: a double row of bins formed by wire mesh and stacked to the ceiling with discarded furniture, books, cartons, galvanized metal garbage cans—none of it of any use. Periodically, the fire department made an inspection, declared the premises in violation, and everything was cleared out. In weeks, the clutter built up again. A narrow passage between the storage cages led past the furnace room and onto the back stairs; one flight up was an exit to the street. Alyssa felt for the side of the elevator door and with her right foot tapped for the threshold she must cross. How could the power have come on just for the elevator and not for the rest of the building? she wondered as she stepped out.

No sooner was she clear than the door hissed shut behind her and the elevator started up.

Groping for the wire mesh as a guide, she stumbled over something, a box, where there should have been clear space and caught herself just in time to keep from falling. This was what it was like to be blind, Alyssa Hanriot thought and began to shuffle forward inch by inch.

As she made progress, she gained confidence. Then, moving more quickly, she heard a soft but distinct click. A door latch? It had come from up ahead. She was sure of that. Whatever it was, whoever had caused it stood between her and the stairs to the street.

"Who's there?" She tried again, fighting to keep her voice steady. "Who is it? What do you want?"

No answer.

"Please, who are you? What do you want?"

Still nothing. She did the only thing she could—resumed the inch by inch shuffle forward. And when she thought she might have imagined the noise after all, Alyssa heard a low grunt and she was grabbed from behind—a hand slapped over her mouth, the sharp point of a knife at the side of her neck. She was cut and could feel the warm blood oozing.

The scream never left her throat.

It wasn't much of a cut, a prick really, but then her head was arched farther back and the knife went in a little deeper. It was done almost delicately, Alyssa thought through her terror, like a surgeon. His body was pressed close as he hugged her to him and she could feel his size and his strength and knew that he was amusing himself. His feet were planted on either side of hers; he held her in the vice of his body. Struggling would be useless.

"What do you want?" She formed the words with as little lip movement or play of neck muscles as possible. "What do you want?" she asked as she raised her right foot and brought the spiked heel of her best dressy shoes, shoes she'd worn for her date, down hard on his instep.

He screeched in pain and rage. But he let her go.

"Bitch," he groaned.

Stumbling forward, Alyssa knocked over a metal garbage can. Next a rancid, mildewed mattress stood in her way. She managed to heave it to one side. She reached the foot of the stairs and he was on her. Literally. A vicious slap sent her sprawling on the steps and he spread-eagled on top of her. From somewhere, a ventilator or the bottom of the door, she felt a cool draft; a thin line of blue light glinted off the blade he held high.

She squirmed under him, writhed, and struggled against his weight but couldn't budge him. Alyssa was physically

timid about inflicting pain. She had never before harmed anyone, but now she became wild, crying with frustration and
terror. She turned her head, and her cheek brushed against the
hand that gripped her shoulder. Stretching just far enough, she
opened her mouth and sank her teeth into it. She tasted his
blood. He pulled the hand away, but his body didn't move. It
pressed on her. She could feel his erection. It made her retch.
Her stomach heaved. She hoped she was going to vomit right
into his face.

With his free hand he grabbed her hair and yanked, pulling
her head back and once again arching her throat. This time he
lowered the knife and held it in front of her where again the
blade caught the light.

Out of pure instinct, Alyssa bent her right knee and with
the demonic strength of desperation, thinking only of her own
life, rammed him in the groin. He shrieked. As he rolled off
her, he brought the knife down. She had rolled too and was in
the act of scrambling to her feet so that it caught her behind
her left shoulder.

Holding the banister, he slowly pulled himself upright.
"Bitch," he snarled as he stood over her.

Outside, a car screeched to a halt. Doors slammed. Footsteps pounded.

He leaned over to retrieve the knife. Then he turned and
lurched down the passage to the elevator.

Alyssa couldn't move. The pain when he pulled out the
knife was the worst of all. She could feel the gush of blood, a
geyser of blood. A terrible lassitude came over her. She
wanted only to sleep.

Officers William Ellison and Raul Hernandez approached
the dark and silent Senior Citizens' Center with caution. Guns
drawn, they rang the front bell. No answer. They tried the
door. Locked. Circling the building they repeated the procedure at the rear. It was twenty-nine minutes since the complaint had been logged, an unacceptable lag in response time,
which routinely averaged eleven minutes. They had been sent
to the wrong address. Checking back they learned the complaint came from the Senior Citizens' Center and on their own
initiative proceeded there. However, there was no sign of the

reported prowler and by now the woman who called in had, apparently, gone.

Officers Ellison and Hernandez were veterans. They would have gone in for further investigation if they could have found means of entry or if there had been someone present to authorize a break-in. The department was touchy about destruction of private property.

So they rang a few doorbells. Nobody had heard or seen anything out of the ordinary. All seemed quiet and at peace.

It was 11:09 P.M. when they left.

At the sound of the car Freda Easlick got out of bed and without turning on a light padded to the window for possibly the fifth time in the last two hours. The car passed and kept on going as the others had. Her nervousness and anxiety increased with each disappointment. Too agitated to go back to bed, she pulled over her boudoir chair and sat, still in the dark. If Junior came home and saw her light on he'd know she wasn't reading or watching television, but waiting up for him. He'd be angry. She didn't want to upset Junior.

She was borrowing trouble, Freda Easlick told herself, but she couldn't help it. Roy Junior was all she had in the world.

Freda Easlick was fifty-one and a widow, a full-bosomed, improbably brilliant redhead, with an indomitable will. She had been brought up the old-fashioned way—to be a wife, make a good home, produce and raise children. It was her purpose in life, her ambition, and she'd intended to be a success at it. She anticipated and was prepared for a large family. Unfortunately, after their firstborn, her husband, Roy Senior, suffered an attack of the mumps—a child's disease with devastating results for an adult. It left him sterile. All the maternal and organizational instincts and energies narrowed in to focus on Roy Junior. Her ancillary interests consisted of decorating the house and sessions with her psychoanalyst, dietician, hairdresser. She was happy, or thought she was, till the disaster. Roy Senior couldn't deal with it. He had a heart attack and left her on her own. For a while she too was looking for a way out, then she pulled herself together. Thank God, because now she had Junior back.

The Five Towns linked the privileged communities just across the bridge from the southern shore beaches of Long Island and carefully separated them from the Rockaways. It was an unusual area—not strictly a bedroom community, not suburbia; not a beach resort, nor a provincial small town. Rather it was an amalgam of all these. There was an elegant shopping area consisting of branches of the large New York department stores and select, individually owned boutiques. On the one hand, wives shopped with little restraint; on the other, they demanded good value for their husband's money. Children were better integrated through the schools, but they shared the big-city problems of drugs, alcohol, and early sex. People were snobbish, keeping to themselves, mixing only within their economic strata. They knew the people who lived on their block. They said good morning, nice day, as they got in and out of the car. They acknowledged those a block to the north and south; they waved as they drove by but didn't speak.

Without speaking, everybody knew everybody else's business and they certainly knew everything about Roy Easlick. That included the Five Towns and beyond, well beyond. They knew why he went away, but no one offered sympathy to his mother. In a sense, that had made it easier. Even one halting word of comfort, the touch of a hand on her shoulder, and the dam of her self-control would have broken. In all the time since Roy's arrest, through the trial and conviction, his mother had not shed a tear, not till he came home again. And she had not let anyone see her cry, not even Junior. She cried alone; wracking, wrenching sobs for all the sorrows in her life. Then she'd stopped. She had her boy back and her job now was to keep him. Crying was a waste of time.

As nobody had said a word to Freda Easlick when Roy Junior went away, nobody spoke to her now of his return. They were aware of it, of course. The account in the newspapers had been merely a brief paragraph on an inside page, but it had been seen and passed on to those who might have missed it. On the block, they watched Roy Easlick from behind their vertical blinds. Probably his new job stimulated their acceptance. Working at a bank was almost a guarantee of respectability. Being an officer in the international division put one beyond reproach.

So why was she worrying herself sick? Freda asked herself. So he'd been out late a couple of nights with the other trainees. He'd had a little too much to drink. He'd been through a lot and was entitled to some relaxation. And tonight was, after all, special. It marked the end of the training course, a sort of graduation celebration. So he was celebrating. Nevertheless, her heart pounded and she was alternately hot and cold at the sound of yet another car.

This one slowed as it turned the corner. She peered. It looked like . . . it was! Freda Easlick breathed a sigh. Then a new anxiety took over. He drove so slowly. She watched as he made a careful, wide turn into the driveway. The garage door went up, but he didn't drive in. He did turn off the engine and car lights. By the street lamp she could see he had dropped his head on the steering wheel.

The radium readout of the digital clock was 3:41 A.M.

CHAPTER TWO

The alarm was set for 5:45 A.M., but an inner alarm woke Gary Reissig first. He extended a bare arm out from under the warm covers and turned it off. Next began the delicate maneuvering to disengage himself without waking Lurene. She lay on her stomach resting half on him and half on the mattress; her left arm flung across his chest, her left leg twined around his left leg. Her face was nestled against his shoulder; all he could see was tousled silver-blonde hair, but he felt her breath —a warm, sensuous current in his ear. As he moved away from her, she turned restlessly and with a soft, lascivious smile on her pouting lips flung herself over on her other side. As she rotated the covers fell away from a perfectly smooth, plump bottom.

Gary Reissig grinned. They slept with the windows wide open and the heat hadn't come up yet. The room was cold but he was hot. Resisting the impulse to lean down and kiss the twin cheeks, he pulled the blanket up over his wife, reached for his robe, and put it on. Better get away while he could.

But he stayed, the fatuous smile still in place as he surveyed his bride of three months. Let her sleep, why not? He looked around the room—at her blue satin panties, the wisp of lace she called a bra, the sheer nightgown she'd taken out of the drawer but he'd not given her a chance to put on. These and his own shorts, tie, shirt, socks and trousers strewn on the floor were the only traces of last night's argument and subsequent reconciliation. He picked them up one by one. Before, Joyce would have been the one to do the picking up. No. Their clothes wouldn't have been flung around like this. With Joyce there would have been no argument in the first place, not over a used car certainly. Joyce had never complained, never demanded. For a long moment as he looked at his new wife in her sultry slumber, Gary Reissig's grin faded. He felt suddenly guilty, as though he were cheating on Joyce.

He shook it off. Gary Reissig was thirty-seven; a detective first grade, working out of the 101 in Far Rockaway, Queens. He had served twelve years, eight of them as a detective. He was blonde, medium height, solidly built with broad shoulders, a thick chest, and narrow thighs. Most of the other cops, even those who lived near the broad white beaches that were the pride of the city, stayed pale. Gary had a year-round tan. Born and bred on the Rockaway peninsula, he loved the outdoors—swimming, sailing, and fishing in the summer; in the winter fishing off the jetties, skating, sometimes even cross-country skiing over the dunes. After the years of exposure, his round, open face was seamed and leathery. He would have looked a lot older but for his vigor, the bounce in his step, the laugh that rumbled up from the pit of his stomach.

Gary got his sense of humor and his optimism from his father. Charley Reissig had been an aviator in World War II. Flyboys, they called them. The appellation was suitable. Charley Reissig was the quintessential flyboy. He braved the dangers of raids, even of being downed in enemy territory and having to make his way back via the underground, jauntily. Long white silk scarf, traditional in World War I, flung around his neck, Gary's father laughed his way through. After the war, through the short charged years with the Air Circus while Gary was an infant, and then when his mother insisted he settle down—literally as well as figuratively—through the long years at the gas station, Charley Reissig went on laughing. And everybody laughed with Charley: the guys who pumped gas with him, the guys who hoisted a few or more with him at the bar every night, his son more than anyone.

Gary's steadiness, his sense of responsibility, came from his mother. Anna Hauser Reissig admired her husband's spirit. She loved him for what he was. It hurt her to have a part in clipping his wings. She understood the drinking that often went beyond control. When she cried, she cried alone where neither Charley nor her son could see. The war had opened doors for women to step outside the home to earn money. Anna Reissig was not prepared to leave her son unattended, much as the money was needed. She concentrated on stretching what Charley provided. As a girl she had been taught to play the piano as one of the social graces; now she began to take pupils. By the time Charley was killed in an explosion of the storage tank under the pumps, Anna Reissig had established herself as a teacher with a comfortable income. Their physical living arrangements at least were not disturbed.

The lesson was not lost on Gary. In Vietnam, he too was a pilot, but he had no inclination to go on flying afterward, not as a commercial pilot and certainly not in the military. His father's insouciance made him reject a nine-to-five job; his mother's stability demanded a commitment. He found both needs satisfied in the police department.

Joyce Crouse, his first wife, had been his childhood sweetheart. Before their marriage and after her death, Gary had not slept with another woman. He had not thought seriously except about one other—and he'd admired her rather than loved her. At least, he supposed that was the way it had been between him and Norah Mulcahaney. Actually, he'd allowed himself to be overwhelmed by her. His lips twisted ruefully—it was an odd time to be thinking about Norah, with his wife's panties and bra in his hand.

The grin returned accompanied by a low chuckle that threatened to explode into a laugh; he stifled it for fear of waking Lurene. Lurene was not at her best in the morning; before eleven she simply didn't function. That left him to get the children's breakfast and see them off to school. On the weeks he worked the four to midnight, it was no problem; he simply walked them to the corner and waited with them for the school bus. When he had the morning tour, he drove them to school himself and saw them safely inside. He didn't mind. In fact, he enjoyed it; it gave him a larger share in their lives. It didn't occur to Gary that Lurene was shirking her responsibility. Taking on another woman's children would be a problem for any young bride; children like Anna and Robin—one deaf, the other retarded—were a special difficulty. He couldn't expect Lurene to change her lifestyle overnight. He had to be patient with her and make his share of the adjustments. It was enough that she loved the kids and Anna and Robin accepted her.

He had showered and shaved and was pulling on his favorite plaid slacks and dark-brown corduroy shirt when the phone beside the bed jangled. Damn! He snatched it up with an anxious glance at Lurene. She rolled over on her back and snored lustily.

"Reissig," he whispered. "Yes, Captain, I'm here." He had to speak up for the captain. "Yes sir, I'm leaving now." He replaced the receiver, leaned over, and shook Lurene gently by the shoulder.

Waking, she blinked up at him.

"I have to go to work. You'll have to take the kids to day camp. Call a taxi. I'm sorry."

"No problem. Don't worry about it," she murmured, slipping into the Southern drawl she tried to suppress—and which he loved. "No problem," she repeated and puckered for a kiss.

It wasn't easy to keep it brief. "Thanks, honey."

She was going to be fine, Gary thought. Everything was going to be just fine. As he backed the old station wagon out of the driveway, Gary Reissig was humming contentedly off key.

The department was going through another of those periods of moral and financial misconduct that seemed to erupt regularly. Gary wasn't sure whether this one was a dormant canker festering or a new infection. After each scandal with its sequence of revelation and investigation there was a lull. The PC, whichever one it happened to be, would claim the bad cops had been weeded out and the code of ethics reviewed and strengthened; henceforth it would be rigidly enforced. Only the good men remained, he announced. Then the cycle started again.

This time, the instances appeared isolated. A bad cop carousing on duty ran down a pedestrian and killed her, a seventy-two-year-old woman. He left the scene. Gary remembered the case very well because, unfortunately for the rogue cop, Lieutenant Norah Mulcahaney, commander of Fourth Division Homicide, which had jurisdiction, took a personal interest. Stunned by the callousness of the crime, she not only turned up a witness but convinced the witness, a timorous old man, to give evidence against the cop. It was not a popular act in the department, but in the end it was seen not as a betrayal of one officer but as a vindication of all the others. Public outrage had barely subsided when another, also apparently solitary incident was revealed: a cop shooting another cop over the first one's wife. "Bad cop" stories proliferated: drinking and whoring while on duty; skimming confiscated drugs and selling them; making off with whatever goods the thief had left at a burglary scene. Victimizing the people they were sworn to protect. The good cops cringed but closed ranks. The brass stonewalled it and let the word seep down that the guilty must not be shielded; the code of silence must no longer be observed. Cops were ordered to snitch on their buddies or share the guilt. Nobody expected the order to be obeyed.

Every cop in every precinct walked on tiptoe. Every commander held his breath. *Not one of mine, he prayed. God, don't let it be any of my men.*

The 101 at the border of Queens and Nassau counties was clean, and Captain Harold Boykin meant for it to stay that way. The 101 was tough duty; not the worst, but a man had to watch his back. The precinct covered a low-income and high-unemployment area, a black and ethnically mixed community. Alcohol and drug addiction were stimulated by idleness. The urban core consisted of ravaged streets, rows of empty and deserted stores, and vandalized buildings. Even down along the ocean front, the once fine old mansions had fallen in decay. Nevertheless, at this point at least, the cops of the 101 remained in control of the area and of themselves. The unspoken tenet: Keep your own nose clean and you won't have to worry about anybody else's.

With the commander it was another matter. Hal Boykin was a good cop who had come up by hard work and dedication, who deserved the appointment but willingly admitted he couldn't have gotten it but for his color. Boykin was in the ambiguous position of benefiting from past discrimination against his race and at the same time having to work twice as hard to prove that he deserved to be where he was. That the current police commissioner was also a black man didn't affect Harold Boykin. The PC had his own problems and wouldn't be likely to give Boykin special consideration if he got himself into trouble.

Boykin was a tall, well muscled man with an open, handsome face. An actor could have used such a face as a screen on which to portray his emotions; Boykin had trained himself to keep it blank. As he did now in speaking to Detective Reissig. Reissig was his kind of cop. Thorough. Didn't rely on hunches or take shortcuts. Didn't miss much. He had never known Reissig to overlook a single item of physical evidence. But that wasn't why he'd called him in. Reissig was absolutely honest and could be trusted to keep his mouth shut whatever he turned.

"I don't like the response lag on the complaint," the captain told Gary Reissig as he handed over the patrol report. "I don't question the error in the address; it was unfortunate, but it happens. What bothers me is that they didn't enter the building. They claim they couldn't get in without destruction of private property. Why the hell not? The perpetrator did."

Though his face remained impassive, there was no missing the anger in his voice nor the worry in his clear dark eyes. Hernandez and Ellison were no rookies, so it wasn't incompetence that concerned Boykin.

"They're good men, sir," Reissig assured him. "And squeaky clean."

"I hope so. The woman is in critical condition. After Hernandez and Ellison walked away, she lay on the basement stairs bleeding for close to six hours till the janitor came to work and found her."

"God," Reissig groaned.

"Exactly. I want you to get over there and find out what happened. I want some answers before anybody starts asking questions."

"Yes, sir."

Boykin heaved a sigh. "And God help us all if that woman dies."

Gary looked over the RMP report. It was preliminary but straightforward. The two officers had scouted the building and found no indication of trouble, no signs of a B and E. They questioned the neighbors. On the surface, it couldn't be faulted. Reissig doubted that the UF5 to follow, a more detailed account, would add much.

The second squeal was caught by PO Jack Caffrey. The janitor of the Senior Citizens' Center had called 911 at 5:10 A.M. Caffrey arrived at the scene fifteen minutes later. The paramedics were already there. The victim was unconscious. They had stanched the bleeding, put her on an IV, and were about to transport. Caffrey put in the usual notifications, including a request for forensics to check for possible prints and take samples of the blood splattered on walls and on the banister, and in a pool at the bottom of the steps. As Caffrey was due to go off duty at eight, he passed what he had on to his replacement—as per procedure. Gary considered calling Caffrey at home, then decided to get his own impressions fresh. That was why the captain had sent for him, wasn't it?

First, though, he made a call to St. Simon's. The resident who had treated Alyssa Hanriot on admission was still on duty.

"The knife just missed the heart," Dr. Robert Lumia told him.

"Is she going to make it?"

"The odds are good—barring unforeseen complications, naturally."

"Naturally." Gary recognized the qualification was standard medical caution.

"She's suffered severe trauma. She keeps drifting in and out of consciousness," the young, weary resident continued.

"Frankly, that may turn out to be more serious than the wound and the loss of blood."

Gary was aware the victim of such an attack could be scarred psychologically for life. "Was she sexually assaulted?"

"No," Dr. Lumia replied flatly.

"When can I talk to her?"

There was a pause. "When she wakes up without screaming."

By 8:30 A.M., Gary Reissig had pulled out of the police lot on Mott Street and was heading along Seagirt. The morning was crisp and bright; the ocean calm, waves rippling to the shore in military rows and breaking with a lacy froth. He parked at the crumbling curb of a weed-and rubble-choked lot. Accustomed as he was to it, Gary never ceased to marvel at nature's splendor and at the ugliness man allowed to develop alongside. He got out of the station wagon and strode up to the front door of the Senior Citizen's Center.

A placard gave the hours as 10 A.M. to 10 P.M. He rang anyway. Not expecting an answer, he wasn't discouraged when he didn't get one and went around to the back. There was a night bell. He tried it. After a while, he heard footsteps inside. The door was opened by a stout, baldheaded man wearing gray fatigues.

"Who are you? What do you want?"

Gary flipped open his shield case. "Detective Reissig. If you're Emil Holzman, I want you."

The lights were dim but adequate. Heavy dust clung everywhere except on the landing where they stood and on the flight of stairs leading down. There it had been disturbed beyond the possibility of any kind of reconstruction of events. To the left, on the flight going up, however, a set of footprints could be clearly delineated—a man's size ten, toes pointing down.

"Did you just come that way?" Reissig asked.

"No, sir. They told me not to use those steps and to make sure nobody else does either. That's where I found her. That's where it happened."

So why hadn't it been roped off? Gary wondered. Not that

roping if off would do much good without a guard posted. "You came in through this door?"

"That's right. I nearly fell over her. I mean, it was dark and I nearly didn't see her. And when I did . . . I couldn't believe what she looked like—such a pretty girl, covered with blood, her face swollen, a mess. They said he not only cut her, he beat her. She was such a nice girl, nice with everybody."

Though his small gray eyes glittered with the unaccustomed excitement, and his own newfound importance, real grief and concern could be seen there too.

"It must have been a shock for you, Mr. Holzman," Gary said.

The janitor was surprised. "Yes, Detective, it was. We were friends, me and Allie. It was a real shock. Is she going to be all right?"

"I hope so."

Gary descended slowly, taking care where he put his feet. On the fourth step from the bottom he noticed some dark splotches and followed them down to the basement floor. Turning his flashlight on them, he bent to touch them lightly with his fingertips: still wet, tacky. Concrete soaked up a lot of the blood, but the victim had lain there too long and bled too heavily for all of it to have been absorbed. Reissig sighed; he was assuming the blood was the victim's but if there had been a struggle, the perpetrator too might have been cut. There could be other traces of him—fingerprints, fragments of skin, threads of clothing, hair. Where was the forensics wagon? He'd better put in a second call and let them know the captain was taking a special interest.

"Any other access to the basement?" he asked Holzman.

"Not from outside. But you can come down in the elevator."

At that moment, Gary heard the whirring sound of the machinery from back near the stairs he had just descended. At the front of the passage the call button lit up. He examined the passage carefully. It was relatively free of dust. He looked for bloodstains and found none.

So, he thought, the victim, Alyssa Hanriot, came down in the elevator and headed for the back exit. Why she didn't go out the front was one of the questions he'd be asking her—he hoped he'd be asking her. At the foot of the stairs, she was jumped and thrown down. The attack was interrupted by the arrival of the RMP. The perpetrator heard it. While Hernandez and Ellison were trying to decide if they should break down the door, the perp fled by way of the elevator and up to the first floor. So far okay. Except . . .

"According to the report from the responding officers, all the lights in the building were out last night. The place was completely dark. Did you turn them out?"

"No, sir, not me. I go home at four in the afternoon. Whoever locks up at night is supposed to turn them out before leaving. Last night, that was Miss Hanriot. Funny you should mention it. I meant to tell the other cop, but in the excitement and all it slipped my mind. You know how it is. I meant to tell you and I forgot."

"Sure." Gary waited. "So tell me now."

"Oh, right. Well, like I said, I go home early, but I also come in real early in the mornings—for the garbage collection and I like the quiet—you know? Anyhow, the place is still dark and I turn on the lights as I need them. Only this morning when I went for the switch—right here inside the door—it didn't work. Everything had been turned off at the main box. Now, I couldn't figure Allie, Miss Hanriot, doing that. I wouldn't have figured she even knew where the fuse box was."

"Show me."

Holzman leaned over the banister and pointed to the alcove opposite the down flight. It housed the elevator machinery Gary had just heard in operation and a row of metal boxes containing the various circuit breakers. Gary opened them one after the other. "And each one was tripped?"

"That's right," the janitor told him. "Except for the elevator switch. That was in the active position."

Gary's tan face was grim. If the perpetrator had thrown the switches, and who else could it have been, then he was familiar with the building, in fact very knowledgeable about it. Of course, he could have simply walked into the place during the day, any day, with no questions asked and stayed on till after closing. Alone in the building, he could take a good look around. But if he knew so much, enough to knock out the lights but keep the elevator going, he could sure also gain access without leaving evidence of illegal entry. Hell, he might be somebody connected with the place. He might have keys. That exonerated Hernandez and Ellison. The captain would be relieved.

For three days and nights Alyssa Hanriot drifted in and out of consciousness. Each time she was awakened by her own screams as she relived the trauma of the attack in the basement. She screamed as once again she saw the knife poised at her throat, screamed as she raised her knee, screamed again and again till the nurse came running. Soothed, reassured, she lapsed into that state which was neither coma nor sleep but a retreat by which nature sought to heal. The doctors were afraid to sedate her and push her down so far she might not come out of it again.

On the fourth day, she awoke quietly, normally, remembering nothing—for a moment. She had no idea where she was and didn't care. With the sun shining in at the window and across her bed, Alyssa was content to lie in its warmth and feel safe and cared for. As she snuggled deeper into the cocoon of bedclothes, she became aware she was connected by a tube in her arm and one down her nose to plastic bags hanging from a high metal stand well above her head. So, she was in a hospital. She had no recollection of being brought there. As she shifted position to look around the room, a sharp twinge in her left shoulder revived a visual memory—the flash of a knife blade in a single ray of blue light, a heavy weight, and a smell, a foul odor she couldn't identify but which was there at that very instant. Then she remembered it all, but she didn't scream. She felt for the call button beside her pillow and rang for the nurse.

"Well," Tess Cummings smiled with genuine pleasure. "You look much better. How do you feel?"

"Dopey."

"You've slept a lot. That will pass."

Alyssa nodded. "Where am I?"

"St. Simon's."

The room was small, barely accommodating the standard hospital bed, a single straight chair, the bureau. The walls needed painting and the window hadn't been washed since summer. Alyssa knew St. Simon's: It was old, but not old-fashioned; they put their money into equipment, not decor.

"How long have I been here?"

"They brought you in three days ago."

Alyssa sighed. "Did they get . . . him?"

Nurse Cummings was very much aware of the patient's anxiety and hastened to reassure her. "No, but they're working on it." She felt a tremendous empathy for this girl. Thirty-four, a capable and competent professional, the mother of three, she had been attacked and raped on the way home from work over five months before. Her family and friends thought she was fully recovered and she let them think so. But she was far from whole again. It would take a long period of tranquility, of unbroken, humdrum routine, to restore her to normalcy. She knew, though, she would never be completely the same again. The experience would remain always a part of her emotional makeup. Tess Cummings would have liked to put her arm around this girl and talk to her like a sister, share her problems and fears. But suppose it was too soon? Suppose she said the wrong thing?

"The detectives have been around to see you. I'm supposed to notify them when you feel up to answering questions."

"Any time."

"You're sure? It won't be easy," the nurse warned out of her own experience. The questioning she had undergone had been almost as traumatic as the attack.

"Might as well get it over."

"Good. Just remember, they're on your side. Oh, and your boyfriend's been calling. Every night. From out of town."

Neil. She hadn't even thought about him. How had he found out? Probably he'd called Saturday morning to say goodbye. Not getting an answer, would he have called the police? Or had the police contacted him? And he still went on his trip? She sighed. After all, what could he have accomplished by staying?

The phone rang.

"That's probably him." Beaming, Tess Cummings withdrew to give the patient privacy.

Alyssa reached for the receiver and picked it up. "Hello, Neil?"

There was a moment's silence.

"How are you?" the caller asked in a soft, breathy voice.

"I'm all right. I'm fine. Who's this?"

"That was a nasty experience you had."

"Yes. Who is this?"

"You're lucky to be alive."

CHAPTER THREE

Gary Reissig dropped everything when he got the call.

He found Alyssa Hanriot sitting up in bed. Her skin was sallow; violet shadows under her dark eyes emphasized their size and depth. Her hair was woven into a single plait that hung down her back. She looked drained, as indeed she must be. But the IV tube was gone from her arm and the gastrointestinal feeder from her nose. A breakfast tray was pushed to one side, the empty dishes indicating she had eaten well.

"Good morning, Miss Hanriot." Gary gave her a wide smile. "I'm Detective Reissig. How are you feeling?"

"Okay. Shaky."

"That's to be expected."

"And scared," she added, watching to see how he would take that.

"Naturally. You went through a terrible ordeal. But it's over."

"You think so?"

That stopped the flow of genial and standard assurances. "Don't you?" he asked watching her closely. She merely shrugged and licked her lips. "Have you any reason to believe this was anything other than a random attack? Prior to it had you noticed anyone watching you, following you?"

"No," she admitted.

"Then why do you think the attack may be repeated?"

"I got a phone call. Two phone calls. One at the Senior Citizens' Center on the night it happened and another this morning, here."

"Threatening?"

She started to say yes, then changed her mind. "The intent was to scare me."

"Let's go back to the beginning. Can you? Can you talk about it?"

Alyssa Hanriot swallowed and nodded. "It was my last night at the Center. Everybody had left; I locked up, and I was upstairs on the fourth floor clearing out my desk. I heard a sound, like a door rattling, like somebody was trying to get in. I was sure nobody could, but still I had this uncomfortable feeling so I called 911. I waited about fifteen minutes, but the patrol car didn't come and I decided whoever it was had gone and I could leave. I was nearly out my door when my phone rang and a man warned me not to go." She stopped and looked expectantly at Gary.

"Go on."

"I called 911 another time. While I was giving the information to the police operator, I heard footsteps in the hall. I had already put out my lights so I crouched behind my desk till he passed. Then I made a run for it."

"You took the elevator."

"Yes, but it got stuck between floors. And the lights went out. When the elevator started moving again, the lights didn't come back on."

"Was there a long wait between the stopping and the starting?"

"Not long. It's hard to judge. I was so scared."

"Go on."

"Well, I'd punched the lobby button, but I could feel the elevator was going past it. Actually, I thought it was going to crash, but it stopped at the basement smoothly enough and the door opened normally."

"Were the lights on in the basement?"

"No, and not in the elevator either. It was all pitch black."

He didn't like the way it was shaping up. The perp was evidently standing in the utility room manipulating the power. He waited till she got on the elevator, then he cut off all the juice. When he figured she was scared enough, he started the elevator moving. He played the fuse box like a console. He brought her down to the basement where she had only one place to go—toward the stairs leading to the street exit. The light panel and elevator machinery were located under those stairs. All he had to do was step out and grab her.

Gary didn't want to add to her anxiety, but he had to ask, "Have you any enemies? Is there anybody who wants to harm you?"

"Nobody."

"Can you describe the man who attacked you?"

"It was dark," she reminded the detective. "I couldn't see my hand in front of my face. Literally. He knocked me down and got on top of me and so I can tell you he was big and very heavy."

"Tall? Short?"

She considered. "Well, tall, I suppose."

"That doesn't give us much to go on."

"I'm sorry," she said with a touch of asperity.

"No, *I'm* sorry," Gary was quick to apologize. "Believe me, it wasn't a criticism. I want to get this guy—for your sake and for others he might hit on. You said you got a call here this morning. You think it was the same man?"

"He asked me how I was feeling. He said I was lucky to be alive."

"How do you know it was him? Did he say so? Did he say he was the one who stabbed you?"

"No."

"Did you recognize the voice as that of the man who called you at the center?"

"No, but who else could it have been?"

"A nut, Miss Hanriot. A psycho. The streets are full of them. Most are roaming around without shelter. Some have homes, jobs, and are accepted as normal functioning members of society. The story about your attack was in all the papers. He could have read about it. He called the hospital and asked for you and they put him through without question. I'll make sure they don't do that anymore."

"Thank you."

She wasn't satisfied; he could see that and he didn't blame her. "It's highly unlikely the same man is involved. People who get their kicks on the telephone don't usually have the guts to take overt action. You'll be okay." Unfortunately, Gary wasn't as sure as he sounded. "If anything more occurs to you, if you think of anything at all, no matter how trivial, that you haven't told me, please call." He was about to hand her his office card, then he put it down on the bedside table and scribbled his home number on it as well.

Alyssa Hanriot wanted to accept Detective Reissig's explanation of that second phone call at least. He was the pro, she reasoned. He dealt with these things every day.

Neil Jaros did accept it because it was rational and because any other interpretation was unthinkable. Jaros was a prosaic young man, though not as young as he looked. He was five feet nine, with bright inquisitive blue eyes, and dark hair beginning to turn gray. He jogged, swam determined laps in the YMCA pool, and watched his weight. But it was his lack of imagination, his refusal to delve below the surface or to take responsibility, that kept his face fresh and unlined. He worked for Kinderson Associates, a sports promotion firm. It was a job both glamorous and routine. He dealt with the superficial. So what? Not everybody could be a doctor or a missionary. But he had gone as far as he could with Kinderson. He knew it, had known it for a long time, but was just starting to worry about it.

Neil Jaros had been dating Alyssa Hanriot for about two and a half years. He had wanted to marry her right at the start; she was the one who had temporized. She needed time, she'd said, though she'd just returned from a stint with the Peace Corps, which he felt should have provided her with plenty of time to decide what she wanted from her life. She was *still* temporizing. Forced to accept the arrangement, Jaros had grown into it. Now it suited him. Her habits, her hangups, had passed from endearing to tolerable to irritating. Jaros found her insistence on getting involved in other people's troubles particularly annoying. So now she had an experience of her own to brood over and dramatize.

He had flown in from Cleveland specifically to be with her when she was discharged and to see her home. After that, he intended to go right back. That should show her he cared and take the sting out of what he had to say.

Alyssa was dressed and in a wheelchair waiting to be officially discharged and Jaros waited with her.

"Try to forget about it, Allie," he counseled. "People get mugged every day. Unfortunately, it's a condition of our society that we all have to put up with. You're lucky it wasn't any worse. You're lucky to be alive."

She sucked in her breath. Ordinary words, but *his* words. She hadn't told Neil about the call. She paused on the verge of doing so now, but he'd only point out that she couldn't get hurt over the telephone, all she had to do was hang up. He'd be right, of course. Tears welled up.

Seeing them, seeing how she huddled in on herself, Jaros felt unfamiliar pangs of compassion. He'd been too brusque. He'd meant only to shake her out of self-pity, but he'd been too stern. As for the rest of what he had to say—this wasn't the time. Bending down, he kissed her on the lips. It had been intended for consolation, but he lingered and the intensity increased.

"I could stay overnight, if you want," he murmured. "There's an early-morning flight I could get. I didn't carry any luggage so I could leave directly from your place."

"You've already missed a couple of meetings on my account. I don't want you to get into any trouble."

"If it'll make you feel better, I'd be glad . . ."

"No, no, I'll be okay. Honestly. You go on back tonight. That way you'll be there and get a good night's sleep before the conference. You'll be sharp. It's enough that you came. It really is."

He smiled at her. She was sensible. She had her priorities right. It was one of the qualities that had attracted him initially. Still, he was disappointed. And surprised at how disappointed.

Neil Jaros took Alyssa home and got her settled. After some restrained lovemaking in which she participated with a marked lack of enthusiasm. Neil Jaros said goodbye and Alyssa was able to lock the door behind him. She sighed, a great deep sigh, and kicked off her shoes. It was good to be home and alone. The apartment consisted of two rooms and a kitchenette. It was tiny, cluttered with her mother's massive furniture. There were mementoes everywhere, some brought tears, others joy—each was a reminder of her mother's love. The best thing about being home, Alyssa thought, was Theo. Theo was a domestic short-hair, an ordinary striped black and gray cat with white stockings and yellow eyes. Theo had been cared for by a neighbor while Alyssa was in the hospital. He had been returned to the apartment, but would not show himself while a stranger was there—and to Theo Neil Jaros remained a stranger no matter how many times he came around. So now that Neil was gone, Alyssa sat in Theo's favorite chair and waited.

Silently, materializing out of nowhere, the little cat was there, rubbing against Alyssa's leg and purring his welcome.

She picked him up and held him close to her cheek feeling the rough little sandpaper tongue licking. Suddenly, the creature's affection unlocked the gates of her tension and she began to cry. These were not tears of terror but of relief. It was over. She was home. The cat looked surprised and then began to lick the salt tears. Alyssa laughed and holding Theo in her lap, closed her eyes and fell asleep.

She heard the phone ringing in the bedroom. It must be part of her dream, she thought, and she kept her eyes closed. If she went on sleeping, the phone would stop ringing.

But it didn't.

Reluctantly, she opened her eyes. The lamps were lit and outside it was still dark. She looked at her watch: 3:20. Who would be calling at this hour? She put Theo down and made her way to the bedroom and the relentlessly ringing telephone.

"Hello?"

"Feeling better now that you're home?"

She caught her breath. "Who is this?"

"Now come on, Alyssa. You know who this is. Or maybe you don't recognize my voice. It's been twenty months. Twenty very long months for me, Alyssa."

She gasped and began to tremble, the new strength, the sense of security all gone.

"Guess," he urged. "Or shall I give you another clue?"

"No. It can't be. It was supposed to be five to fifteen years."

"They gave me time off for good behavior. That's a joke, isn't it? Between you and me."

"Where are you?"

"Close. Very close. And I intend to stay close to you from now on, Alyssa. Every day. I don't intend to let you out of my sight."

There was a pause so long Alyssa thought he might have hung up. She started quietly to hang up too, but almost as though he'd planned it exactly like that, he resumed, not in the breathy hoarseness of before but in a voice that was strong and intense.

"I'm not through with you yet. I meant to kill you Friday night in that basement. I had it all planned, then the police interrupted. So now I've changed my mind. I'm going to make you pay for all the suffering you caused me. Twenty months, Alyssa, twenty months of my life you took away from me. You're going to pay for every hour and every minute of it."

Then he hung up, firmly, definitely.

Alyssa was paralyzed. It was several moments before she could put the receiver down. Then she started to shake again. What should she do? She had to tell somebody, get help. Neil? He was in Cleveland by now. She couldn't ask him to come back a second time.

As she sat shivering, cold and in fear, Alyssa realized she was also sitting in the dark. She reached out and put on the lamp—let it be a symbol, she thought. Then she got up and went to the bureau where she had put her purse. She went through her wallet pulling out credit cards, driver's license, library card, everything till she found it. Still shaking, she went back to the telephone and dialed.

The call was answered so promptly she wasn't ready and had to clear her throat a couple of times before getting the words out. "Detective Reissig, please."

"Detective Reissig isn't on duty."

"When will he be in?"

"Eight A.M. What is this about? Can somebody else help you?"

"No. That's all right. I'll call at eight."

That was almost four hours from now, she thought disconsolately. Too long. She couldn't wait. She turned the card over and stared at the number he had written across the back. His home. He wouldn't have given it to her if he hadn't meant for her to use it. Any hour, he'd said.

Gary's first concern was to stop the phone ringing so it wouldn't disturb Lurene. He did that by picking it up right away. "Reissig," he whispered as she stirred beside him.

"This is Alyssa Hanriot, Detective Reissig. I'm sorry to disturb you but . . ."

"What is it, Miss Hanriot? What's happened?"

Suddenly, Alyssa was embarrassed. Nothing had happened to warrant waking this man in the middle of the night. "I got a phone call a few minutes ago."

"You mean like the other one?"

"Yes. Except this time I know who it was."

He had been clinging to sleep, but now he cast off the last warm tendrils and, swinging his legs over the side of the bed, sat up.

Behind him, Lurene muttered, "Can't you take your conversation into another room?" And turned over.

"Sh . . ." He motioned for silence as he continued. "You recognized his voice?"

"No, he told me who he was. He's out after only twenty months. The sentence was from five to fifteen years. How could he get out in such a short time? How is that possible?"

"You mean out of jail?" Gary clenched the receiver so hard his knuckles whitened. "Who are you talking about? Who just got out of jail?"

"Will you please go and conduct your interrogation somewhere else?" his wife asked him.

"In a minute." He patted her shoulder, but his attention was with the woman on the phone. "Miss Hanriot, you're not in the hospital now; you're home, right? Okay, you stay there. I'm on my way." He hung up, jumped to his feet, and headed for his closet.

"Now what?" Lurene demanded. "Where are you going?"

"To work. Sorry, honey. I'm leaving the alarm on so you'll be sure to get the kids ready for school."

"Again? That's twice in less than a week."

Gary parked at the curb in front of the common patio around which the four sections of the garden complex were clustered. As he got out he noted the movement of a curtain on the top floor of a building. Her building. She was keeping watch. Scared. He waved reassuringly and went inside, rang, and was almost immediately buzzed in. There was no elevator, so he climbed to the fifth floor. She was waiting behind a locked and bolted door.

Now that she had him there, Alyssa Hanriot didn't know where to begin. She had washed her face and combed her hair, but she couldn't as easily get her thoughts and feelings in order. "Thank you for coming, Detective Reissig. I'm very grateful. I didn't know where else to turn."

"Part of the job, Miss Hanriot," he smiled.

Her response was wan. "I put on coffee. Would you like some?"

He had seen Alyssa Hanriot only that once in the hospital. Depleted physically by the severe loss of blood, she'd also been emotionally drained. Tonight, on the phone, she'd been close to hysteria. He watched her as she scurried off to the kitchen. She seemed to have calmed somewhat and it would be his job to get her all the way down to a level where she could rationally and factually answer the questions he must put to her. While he waited, he took in the place: it was small, boxlike, a room crammed with inappropriately large and old-fashioned furniture—inherited, of course. Kept out of sentiment. Or because she couldn't afford to replace it? Reissig chose one of a pair of dining chairs flanking an antique refectory table.

Alyssa Hanriot came back carrying a small tray with the coffee. "Cream? Sugar?"

"Thanks. I take mine straight."

"Me too." Her smile was a little more secure as she set the tray down and served.

She was trying, Gary thought. Good. "Okay, Miss Hanriot, who's out of jail and what's his connection with you?"

"Roy Easlick." She spoke the name and waited for a reaction. When there was none, she went on. "I was responsible for getting him convicted. Or so everybody said. Anyway, now he's out. But it's only been a little more than a year and a half. How can that be?"

Gary sighed. "Our jails are overcrowded. To alleviate that, there's an automatic reduction of sentence. I won't go into the formula but it amounts to more or less one third of the sentence. Assuming no flagrant trouble from the prisoner and that, in turn, means additional time off for good behavior."

Alyssa swallowed. "He says he's going to make me pay for everything he suffered."

"Just exactly what was this man convicted of?"

"Child molestation."

Now it came back to him. He had forgotten the name, but not the case. As a parent with two young children, how could he? The outrage he'd felt originally was rekindled, but he suppressed it. No wonder they'd turned Easlick loose at the first possible moment, he thought; child molesters were pariahs even among the prison population. They had to be segregated. To keep them safe was a strain on the prison management and on the guards. They would have seized every legal loophole to get rid of him.

"You'd better tell me all about it from the beginning, Miss Hanriot."

She sighed. "I was working per diem as a music teacher in a private school in Glen Cove, a girls' school—kindergarten through eighth grade. I also conducted folk dancing sessions after school as an extracurricular activity. On the day it happened, I had conducted such a session. We finished at a quarter of four. I took maybe another twenty minutes to half an hour to store away my equipment—turntable, speakers, and so forth. As I stepped out into the hall, one of the regulars, the history teacher was coming out of the students' coat room. I wouldn't have paid any attention except that he looked somehow furtive. He opened the door and peered up and down the hall before emerging, almost as though he were making sure the coast was clear. I shrugged it off. But I had to pass the coat room on my way out and as I did I heard the sound of crying. I opened the door and there were two little girls, two of my pupils, clutching each other and crying.

"They wouldn't talk to me at first. I could see that they'd been warned not to tell what had occurred. I tried to reassure them. It didn't do any good. All I could do was sit with them till their mother came to pick them up. As soon as she saw them she knew that something terrible had occurred. We decided it was best for her to take them home and try to get the story later.

"That night Mrs. Sagarman, the mother, called me. It seems the children finally admitted to having been molested but refused to say who had done it. Every time they got to that part, they balked. There was no way she could get it out of them. She asked me if I had any idea who was responsible.

"What choice did I have? How could I not tell what I had seen? How could I refuse to identify the man?

"When it came to the trial the girls got up in the witness stand. Each in turn was given a doll and told to show in what places the man had touched her." Alyssa paused. "You know how it goes. Each one confirmed the other in the details."

Gary nodded, sick.

"Crying and stumbling, somehow they got through that. Only when it came to pointing a finger at their molester, each one refused. When Roy Easlick was ordered to stand up in front of her, each child became hysterical. Court had to be recessed. The prosecution decided it was no use subjecting the children to further distress. They would never accuse Easlick. That left me.

"They put me on the stand. I identified Roy Easlick as the man I had seen come out of the coat room seconds before I heard the girls crying and went inside and found Nancy and Beth Sagarman clutching each other. I described their emotional condition and their physical condition—clothes rumpled and stained. The defense claimed it was all circumstantial, but the jury linked it to the children's obvious distress when faced with Easlick and convicted."

"So the prosecution couldn't have made a case without your testimony."

She nodded. "Everybody was very appreciative at the time."

"Why do you qualify?"

She sighed.

"All right, let's go back to the attack in the basement. You told me you didn't know who your assailant was. You said you couldn't identify him because it was pitch black down there and you couldn't even make out the general outline of the perpetrator. Do you want to change that?"

Alyssa Hanriot licked her lips, searching Reissig's eyes for an indication of what he expected from her, but she could find no clue. "How can I?" she asked helplessly.

"You also told me you have no enemies."

"I never thought of Roy Easlick. I assumed he was still serving his time. I had no idea they'd released him. I had no idea he was out or that he would come looking for me."

"Take it easy, Miss Hanriot. We're going to work this out."

"What's to work out?" she demanded. "He says he attacked me. He admits it."

"To you, privately," Gary pointed out. "He told you he was just out of jail, but did he give you his name?"

"If he had, it would have been only to me, privately," she mimicked bitterly. "He threatened me, Detective Reissig. He threatened to make me pay for everything he's been through. But I didn't get a recording."

"I'm on your side, Miss Hanriot, believe me. Unfortunately, your statement by itself isn't enough. But that doesn't mean we're giving up. I'll have a talk with Roy Easlick. He won't bother you anymore, I promise."

CHAPTER FOUR

It was too late to go home and try to get some more sleep. He was too wide awake anyway, his mind churning, so Gary headed for the squad. There he looked up the number for Nassau Central Booking and dialed. Soon the various police computers would be linked nationwide and the kind of questions for which he sought answers could be punched up on the precinct terminal. For now, he had to hold while his opposite number in Mineola called up the Release Prisoner File and passed on the information to him: dates of Raymond Easlick's arrest, indictment, trial, and conviction. It matched Alyssa Hanriot's statement. But there was one surprise—Easlick had been out one month prior to the attack.

Ordinarily Gary would have discussed it with his sergeant, but since Captain Boykin had personally assigned him to the case, it was the captain he went to.

"Why did he wait so long?" Boykin asked.

Reissig shrugged. "The opportunity didn't present itself. Or he hadn't made up his mind."

"Okay, I'll buy that. It's announcing himself on the phone I have a problem with. She could be making that part of it up—the girl, I mean. Has that occurred to you?"

"Why should she?"

Boykin rocked back and forth in the swivel chair. "She's off balance, trying to rationalize what's happened. It's easier to deal with a known quantity, to give the threat an identity. She could be lying—to herself as much as to us."

Gary frowned. "We can find out easily enough—put a tap on her phone."

Boykin considered. It meant getting a court order. Finally, he shook his head. "We need more than her say-so."

LOCAL MAN RELEASED
Convicted Child Molester Returns Home

Freda Easlick sat in the breakfast nook of her big, airy kitchen, her coffee cold in front of her as she stared at the item in the newspaper. Upstairs, her son slept.

It was a short paragraph deep in the center of *Newsday*'s thick weekend section, but Freda Easlick knew that everybody in the neighborhood would see it—all her friends, everybody at the club. Of course, they knew already, but that wasn't the point. The point was that they'd accepted Roy's return with very little animosity. At least overt. The few ripples of gossip had spread out and the waters were just about calm again. Now, with these few lines they would be stirred up. No wonder Roy was drinking.

So far Roy was just hoisting a few after work—coming home mellow, as he put it. The frequency and amount would increase. She knew the pattern only too well. This was the second time since he'd been back that he hadn't been able to make it to the office in the morning. She couldn't deny he had a reason for drinking. The elegant, suburban matron struggling with the present reality, searching for a way to save her son, refused to acknowledge that Roy had been drinking long before he went to prison, in fact before the—accusation. When she thought of the terrible events that had befallen them, Freda Easlick focused only on that, attributed everything to that. Not for one instant did she allow herself to ponder on what might have led up to it.

The front door chimes broke into her reverie and brought new anxiety—neighbors and deliveries came to the rear entrance. As she went around to answer, she caught sight of two men through the glass panel and felt a sharp pain in her chest. It was a long time since another pair, much like these, had stood at her front door. She managed a couple of slow deep breaths.

"Mrs. Easlick? I'm Detective Reissig from the One-Oh-One," Gary introduced himself. "And this is my partner, Detective Dogali."

Marconi Dogali was twenty-eight, six foot two, 220 pounds of college linebacker whose pro career had ended with a knee shattered in preseason practice. Recent transfer from Greenpoint, Brooklyn, was not considered an upward career move, but Dogali's family liked being near the beach and he and Gary had hit it right off. Dogali was content to follow the senior detective's lead, and Gary knew his partner was prepared to back him up without question. With his massive bulk, flaming red hair, and beard, Dogali was an intimidating presence. Never mind that the muscle had turned to flab, never mind the agility was gone; he could be a crushing force. A good man to have behind you.

Dogali grinned cheerfully to put the obviously anxious woman at ease. "Is Roy at home?" he asked.

Freda Easlick hesitated. She had learned, the hard way, that it was best to stick as close to the truth as possible. She also remembered that Roy's maroon convertible was in the garage along with her Buick sedan. "Yes, but he's not well. He's resting."

"I'm sorry to hear that. We certainly don't want to disturb him if he's not well." Gary paused. He looked over his shoulder. The designated "private" street consisted of six small mansions ranged in a semicircle behind perfect lawns well screened by shrubbery. There was no one out. Maybe nobody was watching from behind those discreetly half-lowered shades. "Perhaps we should step inside?"

"Oh. Yes. Certainly." Mrs. Easlick pulled back to let the detectives pass her. Then she took the lead again through a tiled foyer to an elaborate, over-decorated living room in mass-produced French provincial. She waved them to chairs.

They sat. The last time, she recalled, the detectives had remained standing. Was this a good sign?

"I hope it's nothing serious, your son's illness, I mean?" Gary said politely.

"No, no. Just . . . he stayed out a little too late last night and had too good a time."

"He hasn't had much chance to enjoy himself lately," Gary observed.

Mrs. Easlick paled.

"We are familiar with your son's record," Reissig explained. "It's our job. That doesn't mean we're condemning him in advance."

"Condemning? Condemning him of what?"

"I'm sorry. I didn't mean to sound threatening. Perhaps it would be better if Roy came down."

"What do you want? He hasn't done anything. Why can't you leave us alone?"

"Sure, Mrs. Easlick. All we need to know is where Roy was last Friday night. A week ago," Dogali said, matching his partner's low-key delivery.

Freda Easlick became very still. "I don't remember. Home, I suppose. I suppose he was home like most nights."

"That would have been the seventeenth, Mrs. Easlick."

Reissig was courteous but insistent and that was not lost on her.

"I was at the company banquet on the seventeenth. Don't you remember, Mom?"

Unnoticed, Roy Easlick had come down the stairs and stood now in the open doorway. He wore pajamas, a dark blue silk robe with burgundy piping and maroon leather slippers. He stood well over six feet, with a large head and large hands and feet. His features were roughly hewn; they had a rugged outdoor look. His light gray eyes, large as the rest of him, were mild and imparted a blandness echoed in the tone of his voice. Not a man one would pick as a molester of children.

"I'm a trainee, or was, at the First American National Bank. The dinner on the seventeenth was a celebration for those who had successfully completed the course. I was one. We broke up at about eleven. That sound right, Mom?"

The color returned slowly to Freda Easlick's face. "Yes, that's right. I do remember now."

"Is that what you wanted to know, Officers?" Easlick asked.

He was very composed, Gary thought. Why didn't he ask what it was all about. He should have asked what he and Dogali were doing there. He waited, but Easlick remained silent. Because he was afraid to ask or because he already knew?

"How about last night? What were you celebrating last night?"

Easlick threw a look at his mother, then sighed. "It's none of your business, but I'll tell you. I had a few drinks with the guys and I got home before ten. The drinks hit me harder than I expected."

He could have made the call to Hanriot from here, from his own room upstairs. He surely had a telephone up there, probably a private line.

"And if you're wondering why I didn't go to work today, it's simple. I have the day off. I don't start my new assignment till Monday."

The relief on his mother's face was open for all to see. Maybe it spurred Easlick to take the offensive, at last.

"Why do you want to know?"

Reissig waited a couple of beats. "Could we talk alone?"

"Oh, no!" Freda Easlick placed herself between her son and the detective. "You're not taking him anywhere."

"Of course not, ma'am. We just want to talk to your son privately."

"I have no secrets from my mom. I've done nothing she can't hear about, nothing that would hurt or embarrass her. I haven't done a thing I'm ashamed for my mom to know. And I never have," he added.

"Whatever you want," Reissig said. "On the night of October seventeenth, last Friday, Alyssa Hanriot was assaulted and nearly killed. She claims you called her on the telephone and admitted doing it."

The mother gasped. The son turned pale.

"Is it any use for me to deny it? She's lying. I don't know why. Naturally, you believe her."

"We came to hear your side."

Easlick threw up his hands. "I'm an ex-con; I don't have a side. God, why is she doing this? What has she got against me? Why can't she leave me alone. She stood up in court, stared straight at me, and gave false evidence. The two little girls never identified me, not even privately, not even to their parents. The parents were honest enough to admit that. There was only this woman, this woman I scarcely knew—I'd seen her in the halls and in the faculty lounge, but that's all. Then suddenly she was identifying me as having come out of that coat room."

"The jury believed her."

He sighed. "Maybe she didn't lie. I don't know. Maybe she made a mistake and the more she repeated the story, the more she became convinced in her own mind that it was me she'd seen."

There were instances like that, plenty of them, Gary knew. It was one of the dangers of repeated interrogation, confirming a witness in error.

Easlick went on. "But this time she's making up the story out of whole cloth."

"Not exactly," Gary retorted. "She was attacked. Knifed. She lost a tremendous amount of blood. She almost died."

"All right, but it wasn't me that did it. Look, I've served time. At this point nobody cares whether I was guilty or innocent. You're both detectives and you know what being jailed as a child molester means, how you're treated. Mass murderers spit on you. You think I want to take the chance of being sent back? I don't want to have anything to do with Ms. Hanriot ever again, believe me. I intend to stay as far away from the lady as possible." He groaned. "I'd move to another town if I could, but this is my home. I was born here. This is my mother's home. Also, I've got a good job, a really good job and that's a big item considering the tag that's been put on me. I could hardly have expected to get work as a teacher again, not that I wanted it. I'm lucky Stuart Chanin is willing to take a chance on me."

"Who's Stuart Chanin?"

"A vice-president of the bank, a neighbor and an old friend. His hiring me has turned everything around for me."

"You didn't call Alyssa Hanriot last night?"

"Why should I? Don't you understand? I'm in the clear at last. I've got a shot at a decent life. Why should I jeopardize it?"

Gary nodded. "I'd appreciate the names of the men you had drinks with last night. Of course, we'll be checking your alibi for the seventeenth."

Easlick's temples throbbed. "You're going to wreck it for me, aren't you?"

"Not intentionally."

"I'll bet."

"Why would Alyssa Hanriot lie about this?" Reissig asked. "Give me a reason."

"How the hell should I know?" Easlick lashed out. "Maybe she finally has qualms about the evidence she gave. Maybe she realizes at last she might have made a mistake and wants to get rid of me before I can do anything about it."

"Are you planning to do something about it?"

Roy Easlick's broad, handsome face was contorted with frustration. "If I could, I would have done it twenty months ago."

Ed Sagarman was having his first cup of coffee and checking through the weekend edition of *Newsday* when he spotted the paragraph. His hand shook so hard he had to set the cup down but not before he'd slopped coffee into the saucer. He skimmed through the brief account, then read it a second time slowly, lingering over each detail. He glanced at his wife; she was busy loading the dishwasher. He started to speak, but instead got up and went over to close the kitchen door. The girls were still upstairs dressing, but he was taking no chances of being overheard.

"He's out," he announced and his voice was hoarse and throbbing with indignation. "I can't believe it. He's been out a month, a whole month, and nobody informed us."

"Who? Who are you talking about?"

"Who else? Him. Do you need to ask? *Him*. Roy Easlick."

Frances Sagarman gasped. She turned gray under her tan. Thin to the point of anorexia, it made her look like death. Her sun-streaked hair hung lank. Her gold-flecked eyes fogged. Knees buckling, she clung to the counter for support. "How do you know?"

"It's right here." He held the paper out to her.

Somehow she managed to focus where her husband pointed and read the salient facts of Easlick's parole. "Oh, my God. So soon." She reached for the nearest kitchen chair, pulled it around, and sank into it.

Sagarman made no attempt to help or comfort. He didn't touch her. She didn't reach for him.

"I don't know when it came over the wire or how I could have missed it, but I'm not letting it pass. I'm going to the police. I'm going to demand protection. Meantime, we'll have to watch the girls every minute, never leave them alone."

Frances Sagarman nodded, her small narrow face tense. "I'll arrange with Mary Ann—"

"Are you crazy? No baby-sitters. No housekeepers. You and me. Nobody else. We can't trust anybody else."

She licked her thin lips. "He'd be crazy to come near them."

"He *is* crazy. He's sick. That's the whole point. We can't predict what he will or won't do." Sagarman groaned.

His wife reread the item. "It says that he had psychiatric treatment and the doctors pronounced him cured."

"Is that right?" Sagarman dripped sarcasm. "He wouldn't be the first psycho they let loose to repeat his crimes. If you believe that, you're a fool."

She flushed, but didn't retort.

Edwin Sagarman was a quiet man who usually kept his feelings pent up. So did Frances Sagarman, or she had learned to during the past two years. Since the tragedy. There were things they just didn't mention, much less discuss. As a result the silence grew to absorb other matters. The habit of non-communication developed. It was easier not to say anything, to let it pass. Sagarman was over six feet tall, as emaciated looking as his wife, but strong. He was a fitness addict; he ate his yogurt and bean sprouts at his desk then spent the balance of his lunch hour working out on the Nautilus machines. Over a period of years together eating the same food, weaving a skein of shared experiences, married couples come to look alike. Recent events had accelerated the process for Edwin and Frances Sagarman. They looked like brother and sister. They acted like it.

Sagarman was forty-four. His current job as editor of the *Long Island Shore to Shore*, a weekly, was hardly challenging for a journalist of international experience, but he was still remembered and respected. He could return to the mainstream at any time. He never would; deep inside Sagarman knew it though he denied it to everyone including himself. "You'll take off from work as long as necessary. You'll drive them to school and pick them up afterward. No buses." He had himself well in hand again.

Frances Sagarman nodded. She had a good job. She was a lingerie designer for one of the top wholesalers with retail outlets from coast to coast. This was the worst time to be out, but that wasn't what bothered her. "What will I say to the girls? How will I explain so they won't be frightened? I don't think we should tell them the truth."

"No, I agree. It would alarm them." He was thoughtful. "I'll alert the school about the situation, of course, but there's no need to explain anything to Nancy and Beth. You won't be the only parent driving her children to school and picking them up afterward, not once the word gets around. Meantime, I'm going to the precinct. I won't draw one easy breath till this creep is either back in jail or run out of town."

Alyssa Hanriot was scheduled to move on Saturday and she had no intention of postponing it, in fact she could hardly wait. It wasn't only that she was going to a larger place in a better neighborhood, but she was going where *he* couldn't find her. She intended to leave no forwarding address but rather rent a box at the post office so her new address wouldn't be available. Moving to an area with a different telephone exchange, she would be getting a new phone number as a matter of course. It would be unlisted.

With only her few bits and pieces of personal effects left, the move was easy. By midafternoon Alyssa sat amid boxes and barrels exhausted but happy. She unpacked a few kitchen necessities, plugged in the lamps, and made up the bed. Enough. She washed her face, found her makeup, fixed herself up, and went out for dinner to a coffee shop around the corner on Central. It was after eight when she came back. The phone in her new apartment was ringing. Key in hand, she froze.

Who could it be? She hadn't given the number to anyone, not even to Neil yet. In fact, she'd intended to call and do that tonight. Inside the phone continued ringing. Finally, after about a dozen peals, it stopped. She put the key in the lock and went in.

No sooner had she put on the lights and hung up her coat than it started again. She could see it through the open bedroom door where it was placed on the bedside table. She felt like ripping the cord out of the jack and throwing the whole thing out the window. She clenched her fists at her sides. He couldn't hurt her by telephone. There was nothing to be afraid of. Nevertheless, she stared at the jangling machine as at a viper. At last, she went in, touched it. It felt cold and slippery. She lifted the receiver out of the cradle and held it to her ear. But she didn't speak, not a word. Give him a taste of his own medicine, she thought with a surge of courage.

"Hello? Miss Hanriot? This is Detective Reissig."

"Oh, my God," The tears rolled down her cheeks. She shook worse than before but out of relief. She had given Reissig the new number, of course. "I thought . . . I thought . . ."

"Are you all right?"

"Yes, yes, I'm fine. Really. Everything is fine."

"Good. I just wanted to let you know that we've talked with Roy Easlick. He has an alibi for the night of the seventeenth."

"But he told me . . . He admitted . . . on the phone . . ."

"You said the caller didn't give his name."

"No, but he did say he'd been in jail for twenty months. I don't know anybody else who's ever been in jail."

"Well, we've warned Easlick that we're watching him.

We've warned him to keep strictly away from you. If he
bothers you in any way, we can get a court order enjoining
him from further harassment. He won't dare touch you. I honestly believe you can rest easy."

Alyssa said nothing.

"Miss Hanriot? Are you there?"

"Yes."

"If he annoys you in any way, you call me. Understand?
You call me like you did before."

"Yes. Thank you."

"And I'll be in touch as soon as I have any news."

"Thank you." She put the phone down and walked over to
the still uncurtained window. She was too far away to see the
ocean but the cool offshore breeze felt good on her flushed
face and eased her tension. The night was dark, moonless, and
with the lamp shining behind her she was plainly silhouetted.
She didn't think of that or of anything. She was half in a
trance watching the planes from Kennedy climb to cruising
height and then begin the long journey across the sea. Theo,
as usual appearing out of nowhere and sensing her mood,
rubbed against her right leg and meowed his own feeling of
strangeness in the new quarters. Alyssa picked him up and
snuggled him close. Then, just as suddenly, Theo dug his back
paws into her forearm indicating he wanted to be let free.
Theo's tolerance for togetherness was limited.

Part of her edginess and depression was due to physical
weakness, Alyssa decided. As her physical condition im-
proved so would her mental state. Detective Reissig knew his
job. If he said Easlick wasn't responsible for the attack and
the phone calls then she must believe him. And she must also
trust him to find whoever was responsible. From the first moment when Gary Reissig had pulled up a chair to the side of
her bed in the hospital, Alyssa had felt the current of his
concern. She had liked him right away. He'd said he would be
available at any hour and look how he'd come running in the
middle of the night.

A low rumble of thunder in the west was followed by a
gust of wind and a splattering of fat raindrops streaked the
window pane. She pulled it closed and turned away. She was

in a new place that *he* didn't know about. She had the help of a detective on whom she could rely. She was safe. As she crossed the living room toward the kitchen, Alyssa's eyes fell on a white slip of paper half-protruding from under the front door. It hadn't been there before. She would have seen it. Stooping, she picked it up.

YOU SHOULDN'T HAVE PUT THE COPS ON ME. YOU'LL BE SORRY.

The words had been cut out of newsprint and pasted to the single sheet.

She thought she had covered her tracks. Alyssa thought by not leaving a forwarding address at the old place or even informing the post office, she had made it impossible for him to trace her. But, of course, she'd had to tell the moving company where she was going. She'd forgotten about that.

He hadn't.

CHAPTER FIVE

The rain stopped early but it continued gray. Dark clouds scudded ominously across the sky driven by gusting winds, then cleared to reveal patches of blue. Gary Reissig's mood was as changeable—about the case, about Lurene—depressed and then optimistic by turns. As it was a Sunday, the squad room was quiet. Of the detectives on duty most were out on assignment; those there were plodding through their Fives—supplementary detailed reports. Gary studied a photostat of the note Alyssa Hanriot had turned over to him.

"The lab can't get far with this," he complained to Dogali. "The letters were cut out of *Time* and *New York Magazine*."

"Upper class," his partner commented.

"They were pasted with ordinary mucilage on ordinary typewriter paper. Whoever did it wore gloves."

"She could have put it together herself."

"Ah, come on! Why should she do that?"

"She's scared. She wants help. She wants protection. You told her you need hard evidence, something tangible. Something you can show the captain. Presto, she's providing it."

"You don't believe that."

"I'm not ruling it out. I know one thing for sure—she likes you."

"What?"

"She likes you. She wants you around."

"For God's sake, Marc, I just got married."

"She doesn't know that. Or maybe she doesn't care."

"She's not that kind."

Dogali grinned. "If you say so."

Gary scowled. Alyssa Hanriot had called him at home again last night about the note and he'd gone over right away. It hadn't been late, but Lurene had been annoyed all the same, even though he'd returned promptly. Lurene had stayed annoyed for a hell of a long time, he thought ruefully. "Yeah, I say so. The girl is scared, mixed up, but I don't think she's fabricating evidence."

"You think it was Easlick?"

After she'd turned over the note to Detective Reissig, Alyssa felt better. Still, she slept only fitfully. She would look back on that restless night with longing.

Waking on that gray Sunday she was still tired but buoyed with the optimism of a new day and of her own youth. Her new assignment would start tomorrow. Today she could sleep late, have a leisurely breakfast, and spend the balance of the day unpacking. By two, she was more or less settled and decided to do some marketing. She put on slacks and a bulky Norwegian sweater her mother had knitted for her and went downstairs. The clouds had cleared but the wind was still brisk. She decided to try the new shopping mall within walking distance.

Though the mall was small, the market was very large. As Alyssa wandered up and down the wide aisles familiarizing herself with the layout, she began to sense she was being watched. She looked around examining the faces and got some curious, resentful, out-and-out nasty looks back. She flushed. She was developing a persecution complex, she thought. It had to stop.

But the feeling wouldn't go away. Finally, as she stood in the checkout line, she spotted him as he was going out through the automatic doors. Tall, dark, carrying two full brown grocery bags, one in each arm. She saw him only for a couple of seconds and in profile. Nevertheless, she was riveted to the spot.

"Lady? You want to move it?" The man behind her dumped two six packs of Miller Lite on the counter and yelled into her ear.

Alyssa didn't hear; she was watching *him* get into a sporty maroon convertible with the top up. She watched through the store window as the car went past.

"Come on, lady! You in a trance or something? You're holding up the whole line."

By this time Alyssa Hanriot had learned something about how the police worked. She didn't rush right out to the nearest phone to contact Gary Reissig, and she certainly had more sense than to disturb him at home again. Last night her call had been answered by his wife, and though he had been very nice when he came on, sympathetic and kind as ever, she knew she had imposed. So what should she do now? What had happened, after all? Nothing. She wasn't even absolutely sure the man she had seen was Easlick. She hadn't got more than a glimpse of him, and a lot of time had passed since she'd sat in the witness box and pointed at him.

But suppose it was him. What could she complain of? He'd been shopping like her and everybody else. Maybe he'd spotted her, maybe he hadn't. One thing was sure: he couldn't have known she'd turn up in that particular market. She hadn't known herself where she'd be shopping. A new chill coursed through her—unless he had been watching outside the apartment and followed her.

No. That would have meant sitting out front all morning. Not likely. If she were to contact Gary Reissig, these were the points he would make.

So she walked home again. When she got upstairs there were two brown grocery bags on the floor in front of her door. Putting her own things down, she looked inside. Rat poison. Two bags full of boxes of rat poison marked with the skull and crossbones. Clipped to the side of one bag was another note made up of cutout letters.

WATCH WHAT YOU EAT

She went downstairs and threw everything she had purchased into the trash. Then she went to another store, made sure *he* wasn't around, and did the marketing all over again.

After that she saw him everywhere, or thought she did. It was always at a distance, in a crowd. He never tried to approach her. At night, he called. He might start early and call every hour, then skip two or three hours while she twisted and turned in bed waiting. Or he might not start till long after midnight. Varying the patterns, he kept her off balance.

She notified the telephone company. They offered to change her number. She said she'd already done that.

They suggested she contact the police.

She'd already done that.

On top of everything, Theo disappeared. It wasn't unusual. He wasn't neutered and he had his urges. He went, but inevitably he came back, sometimes after several days, sometimes hungry, sometimes overfed, but always content. Alyssa worried because this was a new neighborhood and he might not find his way. She asked around, called the pound, put notices on telephone poles.

Though she tried to hide it, she was nervous and edgy and knew she wasn't making a good impression on the new job. She couldn't go on like this. But she consoled herself with the thought that Neil would be back at the end of the week and wasn't even aware of the irony of being dependent on him. On the third night, the calls stopped at midnight. Of course, she couldn't know that they wouldn't resume, so she lay in the dark, tense and waiting, till finally out of sheer exhaustion she dropped off. At seven in the morning she was jolted awake by the dreaded jangling.

Wearily, sleep sodden and hopeless, she reached for the receiver and held it to her ear without a word, like a subject under hypnosis obeying a command. Remembering how angry her silence made him, she spoke.

"Hello."

"Hello? Allie? Is that you, Allie?"

"Neil? Yes, yes, it's me. Oh, Neil, it's so good to hear your voice."

"I tried all night to call you; well, actually I stopped at midnight your time. I kept getting a busy signal."

She hesitated. It wasn't an easy thing to explain. "There's been trouble on the line."

"I figured that. Listen, honey. I've got good news and I've got bad. The good news is everything's going great. I've signed three new accounts. The bad news is I won't be coming home for another few days."

"Oh, Neil. I was counting on having you back."

There was a slight pause while Jaros recovered from the surprise at the open need she expressed. At another time he might have found it gratifying. "Believe me, I don't want to stay another week, but what can I do? What can I tell my boss—my girlfriend can't do without me?" He chuckled.

It wasn't like him to be openly lascivious. "I need you, Neil." It wasn't like her to plead.

"What's wrong? Something wrong, Allie? There's a problem?"

"No, no. Nothing. You stay as long as you have to."

"That's my girl. I knew you'd understand. I can always count on you. Okay then, I've got to get going; the limo's downstairs waiting to take the bunch of us out to the client's plant. Glad your line's fixed. I'll call you tonight."

"No, don't do that." She spoke instinctively.

"Why not? You're going to be home, aren't you?"

"I—I thought I'd go to a movie," she sighed.

"Oh. Well, I'll take my chances. Love you. Got to run."

She couldn't get back to sleep. She had no commitment till the evening when she was giving a class in yoga, but she'd intended to research the origin of a folk dance she was adding to the adult session. Might as well get an early start. All the while she dressed, she listened for the next call, but the phone remained silent. She ate breakfast with reasonable appetite. It wasn't over, she knew that, but the short respite had done her good. As soon as she opened the front door on her way out and saw the white box tied with red ribbon, her heart sank.

Tears welled up as she bent to pick it up. She knew what was inside.

One of the flyers she had posted on poles and in windows around the neighborhood covered him like a shroud. *Lost: male cat, black and gray, white stockings. Reward*. With a felt-tipped pen she had boldly printed her new telephone number. Why not? He knew it already.

Alyssa wept. All the tears she'd held back for two weeks. Was it only two weeks since the horror began? She sobbed, wracking, convulsive spasms, till she couldn't cry anymore. Then she replaced the lid on the box and carried her pet to the station house.

Detective Reissig was out.

"I'll wait," she told the desk sergeant.

"It might be a long time," Sergeant Reilly liked to keep the area clear. Unless a civilian had specific, urgent business Reilly didn't want him hanging around. But he was a kind man and Alyssa Hanriot was obviously much distressed. "Want to tell me what it's about?"

"I'll wait." She went over to the nearest bench and sat holding the small box on her lap. She rested one hand on it as though to console the small, beloved pet inside.

Sergeant Reilly eyed the box and her, but said no more.

People came and went; police, civilians. Some looked at Alyssa with curiosity, most ignored her. In this place it took a lot to attract attention and more to hold it. Alyssa had no interest in what went on around her. She sat stolidly through the parade prepared to wait the whole day if necessary.

"Miss Hanriot?"

She woke with a start. She couldn't believe she'd actually fallen asleep. However, she wasn't at all disoriented; she knew exactly where she was and why she'd come. The man who stood over her was ruddy-faced, with bushy red hair and a square-cut beard. Marconi Dogali, Gary Reissig's partner.

She looked terrible, Marc thought. When he'd first met Alyssa Hanriot she was still in the hospital and allowing for a natural listlessness, he'd thought her nice-looking in a quiet, understated way. Not his type, but she had her points, one of them those big, dark eyes that now looked haunted. And she was even thinner now than she had been. She seemed to be on the edge of a nervous break-down. "Can I help?" he asked.

"I'm waiting for Detective Reissig."

"He's out on a case. It may take all day. He has your number. Why don't you go home and he'll call you."

She shook her head. "I want to show him something." Instinctively her hold on the box tightened and she looked down.

Dogali's eyes followed hers and he decided he wouldn't ask to see whatever it was. He felt sorry for her and because she didn't make a further appeal, he wanted all the more to help her. "Listen, I'll try to reach out for him. I'll tell him you're here. Okay?"

"Thank you."

She didn't know how much longer she sat there—an hour or all afternoon—she wasn't wearing a watch. If she'd cared, there was a clock on the wall around the corner, or she could have gauged the passage of time by the slant of the sun through the grimy window. All she knew was that Gary Reissig was standing in front of her and looking down.

"Alyssa. Are you all right?"

Her eyes filled, but she held back the tears. "I am now." She raised the box and held it out to him.

"Let's go upstairs." He helped her up, put a hand on her elbow to guide her along the hall and to the elevator. They rose in silence. He passed by the squad room and chose instead one of the interrogation cubicles. Not cheerful, but it was evident she was totally unaware of her surroundings. The need was for privacy.

Alyssa walked directly to the scarred table and gently laid down the small box with its sad content. Silently, she removed the cover, and still not speaking took the paper that covered the little body and handed it to Reissig.

Gary stared at the dead cat. "I'm so sorry, Alyssa. I'm so very sorry." Then he read the flyer. "There was nothing besides this? No other message?"

"No."

"Okay, Alyssa—do you mind if I call you Alyssa?"

"My friends call me Allie."

"I want to be your friend, Allie. I'm going to get this guy —whoever he is. Before anything else, though, I want to make sure you're not bothered anymore. I want you to get some rest without worrying. Is there anybody that can come and stay with you for a while? A friend, a relative?"

She shook her head.

"How about a neighbor?"

"I just moved into the building. I don't know anybody. My neighbor, where I lived before, she has a couple of kids; she couldn't leave them. My boyfriend is out on the Coast on business."

"Okay. You wait here for a few minutes. I'm going to see what I can do."

Captain Boykin was sympathetic but adamant.

"I can't assign a guard because the creep killed her cat!" He shook his head in frustration. "We don't even know for sure he's the one who did it."

"Who else?" Gary responded. "He's trying to terrorize her, Captain. And succeeding. It's all part of a campaign. Why don't you come and talk to her? She's right on the edge."

"I have no doubt she is, but what can I do? She says he's harassing her. He denies it. He says he hasn't been near her. Who are we going to believe? Unfortunately, his word is as good as hers."

"Not to me it isn't," Gary retorted without hesitation. "He's a convicted child molester; she's a decent citizen. She's more; she's a decent citizen who had the guts to stand up and give evidence. There aren't too many of those. If you give me a choice, Captain, I'll take Alyssa Hanriot."

"Shit," Boykin muttered.

"We owe her, Captain," Reissig pressed. "She did her duty and she was led to believe Easlick would be locked up for a good long time. Now suddenly he's out. Naturally, she's scared. Whether it's him or somebody else we owe her protection."

"Suppose, for the sake of argument, I say okay? Suppose I assign somebody? For how long?"

For as long as it takes, Reissig wanted to shout, but he

couldn't say it. It was unrealistic and he knew it. "Let me and Marc tail Easlick. Let us tail him so he'll know we're doing it. Maybe it'll scare him enough to give up."

"You've already warned him," Boykin pointed out. "Look, I feel an obligation to this girl the same as you. It's all very well to say she's a decent citizen and he's a convicted felon, but you know how far that goes in a court. His past record probably wouldn't even be admitted as evidence."

"If she's the victim . . ."

"It could serve as motive, but you can't base your accusation on it. Unless you can get me proof Easlick is the man who attacked Hanriot in the basement of the Senior Citizens' Center, or some hard evidence that he's the one harassing her, stalking her, making overt threats . . ." Boykin shrugged.

"Suppose this guy get tired of playing games?"

The two cops stared at each other.

"He doesn't have the guts," Boykin stated flatly. "None of the perverts do."

"Sometimes they get desperate. He has already attacked Hanriot once."

Boykin took a deep breath. "Okay. Okay, if you can get one of the women to stay with Hanriot for a few nights, go ahead. On her own time, you understand."

Gary ran all over the house. Every female officer in the station had an excuse. He didn't listen. As soon as he saw the look, he moved on. Then he got on the phone and contacted women who weren't on duty—at their homes, beauty parlors, wherever. The pitch over the telephone had less chance of success than a personal appeal. Gary knew it, but doggedly went through the roster.

"Why don't you do it yourself?" Dogali suggested.

"Me?"

"Why not? You can sack out on her couch. I'd do it, but Jan's dance class is giving a recital and I promised to be there. I'm available for tomorrow night though."

Gary thought about it. He wouldn't have to tell Lurene he was doing it on his own time. Let her think it was an assignment. That wasn't right; that wasn't the way to start a marriage. Whom else could he call?

He knew, had known from the start. Norah. Norah Mulcahaney. Not that he expected her to move in with Allie. A lieutenant couldn't be expected to take on such an assignment, but Norah would know somebody. All Norah Mulcahaney would have to do would be to indicate what she wanted and there were people who would run to oblige her.

Gary stared at the phone. He and Norah had broken up almost two months to the day before he married Lurene Benoit. He was dismayed at how promptly the date presented itself. The rest of the chronology flashed up on the screen of memory like a computer readout. Gary Reissig met Norah Mulcahaney about a year and a half ago. She'd been Sergeant Mulcahaney then. He remembered the day she walked into the squad room. Vividly. It had been a day in late July about a year and a half ago—a hot day, a beach day. She'd driven out from Manhattan in typically heavy traffic and the sheen of perspiration made her lightly tanned skin glow. She was late and afraid she'd missed him.

Of course, he'd been told to expect her and he'd waited. Sergeant Mulcahaney was looking for a possible link between a murder committed in the Fourth Zone Homocide Division, her jurisdiction, and a recent knifing in the area of the 101, his. He had been ordered to offer all possible cooperation. That was unusual enough to pique his curiosity, so Gary had asked around about her. Norah Mulcahaney, he learned, had been on the force then eight years, made detective in two and sergeant in four. True, she'd been lucky in catching cases that attracted public attention, but nobody who knew her record could deny she had handled them professionally and with something more—call it flair. Of course, he'd waited.

She'd surveyed the room and headed straight to his desk.

He remembered the brightness of her hyacinth eyes, the rich dark luster of her hair, long and tied back with a coral ribbon that matched her sleeveless linen dress. He also remembered the set of her square jaw. Maybe that wasn't the exact moment Gary Reissig fell in love, but it was close enough. They'd met in July of one year and he'd proposed in May of the next. It was the night Norah Mulcahaney was promoted to lieutenant. He'd proposed and she'd turned him down. He hadn't seen her since.

Be honest, Gary chided himself, Norah had tried to leave the door open; he was the one who had slammed it shut. He had wanted a definite response, yes or no, no temporizing. Was it because he felt inferior in their professsional relationship that he'd needed to assert himself in their private life? Even now he couldn't be sure. But it had been the right move. If he hadn't made a clean break with Norah, he would never have found Lurene. He would never have wandered into that bar. Gary didn't spend much time in bars; his father's history was a deterent. His father had been a heavy drinker and it killed him. Nothing could be proved. The way the detectives had reconstructed the tragedy—one of the pumps at the gas station where Charley Reissig worked was defective, leaking at the base. Somebody had dropped a cigarette. Had to be Charley; he was the only one there. The underground tank was ignited and everything including Charley went up. There weren't enough pieces to do a blood alcohol test, but in his heart Gary believed that if his father had been sober, he would have noticed the leak and wouldn't have been smoking.

Lonely after his first wife's death, the loneliness deeper and blacker after Norah's turndown, Gary found himself slipping into the habit of a few drinks after work. Reaching, seeking, and finding refuge in the artificial conviviality. He believed Lurene saved him. She was working as a cocktail waitress in one of his regular spots, but she didn't belong there. Lurene Benoit was twenty-four, nearly fifteen years younger than Gary. She had perfect ivory skin, dark eyes, and pale silver-blonde hair. She had come up from New Orleans for a modeling or acting career. She had been doing rounds, answering calls, auditioning since she was twenty and she was smart enough to know she wasn't getting anywhere: Time was running out. She had to think of the future. She was what Gary had been looking for, what he needed, what his children needed. Sometimes, when he woke up in the night and looked at her lying beside him, he could hardly believe his good fortune.

Gary hadn't even had professional contact with Norah

Mulcahaney since their breakup. As they worked not only out of different precincts but in different counties, it was not likely they'd run into each other, but there remained the possibility of meeting at some police function. It hadn't happened yet. He'd fantasized about the possibility. There were no grudges, certainly not on his side and he knew Norah well enough to be sure she wouldn't hold any. Meeting by accident was one thing, but going to her for help? Was he ready to take the first step? Actually, all he would be doing would be asking for a professional favor. Norah was his last hope of getting someone to stay with Allie. He could not out of his own personal pride refuse to explore it. He picked up the phone.

"Lieutenant Mulcahaney, please. Detective Reissig of the One-Oh-One."

Maybe she wasn't in. Maybe she was busy on another line, or in conference, he thought, ready to hang up.

"Gary!" Norah's voice came over the wire eager, warm as ever. "What a nice surprise. How are you?"

"I'm fine. How are you?"

"Good. Very good."

There was a pause, awkward for both of them. Norah took the initiative.

"It's nice to hear from you, but I'm sure you have a reason for calling. What can I do for you?"

Gary knew he was blushing and was glad Norah couldn't see it. "I need a favor."

"If I can do it, I will."

Suddenly, it was easy. It was like old times. He plunged into an account of the case. "On October seventeenth a young woman, Alyssa Hanriot, was assaulted in the basement of the Senior Citizens' Center in Far Rockaway. Attacked and nearly killed. She couldn't identify her assailant, she couldn't even give a general description because the lights were out, turned off at the main power source. However, a few days later, while she was still in the hospital, a man called and claimed responsibility."

Norah was immediately interested. "Who did he call? The police?"

"No, her, Alyssa. He called her, but he didn't give his name."

Though Norah said nothing, he could feel her intensity.

"The man did allude to a link between them," Gary went on. "About two years ago, Hanriot gave evidence against one Roy Easlick, charged with child molestation. Due largely to her testimony, he was convicted. Now he's out on parole. Easlick, if that's who it is, has continued to harass Alyssa with more phone calls. He follows her, sends threatening letters. She needs protection. Officially, the captain says we can't spare anybody; we don't have the manpower. I can't do it. But the girl is terrified, Norah. She's alone. She has no family, neighbors, or friends. I've tried everybody I know to get someone to stay with her for a while. I didn't want to bother you, but honestly I don't know where else to turn."

"You did the right thing," Norah assured him. "Too bad you didn't call a couple of days sooner. I would have had the perfect person for you—my roommate, Audrey Jordan. She would have been glad to do it. Unfortunately she left for California to visit her folks."

"That's a shame." So Norah had a roommate now, Gary thought. He was surprised. All this time he'd been thinking of Norah and visualizing her—alone. No, admit it: he had been thinking of her as—lonely. Missing him. Brooding. Whereas she had made a normal adjustment to their breakup. Well, so had he. This was the moment to tell Norah he was married. Tell her about Lurene. It wasn't right to keep silent, but somehow the words stuck in his throat. And Norah was talking.

"I do know somebody else who might be available: Delia Cowan; she's on anticrime. She's a good officer and compassionate. But you can only have her for one night. That should give you time to make other arrangements. Okay, Gary?"

The moment had passed. "Yes, Norah. Yes and thanks. I appreciate this."

"Any time," she said. "Any time at all." Then she hung up.

So it was over, Gary thought. Finished. After three and a half months of marriage it had taken a casual, impersonal exchange over the telephone to put it to rest. He could finally forget Norah Mulcahaney.

In her office, Norah sat, chin resting in the palm of her right hand, and stared at the telephone. She hadn't thought about Gary for months. The sound of his voice had brought back all sorts of memories and emotions. It was good that the call had not been personal, good for both of them. That he could turn to her professionally and she could respond meant that they had both got over—whatever there had been between them.

The case was intriguing, she thought, and obviously Gary was more emotionally involved with it and with the victim's plight than he wanted to admit. Gary didn't usually allow himself to get involved.

Suddenly, Gary remembered that he'd left Alyssa Hanriot alone in the interrogation room for nearly an hour. He jumped to his feet.

"I'm sorry," he said, bursting in. "I was trying to find someone to stay with you for a few days, but we're short-handed. Everybody's carrying a heavy load. However, I did get a policewoman for one night."

"Thank you."

Her meekness stung Gary.

"One night or one week, it is only a temporary solution. As soon as you're alone, he's going to start again."

She dropped her head.

"What we have to do is make him stop for good." Gary put on a show of confidence and energy that he hoped would give Allie strength. "We're going to get the evidence that we need to make a case. But you're going to have to help and that means you're going to have to hang tough, but not for long."

He reached out and took the girl's hands in his. "I know you can do it."

CHAPTER SIX

The next day, Reissig signed out the equipment, an automatic telephone answering machine, then took it over to Alyssa's place. He set it up for her, showed her how to use it, and supervised the recording of the message it was to deliver.

"This is Alyssa Hanriot. I am not able to answer the telephone just now. Please leave a message and I'll get back to you. Start speaking at the sound of the beep. Thank you."

"Don't answer the phone yourself at any time," he instructed. "Not in the day nor at night. Let the machine take over. You'll hear who's calling and if you decide it's someone you want to talk to, you can cut right in." He showed her how to do that. "The caller will have two choices: he can hang up or he can leave a message. Leaving a message will be very foolish because then we'll have a tape not only of what he says but of his voice. We can get a voiceprint from Easlick and compare the two. A match will be as valid in court as fingerprints."

"Suppose he decides not to leave a message, not to speak?" Alyssa asked.

"Probably that's what will happen. In that case, he may keep the phone ringing all night as he has in the past. You're going to have to put up with it. Put plugs in your ears, turn up the television, whatever. But under no circumstances take the receiver off the hook; we want a record of the number of times and the frequency that constitutes harassment. It won't be for long. I promise you."

She was white and pinched, but her voice remained steady. "I understand."

"Good girl. My feeling is after tonight you won't be hearing from him anymore."

"I hope so." At that her voice quavered. "Thank you for everything."

"I wish . . ." Gary frowned as he looked around. He knew she had just moved in and that was why the walls were bare, no carpet had been put down; there was an absence of those personal mementoes that give character to a room. The glow of the lamps should have given comfort against the night outside. Somehow, they didn't. There was no sense of *home*, and Gary hesitated to leave Allie Hanriot not only physically but emotionally alone without anyone to even look in on her during the long, anxious hours ahead. He could move her over to his house for a few days, he thought. God knew there was plenty of space. But what would Lurene say to that? How would she treat Allie? After all, Lurene was a bride of three months with plenty of adjustments still to make. It wouldn't be fair to bring a stranger into her house.

"Listen, how about I stay over with you tonight? You do everything like we planned, but I'll just be here to give you moral support?"

Alyssa stared at him. "I don't know what to say. I don't know how to thank you."

"You don't have to thank me."

"But I can't accept. If you stay tonight, I'll still have to face the same situation tomorrow."

"It won't be the same. We're hoping to end it tonight. That's the idea."

"I know, but I'd still be waiting for that phone to ring. Even if it didn't, I'd still face the possibility—alone. Sooner or later, I'm going to have to face it alone."

He sighed. "Well, if you're sure . . ."

"I don't like it, but I'm sure."

She had guts, Reissig thought. He was also relieved. "I could wait outside in the car."

She shook her head. "Go home. Forget about me."

Alyssa Hanriot made herself dinner, an omelet and a salad, and had to force the light meal down. She was too nervous to read, watch television, certainly to sleep. Fully dressed, she sat on the sofa facing the telephone and waited.

The first call came at 9:00 P.M. Her whole body twitched. The instinct was to jump up, grab the phone, and stop it ringing. She didn't move. It rang the three programed times, then she heard the click and her own voice responding with the metallic echoing quality of a recording.

"Start speaking at the sound of the beep. Thank you."

She held her breath, but there was only the hum of the recorder. After what seemed an interminable time, the connection was broken.

The caller had hung up.

She went limp. Her breath—she only realized then that she'd been holding her breath—went out of her lungs in a rush. Tears sprang into her eyes and rolled down her cheeks. She was shaking. She got up and went into the kitchen for a glass of wine. She was pouring it when the phone rang again. She tensed, turned icy as she listened.

"Start speaking at the sound of the beep. Thank you."

Again a pause filled by the whirr of the recording spool. He hung up. Quickly this time.

Alyssa laughed.

She finished pouring the wine and drank. She drank the whole glass right off, poured another, and carried it back with her to the living room. She sat down facing the phone to wait some more.

The next call didn't come till an hour later. Precisely. Same routine. Alyssa listened to her own recorded voice repeating its message and waited, but with much less tension. He hung up almost immediately. Alyssa laughed louder. She was beginning to enjoy herself.

From then on he called every half hour. She stayed where

she was, relaxed and waiting for the routine to play itself out. Again. She laughed louder and louder.

By 4:00 A.M. she was starting to laugh as soon as the phone rang, before her recorded voice responded. She laughed wildly through the whole sequence.

Gottcha!

The relief and attendant euphoria lasted into the next morning and through her first assignment at the junior high that afternoon. It went well. The sun streamed into the big gymnasium; the children were responsive and seemed to enjoy themselves. Alyssa was very much aware of the presence of the assistant principal at the back of the stands erected for that night's basketball game, and gratified when Mrs. Gebhardt came forward later to compliment her. She was elated, with a sense of accomplishment, as she started for the locker room.

"Miss Hanriot?"

A boy in football uniform called from the far end of the corridor.

"Yes?"

"A man gave me this for you."

Even then she had no premonition. She accepted the envelope and opened it. She unfolded the sheet. Cold sweat broke out over the sweat of her recent exercise.

YOU'LL BE SORRY

The letters were cut out and pasted in the familiar fashion. For a moment she stood immobilized. When she looked up the corridor was empty. She ran to the end and caught sight of a boy in football uniform passing through the exit to the practice field.

There were three separate teams working out—at least they were differentiated by their colors. His wore green and white. And he was small. She remembered wondering why in the world he was going out for football in the first place. So now she thought she'd have no trouble picking him out.

"Are you the one who just handed me this note?"

"Yes, ma'am."

"How did you know it was for me? There's no name on it."

"The man said it was for Miss Hanriot, the teacher direct-ing the folk dancing in the gym. He gave me five dollars to deliver it."

"What did he look like? Can you describe him?"

The child, he really looked too young even for junior high, considered. "He was old. As old as my dad. About your age maybe."

In spite of herself Alyssa smiled. "What's your name?"

"James Reed."

"All right, James, now tell me—did you ever see this man before?" The boy shook his head. "Would you know him if you saw him again?"

James answered promptly. "Oh, sure."

But would he? Alyssa wondered. Under pressure? On the witness stand? She knew only too well the strain that kind of testimony involved. She thanked James Reed and put the note in her handbag. She had not been so casual with the earlier messages. She had handled those by the edges, careful not to smudge fingerprints or destroy other possible clues. That kind of thing was for the movies and television, not real life, she thought as she walked along the perimeter of the playing fields to the parking lot. There was a light breeze that drove small fleets of puffy clouds across the brilliant sky; a salt sea tang wafted across the marshes. She should have known he wouldn't be defeated so easily.

So should Gary Reissig. She'd have to call him, Alyssa thought as she got into her ancient Volkswagen. No rush though. When she got home. She turned on the ignition.

The explosion rattled the car. It was like a backfire but bigger and louder, followed by billowing smoke that seeped from the seams of the hood into the body of the car. The smell was foul. An intense foul smell. The smoke and the stench filled the car. A stink bomb.

Coughing and gagging, Alyssa got out and ran for the edge of a stand of pines to get some clean air. Doubled over as she was, with eyes tearing, she nevertheless became aware of an-other car starting up and pulling out to the street. She straight-ened up in time to catch a glimpse of a maroon convertible, top up, with a dark-haired man at the wheel. The gray in his hair was more evident than on other occasions and he was wearing sunglasses.

"A kid's prank. A kid's Halloween prank," Captain Boykin said.

"Halloween isn't till tomorrow," Gary pointed out. "Besides, she's not only new at the school, she's not even a part of the regular faculty. Why would kids pull a stunt like that on her? How would they even know which car was hers?"

Boykin opened his palms in a gesture of frustration. "The point is, nothing's changed. He still hasn't laid a hand on her. He hasn't physically injured her."

"Except the first time."

"We don't know that was the same man."

Gary didn't say anything.

"We can't put every witness who ever testifies in a trial under protective custody."

"We do it for the organized crime people. We've got a whole Federal Witness Protection Program for them," he pointed out with considerable bitterness. "That involves millions of dollars. All Alyssa Hanriot did was nail a child molester."

"Sure, and I respect and admire her for it. She did us all a favor, and they should never have let the creep out. But my hands are tied. I told you before and I tell you again, bring me some evidence Easlick is the one responsible for all this and at least we can get him on violation of parole. Maybe. At the last count there were fifty-eight thousand prisoners out on parole and two thousand officers responsible for them." He sighed. "Hell, we can try."

The answer, as they both very well knew, was to put Allie under surveillance around the clock. Tail her, watch who approached her, keep a record. Reissig could do it on his own time, but who would take over while he was on duty? Not Dogali, he worked the same shift. Gary didn't even bother to ask for one of them to be switched. He had another idea.

He got Allie a camera—a small automatic Canon FM35, easy to use, and not requiring any special expertise.

"Obviously, now that he can't terrorize you by phone, he intends to increase his personal appearances. So whenever you see him, you stop, face him, and take his picture."

She looked hopeless and forlorn.

"Can you do that, Allie?"

"I suppose so."

"When's that boyfriend of yours coming back?"

"Next week. Thursday or Friday maybe."

Damn, Gary thought. It was on the tip of his tongue to say: Move in with us for a while. We've got plenty of space. What he couldn't say was: My wife would be glad to have you. He sighed. Norah had made it very clear that she could help him out for one night only. He couldn't call her again. Captain Boykin was right: You couldn't baby-sit every witness that ever gave evidence.

Alyssa accepted the camera from Gary Reissig, but she had no intention of using it. She was sure she wouldn't be quick enough or get a clear enough shot. Even if she did, they'd think of some other reason for saying it wasn't good enough to get Easlick put away. She stowed the camera in her bureau drawer. It was of no use to her. What she needed was a gun.

CHAPTER SEVEN

She'd heard it was easy to get a gun, but she had no idea how to go about it. You could buy just about everything on the street, they said. What street? In Harlem, 116th Street was supposed to be an open-air supermarket for drugs and guns of all kinds. But she was afraid to go there.

She'd seen pushers around the local schools prowling the perimeters. Deals went on in the open with little or no subterfuge—no one did anything about it, herself included. It seemed hopeless to try. That was one of the reasons she had been determined to stand up in court against Easlick. It was a chance to do something that would have direct impact. She had been a heroine then. The DA had commended her. And now? Now she was on her own. What she needed to know was: Here, in this elite section of suburbia, were they selling guns along with the drugs? And how could she, an adult and one of the enemy, buy one?

The next morning, Alyssa Hanriot approached the school warily, stopping a block away to observe. Situated on a high grassy knoll, the three-story red brick building with its beige colonnaded entranceway was imposing. The faculty and student parking lots flanked it; tennis courts, athletic fields, and running track were at the rear. The whole complex was enclosed with chain-link fencing. Futile. The gate stood wide open most of the time. Open or closed, it didn't make any difference, she thought, watching the private cars and buses empty and the students stream inside.

"What's your pleasure, dollface?"

The voice was soft, insinuating, and right in her ear. Alyssa jumped. "Nothing." She knew she was flushing. "I mean, I don't want any drugs."

"So what do you want?"

He was no high-school kid, but he was young—say nineteen or twenty. Hispanic. He wore a fine suede leather jacket of a cream so pale and buttery-looking she wanted to reach out and touch it. His large, dark, liquid eyes were shaded by the wide brim of a beige fedora. He was handsome, Alyssa thought—surprised at herself for noticing.

"I want to buy a gun," she blurted.

"Yeah? What for?" Quickly he held up a manicured hand. "Don't tell me, doll. I really don't want to know. Anyway, I don't deal guns."

"Oh." It hadn't been easy to tell him what she wanted. "Maybe you could suggest where I could get one?"

He looked her over with amusement.

"It's for protection."

"Sure." Then he decided. "Maybe I know somebody who could help you. But I'm in business. You got to pay me something—what do they call it? A finder's fee. Yeah, right." He snickered.

"Of course, of course." She fumbled in her purse, located her wallet, and fished out a ten-dollar bill.

"You got to be kidding. You call that money?"

She swallowed and added a twenty.

"If that's the best you can do. The piece is going to run you ten times this."

Alyssa gasped.

"And don't try to pay by credit card, okay?" He was laughing out loud as he went to a phone booth on the corner to contact his friend.

* * *

Alyssa's instructions were simple: drive to the subway station in Far Rockaway, park in the lot across the street, wait.

She was very nervous, not only because of the illegality of the transaction and the amount of money she was carrying—she'd gone to the bank to draw it out—but because of the area.

Downtown Far Rockaway was a slum. First the middle class had fled, then the merchants who had served it and been supported by it. The gutted buildings, the boarded-up stores, the dirt, and neglect were urban blight at its saddest and most frightening. Amid the remnants of a once thriving community, idle gangs stood on street corners or roamed aimlessly. The subway station was the end of the line from Manhattan. It was relatively safe during rush hours morning and evening when used by commuters. In between, it became one of the highest crime sites in the system. Alyssa was grateful she had been told to stay in her car.

It was warm for October and the sun beat on the metal roof, yet she kept the windows up tight and sweated. She was sorry she'd ever started this thing. She was about to turn the key in the ignition and drive away when there was a tap at the rear. She turned in the seat. A black man not much older than the dealer at the school stood beside her car door. He was dressed in similar style but not so expensively. Apparently guns weren't as much in demand as drugs. He indicated she should roll down the window.

"Waiting for somebody?" He leaned an elbow casually on the sill.

"Yes, I am."

He continued to stare at her, assessing her. "I don't have the merchandise you want," he told her finally.

"Oh."

Suddenly, he grinned. "Don't be upset, lady. I can connect you with somebody who does." The grin broadened. "It'll cost you."

She sighed. "How much?"

"How much did you bring?" At the look on her face he guffawed heartily. "Ten percent, ten percent of the price, lady. Same as you gave my buddy, Vanilla."

It was a good name for him, Alyssa thought as she reached for the handbag on the seat beside her. Starting to pull at the zipper she noted a group of young blacks standing on the far end of the lot. They were watching. What was to stop them from coming over and just taking her money? What was to stop this man, leaning so indolently at the car window, from reaching over and grabbing the envelope stuffed with cash out of her hand?

"Don't worry, sweetheart, I'm not going to rip you off. Nobody is. This is business. You'll get what you pay for." Then he added, "Maybe you'll recommend us to a friend?" He waved toward the group and one of them—older, heavier, not smiling—sauntered over. When he got close the two men shifted places. The new man slipped his left hand inside his jacket and showed Alyssa the butt of the weapon.

"This what you're looking for?"

Alyssa's eyes widened. It was black and evil-looking. She gulped. "Yes." She reached.

"Not so fast. Four-fifty."

"I was told three hundred."

"You were told wrong."

"Three-fifty is all I have."

He scowled. There was a long moment when she thought that after all this she wasn't going to even get the gun. Then at a look from the first man, the seller relaxed. "You got moxie, lady. Okay, today's bargain day for you. Sold for three-fifty."

Alyssa licked her lips. She was disappointed. She almost wished he hadn't sold it to her. "Thank you," she said, handed over the money, and felt, rather than saw, the weapon slide into her hand.

"Wait . . ." she called out after the two men fast distancing themselves from her. "Excuse me. Please . . ."

The young one turned. He came back on the edge of anger. "Now what ?"

"Could you . . . show me how to work it? And . . . where would I get bullets?"

He sighed heavily. "It's already loaded, lady. On the house. Anything else we can do for you?"

* * *

Ed Sagarman came home early as he had been doing since the morning he read in the paper that Roy Easlick was out and free. As he pulled into the driveway of the two-story half-brick, half-shingle colonial, he could hear the girls laughing and shouting in the back, and the slap of the ball as it bounced off the pavement and was batted against the wall. They were playing a version of paddleball and Sagarman unlatched the gate of the stockyard fence enclosing the yard. Nancy and Beth were too excited to notice him so he stood to one side and observed them. Their cheeks were rosy with the nip of November and the exertion of the game. Their blonde hair streamed in the wind. Though born two years apart they were almost the same size and remarkably alike. No one could doubt that they were sisters nor that they were his children. They had inherited his narrow face, high cheekbones, lantern jaw. Not desirable assets for girls, but Ed Sagarman's eyes saw only beauty.

"Hi," he called.

Nancy, the elder, gave the smooth rubber ball one final swat putting it past her sister's reach. "My point, my point!"

Beth had already turned and started for her father. "It doesn't count. I wasn't playing."

Sagarman held out his arms and gathered them both to him. He looked over their heads. "Where's your mother?"

"In the house," Nancy said.

The blood rushed to Sagarman's face and he held the girls very close while he struggled to compose himself. "I think you'd better come inside now too."

"Oh, Daddy!" As always, Nancy spoke for both. "Can we finish the game?"

"Have you done your homework? Homework first."

"It's not fair," Nancy pouted. "We never have any fun."

He was stung. Beth never complained, was never sullen. Sagarman loved both his girls equally, but there was a slight edge in Beth's favor—maybe because she was the younger and after her there would be no more: Fran had spent the last three months when she was carrying Beth in bed; the doctor had warned her she might not survive another pregnancy.

"You know the rules. Come on now." With another hug,

Sagarman gently turned them around and pushed the two ahead of him to the back door and inside up the stairs to their room. When he was sure they were out of earshot, he called to his wife.

"Fran? Frances, where are you?"

"In here. In the kitchen."

The carefree tone of her answer aggravated his anxiety and his anger. He strode in and confronted her. "Do you know where the girls are?" he demanded, seething but keeping his voice low and steady.

"Playing in the backyard," she replied. Suddenly she went white. "They are still there, aren't they?"

"Alone. You left them alone. I told you never to do that. What the hell is the matter with you, Frances? Don't you care?"

Though her color returned, the strain remained etched deep. "They're in our own backyard."

"That doesn't mean they're safe. Somebody has to be with them at all times, watching out for them."

"It's not good, Ed. It's not natural. They sense something's wrong. Don't you see what's happening? We're smothering them. We're not letting them have one minute by themselves or with their friends and they're beginning to sense it and wonder why. They're getting scared. Like before. We can't let that happen."

"Oh, God . . ."

"We mustn't let them see we're scared. Children are smart and they'll figure out why. We can't go on like this."

"No." The anger drained. He pulled out a kitchen chair and slumped into it. "No, we can't."

She sat too, opposite him. "I think we're overreacting. After all, he hasn't approached them. He hasn't been hanging around. He hasn't done anything."

"You sound like the police."

"It's the truth. Sick or crazy, he's not dumb and he's not going to bother us. The girls are getting nervous and I'm going to lose my job if I don't show up for work pretty soon. We've got to get back to normal."

Ed Sagarman sighed heavily. "You're right." He got up and started for the door.

"Where are you going? Dinner's on the stove."

"I'm going to take care of Roy Easlick once and for all."

Alyssa knew the area well. It was actually in Queens but as it bordered on Nassau County near the prestigious town of Lawrence, an enterprising builder had applied for and received permission to call it Lawrence West. The snob appeal of the new designation raised both old and new property values. The street on which the Easlicks lived, mother and son, benefited. Once a dead end, it was now designated a "private street" and renamed Crescent Close. It had become the kind of place in which an unrecognized car would trigger calls to the police. So Alyssa continued past and found a spot a block down on Central where she could park in a line of other cars and not arouse curiosity.

Then she walked back.

Between the Easlick house and the adjoining property there was a low retaining wall and a space hidden by a tall privet hedge. It had not yet dropped its leaves so she could sit on the wall and be shielded both from the neighbors and the house itself. Here she would see Easlick when he returned, but he would not see her. She took the newly purchased gun out of her handbag and placed it in her lap.

CHAPTER EIGHT

It was Saturday morning and Gary and Lurene were stepping out the door as the phone rang. They looked at each other. She didn't want him to answer, but he knew he had to. He walked down the long narrow hall to the kitchen and picked up the receiver of the wall extension. She waited at the front, able to hear his voice but not listening to what he said. She didn't need to. She knew even before he came back, without looking at him.

"You're going in, aren't you?"

"I'm sorry."

It struck her that he was pale, that he looked as though he'd just received a shock, but she was too angry to care. "You'd think they could run that place one day, just one day, without you."

They'd intended to go car shopping. Lurene had glowed with anticipation, and Gary had been looking forward to it too. There was no question that Lurene needed wheels of her own; the argument was between a new and a used car. Certainly, he didn't want her breaking down on the road and he did have a small sum of money from Joyce's estate, a nest egg set aside for emergencies or for the children when they grew up. If he spent it, he could make it up—moonlighting as a

80

security guard in some store or office. He owned this house—inherited it from his parents—and if a real need arose he could always get a mortgage.

"What is it this time?" Lurene demanded.

He pursed his lips for a moment before answering. "Homicide." It was all he was prepared to say at this moment. To say more would risk letting his dismay, his regret, his guilt spill out. And she wouldn't understand.

"Oh." For a moment his wife was impressed, but then she shrugged it off. "Why you? Why does it always have to be you? Don't they have anybody else who could handle it?"

"Because it's my case," he answered. Then after a pause added, "Because I'm responsible."

Having said it, a shudder passed through Gary. He felt the strength which he took so much for granted, the reliability of his body to respond to crisis, draining away. He broke into a cold sweat. Over his twelve years on the Job, seven of them as a detective in a high-crime area, Gary Reissig had learned that it paid to go by the book. Sometimes an interpretation had to be made, the rules bent, but never before had he been faced with a situation in which common sense and compassion called for an action which procedure prohibited. That had been the predicament with regard to Alyssa Hanriot. He had been torn and finally opted to stick by the rules. To play it safe.

And he had made a terrible mistake.

How could Lurene understand? There was no time to try to explain. He leaned over and kissed her cheek. "I'm sorry."

She didn't unbend. "Is this the way it's going to be?"

Her intransigency was the second shock, almost as severe as the first. Joyce had never questioned his obligation to the Job. Norah wouldn't have, naturally, being a police officer herself. Gary had no hesitation about his answer, yet it didn't come easily to his lips.

"Yes," he replied flatly. Then, because of the hostility he saw, he modified it. "As long as I'm a cop."

Her retort was quick and stinging as a whiplash. "Maybe you should look for another job?"

He flinched, then went numb. Now was not the time to

analyze, to discuss. He tossed the keys of the station wagon to her. "Go buy what you want."

Gary Reissig found a cab and went directly to the scene. The special teams that roll on a homicide had already arrived, their marked and unmarked vehicles lined up along both curbs. Uniforms had curious neighbors under control and were keeping the entrance to the apartment building clear. Ben Kuser, medical bag in hand, hurried up the front steps. Gary made no attempt to catch up. His steps were heavy and slow, but inevitably took him to the open door of Alyssa Hanriot's apartment. He spotted Dogali, and Marc, seeing him, came over.

How could it have happened? was the silent question each asked of the other. They had accepted the pattern of harassment, focused on it, and lulled themselves into believing the perpetrator of the threats wouldn't take violent action, that the creep didn't have the guts for murder. They had set aside the fact that he had already come close to it in the basement of the Senior Citizens' Center. No, Gary admitted in a rush of honesty and with another pang of self-blame; not *they* but *he* alone had decided Allie Hanriot was not in real danger. As always, Marc had merely followed his lead.

"We'll get him," Marc murmured.

For all the good it would do Allie, Gary thought, and the two of them made their way through the cops and technicians to the bedroom.

She was the cause of all the activity, yet other than being careful to step over her, they all but ignored her. Alyssa Hanriot was on the floor on the near side of the bed lying partially on her right hip, legs drawn up. Her right arm was outflung and her head nestled against the shoulder. A dark blossom of blood over the left breast marked the wound. She wore a gray sweater and gray slacks with black ripple-soled oxfords. Reissig couldn't see her face because Doc Kuser blocked the view.

Benjamin Kuser was a tall, imposing figure. With his dark hair, white face, large piercing eyes under satanically slanted brows, he presented an intimidating appearance. Till he spoke. Then his breezy humor, his enthusiasm for his work changed the impression. For Ben Kuser pathology was both vocation and hobby. Each case presented a challenge. Nothing was ever routine. He lectured on his cherished subject whenever and wherever he was invited, illustrating his points with slides whose technicolor gore was often too much for his layman audience. Ben Kuser carried all before him, forcing them to accept their own mortality.

While he waited for Doc to complete the preliminary examination, Reissig looked around. The phone was off the hook. He was surprised. They had agreed, he and Allie, that though the calls appeared to have stopped they might resume, so she should continue to use the machine. Unless, of course, she had been making a call herself. Was she attacked before she could complete it? Could she have been calling for help?

"Any sign of forced entry?" he asked Dogali.

"No, but the front door was ajar. That's how we came to be notified. One of her neighbors spotted it."

There were two locks on the door—a standard Lockwood and a deadbolt Medeco. Reissig knew from personal experience that Alyssa Hanriot had been meticulous about securing both. Assume, for the moment, she had admitted the perpetrator; an argument had ensued—signs of struggle were apparent. The bureau top had been swept clean. The scarf that had covered it and all the things on it were scattered on the floor —makeup, an open handbag with its contents spilled out. Some were stained by the blood that had soaked into the hardwood and left a dark stain.

Kuser got to his feet and stepped to one side. "What do you make of that?"

He pointed to a scrawl in what at first looked like red crayon. Reissig got on his knees and immediately spotted the open lipstick that had rolled under the bed. He sat back on his heels and looked toward the bureau. "I'd say she was shot over there. She could have grabbed at the bureau top to keep from falling; she got the scarf instead and pulled everything down with her. Anyway, she went down. The perp fled leaving her for dead. But she wasn't dead. Somehow she managed to crawl to the bedside table to phone for help. The receiver fell out of her hand. The lipstick was within reach. She used it to leave a message." Gary stared for several moments at the red scrawl. "She started, but she couldn't finish."

"It looks to me like an *e* and an *r*," Marc said. "Maybe she started to write Easlick and realized she couldn't finish, so she switched to his first name, and couldn't finish that either."

"Want to take a closer look at the wound, Detectives?" Kuser suggested.

"I noticed the powder burns," Gary said.

Dogali gasped. "You mean she shot herself, then changed her mind and tried to get help?"

For one moment, Gary clutched at that. Then he was ashamed. Even if Allie had committed suicide, the responsibility for the desperation that drove her to it remained, in large part, his. He shook his head. "There's no gun. And suicides don't write messages as after-thoughts. They write before they commit the act." He turned to Kuser. "Can you give us an approximate time of death?"

"From the way she's lying on her right side and the extent of the lividity, I'd say six to seven hours. I'll know better after the autopsy, naturally. You might try to find out if anybody heard the shot."

"Just the one shot?"

"That's what it looks like. One shot and at close range. He must have been right on top of her."

Reissig and Dogali exchanged glances. Alyssa Hanriot would not have let Easlick get near her. She wouldn't have admitted him in the first place. Unless . . . could he have climbed in through the window? Gary examined it. There was a fire escape, but the window was closed and locked. "She was the victim of a previous attack, a knifing," Gary told the ME.

"You think he came back to finish the job?"

"I'd call it a strong possibility."

Kuser gave Reissig a long, hard look. Though he liked to show off his own expertise, he knew when to defer to the detectives. "Okay. I'll pass on anything else I get as soon as I get it. If you've seen all you want . . ."

"I want to make sure we have shots covering the area from the bureau to the body and including the night table and the phone." He waved the photographer over. "We'll need closeups of what she wrote or tried to write. From all angles, Phil."

"Done."

"That's it for me, then, Doc."

He watched as the medics prepared the body bag and went about the business of removing Alyssa Hanriot. He watched till the zipper was pulled up and the straps that secured her to the gurney were fastened. When that was done, he began the business of finding the man who had killed her.

"You said a neighbor found her?" he asked Dogali.

"Right. Little woman down the hall. She was on her way to the incinerator chute when she noticed Miss Hanriot's door ajar. She knocked, but nobody answered. Of course, it was early, 7:00 A.M., and she figured the new tenant might still be sleeping. But she didn't feel comfortable leaving the door like it was. So she pushed it a little further and looked in. She didn't see anything out of the ordinary. She called and nobody answered. Finally, she went in."

"She hear anything in the night? Loud voices? Any kind of disturbance? The shot?"

"She says not. She says this is a fine old building with good thick walls. They don't build them like this anymore, she says."

"Yeah, well, we'll talk to her again after the shock wears off. Maybe she'll have remembered something. We'll talk to all of them."

Miss Molly Bright, the spinster who had found Alyssa Hanriot, seemed in good control when she received the two detectives in her frumpy fourth-floor apartment overlooking the street. She was short and dumpy with huge brown eyes magnified by the thick lenses of her gold-rimmed bifocals. She immediately informed Reissig and Dogali that she was eighty-five, blind as a bat without her glasses but never without them because she had plenty of spares. She also assured them she had all her wits and knew what was going on, you bet. The surge of anticipation that remark caused in Gary was quickly snuffed out. Miss Bright repeated her earlier testimony: She had slept soundly through the night—again crediting the excellent construction of the building as well as her daily constitutional, one mile regardless of weather. She could add nothing.

As usual Dogali deferred to Reissig in the interrogation.

"Have you noticed any strangers hanging around the building recently," Gary asked.

The myopic brown eyes glittered. "You mean since the girl moved in. No."

Molly Bright lived up to her name, Marc thought, and shared a moment of appreciation for her sharpness with his partner. When asked whether she'd noticed any strange men going into Alyssa's apartment, her answer was just as shrewd but more discouraging.

"How would I know if they were strangers? How could anybody? She'd just moved in. We didn't know who her friends were or what her habits were. She seemed like a nice enough girl. She kept to herself. That was fine with us." Molly Bright sniffed, knowing she had scored. "I saw you," she told Gary. "You were in and out of there—three times that I can recall. I didn't know you were a police officer." Then, with an impish twist at the corner of her mouth, she added, "I didn't think you were strange."

Gary grinned back. "I appreciate that, Miss Bright."

They didn't get any farther with the other tenants. Mostly they were quiet, conservative, middle-class, elderly couples. The lights in their apartments started going out at ten and nobody much was up after midnight, not even watching television.

They all claimed to have been in bed and sound asleep last night by 3:00 A.M., Kuser's estimate of the time of death. Nobody had been awakened by a shot. If by chance anyone had happened to hear it, Gary thought, it would have been dismissed as a backfire and forgotten. In this neighborhood the nights were quiet; the tranquility was prized and fiercely protected.

Finished with the interrogation in the building, Reissig and Dogali went outside. The street had been cleared of the curious; the official cars gone. Gary looked up and down. The rest of the neighborhood consisted of one-and two-family homes. It was possible not all of the people in those houses turned out the light at ten. Someone might have noticed something, if only a stranger loitering in the hours before dawn.

Alyssa, Gary recalled, had been fully dressed in slacks and sweater. Odd. Also, she would not only have had to open her door to the perpetrator but also to have buzzed him in downstairs. Could he somehow have managed to get a key? Questions kept cropping up and Gary put them into his memo book. All officers below the rank of captain were required to keep a record of what transpired from the start of each tour till the end. It was Reissig's habit to include not merely the events and facts but his own observations, his own questions. He noted the initials the victim had scrawled on the floor in lipstick: *e-r*. He noted Marc's suggestion that she had written the last first intending to write the full name, then discovered she didn't have enough strength and added the first initial. He was about to close the book when another question loomed: What had finally compelled Roy Easlick to take the irrevocable step from harassment to murder?

He glanced at his watch: one-thirty. "Let's grab a bite and then report to the captain. I'm surprised he didn't show up at the scene."

"Oh, he was there," Dogali told him. "First thing. He was the one who said to reach out for you."

They had hamburgers and fries at the nearest McDonald's. It happened to be a small store in the village that looked like a local coffee shop. Gary forced himself to chew and swallow, to take his time, but he was anxious. He appreciated being called; it was his case. He also appreciated being left to do the work without a superior breathing down his back. What bothered him was that he had one strong suspect who couldn't be ignored but against whom he had no evidence. Meanwhile, Marc had two of everything except the coffee. He would have liked a second cup but he sensed Gary's impatience. He wasn't dumb. He knew they didn't have anything on Easlick, but he didn't doubt for a moment they would get whatever they needed.

They rode back to the station house in Dogali's car, naturally, since Lurene was using Gary's. They went in to the captain together.

"What've you got?" Boykin asked.

"Approximate time of death: 3:00 A.M.," Reissig began. "Single shot through the heart and fired at close range, close enough to leave powder burns. Not suicide because the gun is gone. Nobody in the neighborhood heard anything. Nobody saw anything. She scrawled initials on the floor with lipstick: *e-r.* Roy Easlick in reverse." He didn't offer his and Marc's theory mainly because he wasn't all that convinced of it.

"You made sure there were good shots of everything, of course." Boykin knew he didn't have to ask. It was an interim maneuver, like packing a pipe or lighting a cigarette, a device to make time for both of them.

"Yes, sir. We talked to the residents in the building. We'll need to canvass the entire neighborhood." More temporizing.

"Sergeant Winetsky can handle that," Boykin said.

"Everything points to Easlick. We ought to bring him in for questioning."

"We've got to go easy."

Reissig cast a glance at Dogali. "We don't see it that way, Captain. We don't see why we have to use kid gloves with this particular suspect."

"Because if we're not real careful we're going to have every bleeding-heart organization in the country on us."

"We should have brought him in the first time on the assault charge."

"He had an alibi for that, remember? Could be he has an alibi now. Go and find out."

"Yes, sir. And if he doesn't?"

"Then we'll take it from there. And a little reminder, Detective Reissig. I don't want any solo effort on this one. The two of you see him together. I don't want anything to happen that could be misconstrued, or misinterpreted, or misrepresented. You know what I mean?"

Gary stiffened. "I've never tricked or strong-armed anybody in my life, Captain."

"I know that. I want everybody to know it too. This case

will receive heavy media attention. I want to be able to document everything that happens in that interrogation. I don't want to have to answer charges of police brutality or entrapment."

"Why don't we just bring him in for questioning?" Gary urged once again.

"We don't want it to look like we're railroading the guy."

Even Dogali had to protest. "We're treating him like some kind of untouchable."

"Because we want him," Boykin replied. "And we're going to get him. When we do it's going to be legal and it's going to stick."

CHAPTER NINE

"So somebody finally snuffed her," Easlick said.

Though he had not expected regret or even a pretense of sorrow, the total callousness shocked Gary.

"And you thought of me first," he added.

"You threatened her."

"Wrong. She said I threatened her. Oh, hell, you didn't believe me then, you're not going to believe me now."

Reissig and Dogali had rung the bell of the plain three-story brick house and were standing on the front porch. Though it was a Saturday and unseasonably warm, nobody was out to enjoy it. No children played in the deadend street; nobody raked leaves or worked in the yards: They had gardeners for that in Crescent Close. Nevertheless, Easlick suddenly looked over his shoulder as though he could feel watchful eyes upon him and motioned the detectives into the house. Once in, he urged them past the open living room and on down the long hall toward the back.

"I'd rather not disturb my mother," he said.

Too late. Freda Easlick had heard and was standing on the second-floor landing. "Roy? What's going on? Oh, it's you," she said, recognizing Gary Reissig.

"Alyssa Hanriot has been shot, Mom."

She came down. She took her time. "I can't say I'm sorry. What do you want from us, Detectives?"

"We need to know where Mr. Easlick was early this morning."

"Are you suggesting my son had something to do with her death? He never went near—"

"Mom, please. It's easier just to tell them what they want to know."

Gary almost admired Easlick's casual arrogance as he led them back to the living room, which he'd tried moments before to bypass. He waited for both to be seated before beginning.

"All right, let's see. I worked late last night. My office is in Manhattan, as you know. My boss, Stuart Chanin, looked in on me at about 7:00 P.M. Afterward, food was sent down to me from the executive dining room and I ate at my desk. At eleven, the party upstairs broke up and Stu Chanin looked in again. He offered me a ride, but I had my own car. I worked about half an hour longer, stopped for a drink, and got home about one A.M., or a little after. I went straight to bed."

"Can you verify that?"

"I can," Freda Easlick put in. "I heard him."

"Did you speak with your son?"

She hesitated. "No," she admitted. "I was in bed but not asleep. I heard the car. I heard Roy come upstairs and go to his room, which is just down the hall from mine."

Gary nodded to the mother but addressed the son. "After you got home, did anyone call you on the telephone?"

"When was she killed?"

"After midnight." That was as close as he cared to admit for the moment.

"I can't prove I was upstairs in my own bed."

"I can." Again his mother volunteered. "I've had a lot of trouble sleeping lately. I was wide awake last night and well after midnight. I heard him come in and I would have heard him if he went out again."

She would get on the stand and swear to that and the jury would believe or disbelieve according to where their sympathies lay.

"Do you own a gun?" Gary asked Easlick.

"No, that would be a violation of my parole. You do *know* that I'm on parole."

"Be sure that we're completely conversant with your case, Mr. Easlick," Reissig retorted. "That's why we're here."

"You have no right to assume anything on the basis of a prior conviction." Freda Easlick parroted the legalese. "He was innocent then and he's innocent now."

"Don't get excited, Mom."

"These men have no right to walk in here and accuse you of anything based on a prior—"

"We haven't accused him, Mrs. Easlick."

"And now I suppose you're going out to talk to the neighbors."

"It's routine, ma'am."

"You have no right, no right to smear his reputation. It's all happening like before. You're putting ideas into people's heads. Maligning my son. I'm calling my lawyer. You've heard of Franklin Rosenwall, I suppose? Good. Roy, don't you say another word until Franklin gets here. And you two —out. Out of my house. Now. I want you out of my house right now." She was shouting as she pointed a shaking finger.

As they emerged into the bright sunshine, Dogali shrugged. "At least we know he doesn't have an alibi. You'd think he would have cooked up something."

"Maybe he thinks it looks more natural this way." Gary was watching a boy across the street dribbling a basketball up the driveway toward a hoop over a garage door.

"Franklin Rosenwall's heavy stuff."

The boy was shooting with great concentration, deliberately ignoring the detectives.

"So, are we going to talk to the neighbors or what?" Dogali finally realized Gary was watching the kid.

"Right. We're going to talk to the neighbors right now." Let the kid wait, he thought. He had something to tell and the longer he had to keep it in, the more eager he would be.

They worked clockwise. Of the five houses, besides the Easlick house, the first two didn't answer their ring. At the next two they were kept waiting and the resulting interviews were unproductive. That left the house where the boy was playing. Even as they went up the drive, he continued to play.

"Police officers," Gary announced. Both he and Marc flashed their gold shields. "What's your name, son?" Make it official and make it tough, he thought and took out notebook and pencil.

"Billy. Billy Rahr."

"How old are you, Billy?"

The boy scowled as though resenting the question. "Fourteen." He looked older and he knew it. He was one of those kids who shot up to his full growth suddenly, almost overnight, and then had to struggle to catch up emotionally and mentally. He didn't belong with his own age group anymore and didn't fit in with the older boys. His brown hair, cut in a spiky, punk style, bleached blonde at the ends, was an attempt to proclaim his individuality. It didn't look good on him, Gary thought. It didn't look good on anybody.

"Were you home last night?"

Billy Rahr shook his head.

"Oh, of course, it was Halloween. I suppose you were out trick or treating."

His look was one of utter contempt. "That's for babies. Me and a bunch of the guys went to New York for the big parade in the Village."

The Greenwich Village Halloween parade was wild and weird and wonderful and had over a very few years become an institution. It started early and ran late and like all such events spread into rowdiness. No use asking if there had been adult supervision for the outing. "What time did you get back?"

"Midnight," he admitted readily.

So now they were getting to it, Gary thought. Otherwise the kid would have been ashamed to acknowledge that his parents had enough control over him to make him get home that early. "Did you happen to notice if there were lights on across the street?"

"Nope."

"Does that mean there weren't any or you didn't notice?"

"Mr. Easlick's car pulled in about an hour after me, if that's what you're trying to find out."

At his age children were generally good witnesses. They were curious and interested in the world outside themselves. Later on, as they got older, they became less observant and more preoccupied with their own affairs. "It is," Gary acknowledged.

"The woman followed him into the garage."

He meant to surprise them, but both Gary and Marc kept their faces blank. "What woman?" Gary asked casually.

"The woman sitting on the wall. She was there when I got home," he announced with a grin of satisfaction that erased the sullenness, temporarily. "She was sitting right there on the wall between the Easlicks' and the Schumans'." He pointed.

Gary had to walk well over to one side of the driveway to see the four-foot wall running along the privet hedge.

"How come you noticed?"

Billy gave that elaborately casual shrug of the teenager who had no ready answer. "She had real long hair, a kind of light brown color. She was wearing one of those wool ponchos; my sister got one like it on her trip to South America last year—white with black embroidery and tassels."

"Had you ever seen this woman before? Around the neighborhood?"

"Nope."

That had been too much to hope for, Gary thought.

"But I know who she is. I saw her picture in the paper."

It was hard to hide his eagerness, but Gary managed. "Okay. Who is she?"

The teenager pressed his full lips into a hard, smug line. He had already decided Reissig was boss, so he dealt with him. "How much is it worth?"

Despite the years of dealing with kids and drugs, with kids selling whatever they had—what they owned, what they could steal, their own bodies—Gary had not expected this. He indicated the Tudor-style mansion in front of which they stood. "You live in there?"

Billy Rahr, fourteen years old, was thrown off stride. "That's right."

"You've got nice clothes, go to a good school, eat all you want. And you need money? What for? What are you on?"

"Nothing. None of your business. I got nothing to tell you." Tucking the ball under his arm, Billy Rahr started around to the front of his house.

"Hold it, sonny." Gary reached for his shoulder and spun him around. This boy had all the advantages, but he was also subject to stresses unknown to Gary and his generation when they were growing up. He thought of his own two—Robin particularly. Robin was retarded. He would never reach Billy Rahr's mental age, but in a sense that became protection for him. "I'll make a deal with you, kid," Reissig said, holding on to him. "You tell me who and what you saw last night and I'll let your parents find out for themselves what you're on."

"That's low, man. The pits."

"What'll it be? Your choice."

Billy Rahr hesitated. He took a second look at Dogali and decided there wouldn't be any help there. "Okay. It was the woman who was attacked at the Senior Citizens' Center."

Gary let him go. "Alyssa Hanriot. Are you sure?"

If Billy was disappointed that the reaction wasn't greater he didn't show it. "Yeah, I'm sure. My folks haven't stopped talking about her. She testified against Mr. Easlick in his trial."

"All right. Fine. You say she sat over there on that wall for about an hour till Mr. Easlick got home." The kid was sharp and in view of the threat to tell his parents about his drug habit would probably also be truthful. "You said she followed Mr. Easlick into the garage. Before the door came down? Or did she use the side entrance?"

"The side."

"Then what?"

"After a few minutes she came out. She walked down to the corner and turned . . . right . . . and that's the last I saw of her. I went to bed."

"How about the lights?"

"The lights in the garage went on when the door went up. They went off before the woman left."

"And in the house?"

"No lights."

"Let me get this straight," Gary said. "The garage lights

came on as the door went up. The car was driven in, the door came down. Miss Hanriot entered through the side. Shortly after, the garage lights went out. Miss Hanriot left. No lights appeared in the house. Anywhere."

"You got it." Billy Rahr turned his back and dribbling the ball made his way up the driveway to the basket.

Gary trailed. "Did you happen to see Mr. Easlick go out again?"

Rahr didn't answer. He set up the shot—and missed.

Gary caught the ball. "Who are you mad at, Billy? Your parents? Why don't you talk to them about it? Give them a chance to make it right."

He bounced the ball once, then bent his knees and as though he had springs in them, jumped. Slam, dunk!

If you wanted to mount an operation in another jurisdiction you had to clear it with your own boss, naturally, and then with the commander in the other precinct. If you just needed to go in and ask a few questions, if the subject was not likely to become a suspect and require a Miranda warning, protocol wasn't as rigid as it once had been. However, it remained a courtesy to drop by the house and advise the duty officer of what you were doing, particularly if you had at one time been friendly with the whip of one of the overhead units—Lieutenant Norah Mulcahaney, head of Fourth Zone Homicide.

Actually, Gary could have talked with the witness, Stuart Chanin, at his home in Woodmere either the Saturday or the Sunday following the murder, but he rationalized. There were still basic interviews with the victim's neighbors to be concluded. There was the call to Neil Jaros. As it turned out, he had to trace Alyssa's fiancé from the Cleveland hotel that was the address she had provided through stops in Kansas City and Dallas. It took till late Sunday night to make contact in LA. After that, it was too late to barge in on Chanin. Anyway, it would be more productive to talk to the man who had befriended Easlick to the point of giving him a job of consequence in the actual work environment. While there he could also interview the people who knew Easlick, find out what they thought about him; check out his afterwork haunts. If he intended doing that, Gary thought, he must present himself at the local precinct.

Gary's heart pounded as he walked into the squad room of the Twentieth on Eighty-second Street just west of Columbus. Squad rooms didn't have much individuality. This one was interchangeable with any other, including his own, yet there were special memories here. While he and Norah Mulcahaney had been going together, he'd spent a lot of time here. He had got to know the detectives, her friends. He wondered if any of them would be present; what they would say; what kind of greeting he'd get. But the place was nearly empty and the three men present were strangers to him. He went up to the nearest desk. The name plaque read Wyler.

"Reissig from the One-Oh-One." Gary flipped open his shield case. "I'm looking for Lieutenant Mulcahaney."

"Over there." Simon Wyler nodded toward one of the two doors at the far end.

"Thanks." Suddenly, Gary wished he hadn't come. Calling on the phone was one thing, seeing Norah face to face . . . on her ground . . . He had never been in her office before.

"Detective Reissig?" Wyler spoke. "You can go right in."

"Oh? Oh, yes. Thank you." He walked over. At the second of the two doors he paused. Her name was painted on the frosted panel: Lieutenant N. Mulcahaney. He took a deep breath and knocked.

"Come."

She sat at the desk engrossed in what appeared to be a stack of DD5s, detective detailed reports. She scanned through to the bottom of the page before looking up, then Norah Mulcahaney smiled. The light in her deep-blue eyes brightened, her face was transformed. "Gary!" The color deepened.

She looked exactly the same, Gary thought. She still glowed from within with that special quality that was more than physical beauty. "Hello, Norah. It's good to see you."

Not that she wasn't outwardly beautiful as well. Her skin was smooth and translucent. As always her blue eyes were large and luminous. The few wrinkles at the corners of her eyes and around her mouth added maturity. She still wore her glistening dark hair tied back with a scarf that matched her outfit, today a hunter green. The prominent jaw was no less so than ever—only it seemed to Gary that it jutted less aggressively right.

"It's good to see you, too," Norah replied. "What are you doing in these parts? I suppose it must be the Hanriot case."

She was sure of herself. He could sense the confidence. Promoted a mere six months ago, she wore the responsibility well. She was where she belonged, Gary thought. However, the flush indicated she still had some feeling for him. He was surprised finding that out should touch him so deeply.

"You haven't heard? Alyssa Hanriot was murdered Saturday morning in her apartment."

"I'm sorry." Norah knew instinctively and instantly that Gary was blaming himself. "I'm very sorry."

He sighed.

"You figure this man she testified against and who was harassing her, Easlick—he did it?"

He nodded. "Trouble is, we couldn't pin anything on him before and we can't now. We can't show he went anywhere near the girl."

"You couldn't provide permanent protection for her," Norah reminded him.

"I know that," he snapped. "I installed a telephone answering machine for her, but he didn't allow himself to be recorded. Not that I expected he would, but I did expect it would scare him off. It made him angrier. The notes got nastier. He put a stink bomb in her car. He tailed her close, real close. I got her a camera, but she never took a picture."

"It was asking a lot," Norah pointed out.

"My God, I know that," he snapped.

"You did what you could."

Did I? In his mind and with his whole being, Gary cried out. *Did I?*

"Does Easlick have an alibi?" Norah asked.

"Sure, he does, and it's a joke. He claims he was in bed asleep and his mother claims she's an insomniac and would have known if he'd got up and gone out." Gary shrugged. "It doesn't matter; like I said, we can't place him at the scene. On top of that, Allie, Alyssa Hanriot, scrawled something on the floor with lipstick before she died: *e-r*. His initials but in reverse. What do you think of that?"

"Maybe they weren't initials."

"Come on, Norah! What else? A message from the killer?" he asked with open irony.

But Norah took him seriously. "Probably not. You're right. If the killer wanted to direct your attention to somebody else he would have been less cryptic."

Their eyes met; the tension between them was easing as they exchanged ideas.

Norah frowned, took a deep breath, and tried another approach. "As far as you know the last contact that can actually be documented between Alyssa Hanriot and Roy Easlick was at the trial when she took the stand against him."

"Right—" Reissig caught himself. "No. Actually, no." He licked his lips; his eyes brightened. "Alyssa went to Easlick's house the night she was murdered. She was seen sitting on the wall along his driveway waiting for him. He got home around midnight and put the car in the garage, and she followed him in. She came out again minutes later."

"What happened?"

"I don't know. Nobody does."

Norah thought about it. She didn't have to think long. "This man was terrorizing her. At least, that's what she said."

"She wasn't lying."

"I'm not suggesting she was," Norah retorted. He was very touchy, not like himself. "What I'm wondering is why she went looking for a man of whom she was understandably frightened, so frightened she was asking police protection?"

"I don't know."

"She visits him, then a few hours later he somehow manages to get into her apartment and kills her. She leaves a dying message that seems to point to someone else."

Gary wiped his brow. "I can't figure it."

"Maybe you can't figure it because you're only looking in one direction. You've already made up your mind who the guilty party is."

"There is no other direction. Alyssa Hanriot was decent

and straight. She didn't have an enemy in the world."

He knew better than to make a statement like that, Norah thought and decided it was one more indication of how deeply troubled he was. Gary was thinking only of himself and the only thing she could do for him was to shake him out of it. "It's your case. If opening up other lines of investigation seems futile or too much work . . ."

"Are you accusing me of being lazy?"

"I'm discussing the case. That's what you came for, isn't it? If you didn't want to discuss the case, why did you come?"

Their eyes met and held. There was a long silence. The hostility eased.

"I came because I wanted to see you, Norah." Despite himself, or without realization, there was tenderness in the way he spoke her name.

She was the first to look away.

"And I'm glad I came."

She sighed. Settled back in her chair. "Me, too."

"You look wonderful, Norah. Never better. Things going good for you?"

She nodded. "You don't look so bad yourself. Still got that great tan. Put on a little weight though," she teased.

Now was the moment. His tongue flicked out nervously, licking his lips. He couldn't put it off any longer. "I'm married."

"Oh."

Suddenly, Norah's hands were clammy. She had a sharp pain in her chest that made it hard to breathe. "I didn't know. Congratulations."

"Thanks." It was out and he felt a lot better. "I wanted to send you an announcement, but . . . it was very spontaneous . . . just a few friends . . ." Damn. That was a mistake.

Norah ignored it. "What's her name?"

"Lurene. Lurene Benoit. She comes from New Orleans."

"How did you meet?"

He didn't want to say he'd met Lurene in a bar where she'd been a cocktail waitress. Nothing wrong with that, but he didn't want Norah to have even an inkling that their breakup had started him drinking. "Through a friend."

"And everything's fine at home? The children like Lurene? How about Mildred?"

"Lurene is very good with the children." Mildred was the mother of his first wife, who had gone on living with Gary and looking after Robin and Anna after Joyce's death. "Mildred's moved to Florida. We wanted her to stay, but she said it wouldn't be fair."

Norah nodded. "So what does Lurene do?"

"Nothing." He caught himself. "I mean, she's got plenty to keep her busy taking care of us and the house. She likes the beach, gardening. She's a wonderful cook. She's blonde and gorgeous. Everything I ever wanted."

And that I couldn't offer, Norah thought. Naturally, he didn't mean it that way; he was extolling the virtues of his bride as it was right he should. "I'm happy for you, Gary. I really am." Having said it, Norah straightened in her chair. "So. What can we do for you here at the Two-Oh?"

And Gary replied in the same businesslike manner. "Easlick works at the main office of First American National on Broadway and Eighty-sixth. I'd like to talk to the people there and maybe canvass the neighborhood bars. See what I can turn up."

"You want me to assign somebody to go with you?"

"If you prefer it, but it's not necessary."

"Captain Jacoby is out with the flu, but I don't see any problem. Naturally, if it turns out a stakeout or surveillance is required, you will advise me?"

"Of course. I appreciate the courtesy, Lieutenant." He couldn't bring himself to use the informal "Lou"; that would have put him on a level with everybody else and he wanted to remain special. On the other hand, he couldn't leave it like this, cold and formal, either. "Maybe you could come out for dinner some time, Norah?"

"How long have you been married?"

"Since July seventeenth."

He hadn't wasted much time, Norah thought. Was that a twinge of hurt pride she felt, or did she still care—a little? "That's hardly long enough for your bride to get settled. I suggest you wait a while longer before confronting her with old girlfriends."

He took the hand she held out, squeezed it, and grinned. "I don't want you to think I don't appreciate your suggestion about the case."

"That's all it was."

"It was a criticism," he acknowledged. "And justified. The thing is—there are no other suspects. There is nowhere else to look—not in Hanriot's past, not before she became involved with Easlick, and not since."

"I can't buy that."

"If it had been Easlick who was shot that would make it a whole other ballgame. There'd be no problem finding people who have it in for him, starting with the parents of the two little girls he abused."

"Why *not* start with the parents?"

"They wouldn't harm Alyssa Hanriot. They were grateful to her. The children were too frightened to testify. If she hadn't come forward and taken the stand there would have been no conviction."

"How about the people who were on Easlick's side, who believed in his innocence? There must have been some."

"I don't know. I hate to think what reopening the case will do to those children."

Norah sighed. "The seeds of Alyssa Hanriot's murder are in that trial. You can't ignore it."

CHAPTER TEN

Stuart Chanin rose and came around the desk to shake hands with Detective Reissig as though he were greeting a valued client.

At thirty-two, Chanin was already vice-president, international division, of First American and considered still on the way up. Birth and social position had been his springboard and smoothed the way; the rest of his rise would depend strictly on his own efforts. Chanin had big ideas, big plans. He intended to make it to the top, not just to the presidency of the bank but beyond—he set himself no limits. Stuart Chanin was six foot two, built on a sturdy frame. His head was narrow, but it had a high, domed brow. He looked older than his years—his white skin already hinted at the brittle texture of parchment and his hair was thinning and prematurely gray. But he possessed a driving energy. He was never still, never idle. He was an expert skier, squash player, golfer, a life master in bridge. He supported the opera, was on the board of the Metropolitan Museum. As yet Stuart Chanin hadn't married, but marriage was on the agenda. He knew the image he wanted to present would not be fully realized until he had a wife and family. He intended to make a choice soon.

Reissig had recently read a *Time* magazine profile on

Chanin. He'd been interested because they both came from the same area. There the similarity ended, Gary thought without resentment.

"Sorry to bother you, Mr. Chanin, but I would like to ask you a few questions about one of your employees."

"Roy Easlick," Chanin sat down behind his imposing desk. "You were expecting this."

"I heard about the murder of the woman who testified against Roy at his trial. Naturally, he would be a suspect. I must tell you, Detective Reissig—I don't believe Roy had anything to do with her death. I believe he's as completely innocent now as he was then. But that's another story."

"Perhaps not. What makes you think Roy Easlick was innocent of the charge of molestation?"

"It's a gut feeling. I know Roy. We grew up together. Well, that's not exactly accurate. We did go to the same school, a private school, and that's a bond. We played soccer and were in the debating society together. On graduation I went to Harvard and he was admitted to Hofstra." He immediately added, "His mother wanted him to attend a school nearby and live at home."

Gary understood the explanation was intended to take out any deprecatory sting.

"What I'm saying is that Roy is no sex maniac or murderer. I'm not going to question Miss Hanriot's motive in testifying. She heard the girls crying and she saw somebody come out of the coatroom. Only it wasn't Roy."

"Mistaken identity?"

"It wouldn't be the first time."

She wasn't ten feet away, Gary thought, but didn't argue.

"If she was wrong, if she did accuse him falsely, Easlick would have all the more reason to seek revenge. Easlick's innocence wouldn't change anything."

"That's a matter of opinion."

"Do you read the papers, Mr. Chanin?"

"I read the *Wall Street Journal*."

"Two weeks ago Alyssa Hanriot was attacked, stabbed and left for dead in the basement of the Senior Citizens' Center on Seagirt. Shortly after, while she was still in the hospital recuperating, she claimed to have received a telephone call from Easlick, who took responsibility and threatened further reprisals."

"The operative word there is *claimed*, isn't it?"

"You think Miss Hanriot lied?"

"That's not for me to say. It doesn't make sense for him to contact her, much less attack her. Roy spent nearly two years in prison. He's a sensitive man; the experience must have been traumatic. Now he's out on parole. Why would he take the risk of being sent back?"

Easlick's own argument, Gary thought. And a good one. "Because he thought he could get away with it. Why *should* Miss Hanriot lie?"

"Because she thought you would believe her."

Gary dropped it: They were getting nowhere except to establish antagonism, and that wouldn't help. "Why did you hire Roy Easlick?" he asked. "He has no experience in banking."

"His mother asked me to help him. She also asked me not to tell him." Gary's nod was an indication he would respect that wish if he could. "Also, I subscribe to the belief that a man can make a mistake and learn from it. It's to society's advantage to give the prisoner a second chance. Though we agree in theory, we don't support the practice. The ex-con is branded. The police never forget. You roust him for every crime that can possibly be laid on his doorstep. You're doing it now."

"If I told you we were bending over backward to protect Mr. Easlick's civil rights, would you believe me?" Reissig asked in full appreciation of Captain Boykin's caution.

"I'm glad to hear it. As far as I'm concerned, I don't regret hiring Roy. He's doing a good job. He's producing. As for his behavior—it's unexceptional."

"He says he worked late Friday night."

"He did. We were having a director's meeting and dinner upstairs and he prepared some material I needed. He delivered it to me just before seven. When we broke up, a little after eleven, I saw the light was on in his office and I looked in on him. He was still hard at it. I told him it was time to close shop and I offered him a lift, but he had his own car."

A repetition of Easlick's account. "That was the last you saw of him—here, shortly after eleven?"

"Yes."

Had the news stories mentioned the time of Alyssa Hanriot's death? Probably. Anyhow, Gary saw no reason to keep it secret. "According to the preliminary findings, Miss Hanriot was shot at about 3:00 A.M."

"I can't vouch for what Roy did after . . ." Chanin stopped in dismay. "Are you asking me for an alibi, Detective Reissig? I'm afraid I don't have one. I don't know many people who would have an alibi for three in the morning. Unless one frequents the discos or is having an affair."

It was a feeble attempt at humor and not his style, Reissig thought. Stuart Chanin had tried hard to defend Easlick on the grounds of friendship and at the same time he had been careful to disclaim the friendship, impose limits on it. He had proclaimed belief in Easlick's innocence and also suggested he would have hired him anyway. Maybe he was one of those people who were loath to cast the first stone. It was Gary's experience that they usually found someone else to do it for them.

Gary didn't give much weight to Chanin's opinion that Easlick had been convicted on a bum rap, but he did respect Norah Mulcahaney's suggestion that he look into the original case. The first step would be to talk to the parents of the two young victims. When he called ahead to make sure the Sagarmans would be home, Frances Sagarman told him that in fact her husband would be late.

"It's the night they put the paper to bed," she explained. "It's a weekly, so unless there's a late-breaking story—and there hardly ever is—he should be home by ten."

The Sagarman house was new, a two-story colonial set on a handsome half acre. It was nicely landscaped in front with a frontier-style fence closing off the backyard. Peering over the top, Gary could see in the light of the street lamp a brightly painted red and yellow children's gym. At ten precisely he walked up to the front and rang the bell. Frances Sagarman opened the door and led him to the living room where Edwin

Sagarman was expecting him. He scrutinized Reissig's ID with care.

"You're from Queens," he observed. "I thought you'd be from Nassau."

"Why?"

Sagarman was thin; his flesh hung loose from a massive frame as though he'd recently lost weight. He had a sharp nose, large ears, and lank, dark brown hair. Despite a deep tan, he didn't look healthy. He was wearing a gray sweat suit and slippers. A half drunk highball stood on the table at his elbow and a large crystal ashtray was half full of butts. He was deeply disturbed and made no attempt to conceal it. Gary couldn't blame him. What had happened to his children was not something a parent was likely to get over quickly. Or ever to forget.

"I'm a resident of Nassau County." He coughed, a hollow hacking that grew into a spasm convulsing him and making his eyes tear. It left him limp. He had to take his glasses off and wipe them. A swallow of the highball served to calm him, then he picked up a live cigarette from the ashtray.

Frances Sagarman watched, but said nothing. When she was sure the attack had passed, she turned to Gary. "Can I get you something?"

She was thin too, almost gaunt. Her blonde hair stringy, her tan faded to an unattractive yellow. She had been pretty once, Gary could see the traces, and could be pretty again if she would put on a few pounds and take a little trouble. She was obviously under strain, but he had the feeling she was more upset over her husband's distress than the actual situation.

"A cup of coffee would taste good, if it's not too much trouble."

"Won't take a minute." She seemed grateful for an excuse to get out of there.

"They didn't tell you?" Sagarman continued as though there had been no interruption. "The Nassau police didn't tell you that I went over there to the precinct, that I lodged a formal complaint against Easlick's presence in the community; that I demanded protection for my family? They refused. They said I had no cause. Apparently, they intend to wait for Easlick to molest my children or some other children before doing anything." He ground out the stub, reached into the pocket of his sweat shirt, produced a crumpled pack and lit up again. "Well, they got more than they bargained for."

"How do you mean?"

"I'm talking about the murder of Alyssa Hanriot. That is why you're here?"

"Yes."

"So now you'll lock him up and we'll be safe again. For a while. I'm only sorry about that poor girl. She had guts. She did her civic and moral duty and I tell you it couldn't have been easy to get up on that stand and face that creep and tell it right out—what she saw. The shame is ours that we couldn't protect her. This is the thanks she got. This is how the community rewarded her."

Quietly, Frances Sagarman slipped in with the coffee, handed Gary his cup, and went off to sit at the side.

Gary sipped and waited but it seemed Ed Sagarman had run down.

"You think Roy Easlick committed the murder?"

"Who else? He threatened her."

"You know about that?"

"I'm in the news business, Detective Reissig. My paper is only a local sheet, but this is a local story and that means it's very big news to us."

"Then you know there's no proof it was in fact Easlick who was harassing Miss Hanriot."

"I'll say it again: Who else?"

"That's what I'm trying to find out."

"He threatened her in court," Frances Sagarman offered from her corner. "When the verdict was delivered, he yelled at her: This is your fault and I'm going to make you pay. Everybody heard him."

"Since then, since he got out, do you, of your own knowledge, know that he made threats against her?"

Sagarman spoke for his wife. "Neither of us had any contact with him. That's the last thing in the world we would want."

"Were either of you in contact with Miss Hanriot? Did you speak with her? Did she tell either of you Easlick had threatened her?"

Ed Sagarman sighed. "We had no contact with her since the trial."

Frances Sagarman merely clasped her hands tight and looked down.

"Then on what did you base your complaint to the Nassau police?"

"My God, don't you people have any feelings? Easlick was and continues to be a danger to my girls. Oh, I don't think he'd go after them again; I don't think he's that dumb. But they're bound to find out he's in the area; they might even catch sight of him. And that would bring it all back. It was a horrible experience for them. They were not only emotionally traumatized, but infected . . ." He paused. "They needed medical and psychiatric treatment. I don't know if you have children of your own, Detective Reissig, but a wave of rage and frustration comes over a parent in such a situation. You want to get your hands on the man. You want him castrated. You want to do it yourself."

"I do have children of my own, Mr. Sagarman, and I understand. But I have to ask you where you were at 3:00 A.M. on Saturday."

"That's when she was killed, isn't it? Why don't you say so right out?"

"Where were you, sir?"

"Do you think I would have harmed a hair on that girl's head?"

"Just answer the question."

"I can't believe this is happening. I can't believe you're here, in my home, asking me . . . all right. All right. I was here, of course. Where else would I be? I wouldn't leave my family alone and unprotected in the middle of the night. Why don't you ask my wife? Go ahead, ask her."

It flustered Frances Sagarman to have their attention focused on her. Her right hand picked nervously at the fabric of the chair arm. "Yes. Yes, of course, Ed was home. In bed. Sleeping."

"How can you be sure?" Gary asked, but gently. "Were you awake at 3:00 A.M.?"

"No, but . . . I know he was there." She swallowed a couple of times. "I would have known if he wasn't," she proclaimed defiantly.

"Have you ever awakened in the night and found the place next to you empty, Mrs. Sagarman?"

"Well, yes. Certainly. Everybody gets up in the night sometimes—to go to the bathroom, or read, or get a snack out of the refrigerator. But being out of the house, that's different. I would have known if Ed was out."

He wouldn't shake her and there was no need to try, not now, Gary thought. He returned to the main thrust of questioning. "Do you know anyone who didn't view Alyssa Hanriot's testimony in the same way you did?" he asked Sagarman. "Who believed in Easlick's innocence and blamed her for getting him convicted?"

"No," Sagarman replied. "Why are you trying so hard to get him off?"

"I'm trying to make sure we have the right man."

"You do. Believe me."

When Gary got home, Lurene was already in bed, but awake. Her blonde hair was loose on the pillow framing her pale face and shimmering in the light of the bedside lamp.

He sucked in his breath at the picture she made. "I'm sorry I'm late," he said. "You shouldn't have waited up."

"Yes, I should." She held her arms out to him. The covers slipped down revealing her bare breasts.

Later, much later, he asked her, "Did you get the car?"

"Uh—uh."

"Why not?" It was three days since he'd tossed the keys of the station wagon to her and told her to go and buy what she wanted.

"I decided we should do it together. We don't do enough together," she murmured, her warm breath in his ear.

As once more he intertwined his legs with hers, the phone rang.

Damn, he thought, let it ring. Then with a sigh, he picked it up.

"Yes? Oh, Mr. Jaros. Where are you?... Back in the city ... No, no problem, I did ask you to get in touch as soon as you were home. We certainly do still need you for the identification.... Tomorrow morning. Either my partner or I will be in touch and set up a time.... Yes, in the morning.... We'll call you." He was getting impatient. "Right, Mr. Jaros.... Thank *you* and good night."

At last. He hung up. He rolled over to Lurene. She was lying on her back. Snoring.

In the living room of his very modern and very lonely apartment, one of a row of new condo townhouses along the shore, Neil Jaros hung up the phone. He was drenched in sweat. He turned on all the lights and turned up the radio but it didn't dispel the shadows or fill the silence. Gary Reissig had caught up with him on Sunday after a day of meetings—at lunch, dinner, and what was supposed to be a night of pleasure. The detective had informed him of Allie's death and asked if there was family to be notified. Neil didn't know of any. The detective then asked if he would claim the body. Three thousand miles across the country, Neil Jaros had started to shake.

"I suppose so," he'd said and was instantly aware of how callous he'd sounded. "Yes, sure," he amended. "I'd be glad to." Oh God, that wasn't right either.

The first available flight out wasn't till Tuesday. The hours spent waiting, thinking of what lay ahead were the worst Jaros had ever spent. He'd have to pay for the funeral, but that wasn't what bothered him, not the money part. Detective Reissig had explained that Allie's neighbors had identified her, but since she'd only recently moved, identification by someone closer, who had known her longer, was desirable. How could he have said no?

How was he going to bring himself to look at her?

CHAPTER ELEVEN

Gary awoke to what the Irish call a "soft morning," gray with a gentle persistent warm drizzle that soaked the earth and nourished it, preparing it for winter. A good day for staying in bed, he thought and snuggled closer to his wife and her warmth, the smell of their encounter still redolent. But there would be other nights and other mornings, he thought. There would be many long winter nights to share. His favorite season lay ahead. Smiling with a sense of satisfaction and well-being, Gary flung the covers back.

He checked in for the shift, advised Dogali that Jaros was back, and asked him to set up the visit to the morgue. Then he relaxed, pulled out the bottom drawer of his desk, propped his feet on it and gave himself up to some leisurely thinking.

What *had* Alyssa Hanriot been doing at the Easlick house? Waiting for Easlick to come home, obviously, but why, for what purpose? Frightened of him as she was, what had spurred her to seek a confrontation? Billy Rahr had seen her waiting, had observed her go in and come out almost immediately. What else had he seen? Possibly Easlick going out after her? Suddenly, Gary felt a hot wave of anxiety followed by a prickly chill. He put his feet down and slammed the drawer shut.

Dogali jumped.

"I'm going over to the school."

"Want me to come?"

"I don't think so. You go with Jaros to view the body. I've got to talk to the kid, to Billy. Right away. And alone is better."

Gary arrived well before the start of the school day. The rain was still coming down, not hard enough to deter those who had business with the children. He spotted them right away— youths strolling casually to take up allocated posts at the perimeter of the school property. They were dressed mostly in jeans and leather jackets. One, making no concession to the weather, kept to his trademark—a pale beige three-piece silk suit nipped at the waist Italian style, topped with a cream fedora. The jacket sleeves were pushed up above the elbows —of course. Vanilla, he was called. Gary knew him from previous encounters; the others he recognized by instinct: saboteurs of our society, sellers of poison, debauchers of the young. The Reverend Martin Luther King, Jr., had put it precisely when he warned that if we allowed the continued use of drugs we would reap "the whirlwind of social disintegration." The enemy, Gary thought, was not Russia or international terrorism, but our own apathy. He knew the pushers and they knew him, but for today at least his business was not with them and they knew that too. Nevertheless, the youths would not deal openly in front of him. It was an uneasy hiatus.

Gary watched as the orange school buses released loads of chattering, laughing, energetic boys and girls. They were like birds, he thought, flapping their wings, cawing and chirping and shrieking in their last moments of freedom. In less than ten minutes, all but a few stragglers were inside.

Had he missed Billy? In that melee, he might have, but somehow he didn't think so—the boy was tall, had a distinctive hair style even among his peers and a characteristic loping gait. Gary got out of the car and crossed the street to the main entrance.

"Excuse me, which way is the administration office?" He showed the guard his ID.

Following directions, he found the office easily. As he entered, the bell for the first class rang and students poured out of home rooms and into corridors. Gary closed the door behind him, shutting out the hubbub. The woman at the reception desk didn't look up.

"Excuse me. I'm looking for a student, Billy . . . William Rahr."

"He's in class." She went on with whatever she was doing.

"I was waiting outside for him. I didn't see him."

She sighed lugubriously. "So you missed him. What do you expect me to do? I can't take him out of class."

"I want you to check with his home room teacher. I want to know if William Rahr, Jr., is in school today and I want to know it now." He leaned over and held his open shield case in front of her face.

She was around forty, stout, and not in the least intimidated. "Why didn't you say so? All right, I'll check it out." She punched a couple of keys on the desk terminal and within seconds the information appeared on the screen.

"No, as a matter of fact, William Rahr, Jr., was marked absent this morning."

Gary had already seen it for himself and was on his way out.

"Do you want his home address?" the woman called after him.

"I have it," he threw over his shoulder, then he thought—what the hell, and added, "Thanks."

Outside, the pushers were gone. Usually, he knew, they hung around waiting for latecomers and the neighborhood trade. He had ruined their morning, Gary thought. It wasn't much in the overall picture, but it did give him a moment of satisfaction.

Cornelius Perette lived at the far end of Crescent Close. Cars that ignored the "Private Street" sign and entered had to make a U-turn in front of his house to get out again. It was a source of constant irritation. If it had been up to him, there would have been an electronically controlled gate, but he couldn't get the other residents to take on the expense. However, he wasn't giving up. "Corny" Perette was a feisty sixty-eight, still commuting to work every day. He had no thought of retirement. He owned a seat on the American Stock Exchange and nobody could tell him what to do or when to do it. Corny got up every morning at five-thirty, had his breakfast alone in the kitchen, and drove himself to Wall Street. The market didn't open till nine-thirty, but he valued the private time before the opening bell, before the telephones started ringing, and his secretary started hovering over him. She treated him as though she were a privileged aunt. One of these days she was going to retire and he'd replace her with some young chick who'd be afraid of him.

On the "soft" gray morning of November fifth, Corny Perette got up as usual. It was still dark, sunrise wouldn't be till around seven and the old-fashioned street lamps were still lit. As he stood at his window putting on his robe and looking toward the east for that first rim of light, Perette noticed what he thought at first was the fog rolling in eerie silence down the street. Then he realized it wasn't coming from the south and the sea. It was a thin plume, low along the ground, and it emanated from the Rahr house, seeping out from under the garage door. Smoke, he thought. Fire!

He called the fire department, and then, still in robe and slippers, went across the street to rouse the family.

The morgue wagon was in front of the Rahr house and with it the usual assortment of patrol cars and official but unmarked vehicles. The house, blinds down, had a closed, withdrawn look. However, the garage door was up and all activity centered there. Gary approached the first uniform he saw.

"Reissig from the One-Oh-One. What've you got?"

"Kid died from carbon monoxide poisoning."

"Billy Rahr?"

"Yeah, that's the name."

Gary sighed. "Who's in charge?"

The uniform pointed to a burly figure in tan slacks and a yellow slicker. Sergeant Ansted; he and Gary were fishing buddies. "Yo, Vic," he called and went over. "I talked to the boy on Saturday. What happened?"

Ansted motioned him inside.

There wasn't much to see. The garage was unusually neat and clean—no dilapidated furniture, no cartons, lawn mowers, rusting tools, or fertilizer bags. A dark blue Mercedes and a smaller white Volvo were parked side by side. The activity centered on the Volvo, but Gary was interested in the canvas-shrouded form lying on the cement floor half in and half out of the opening. "Mind if I take a look?"

Getting his friend's nod, Gary lifted a corner of the canvas. Billy Rahr seemed younger in death, without the strain of his habit: vulnerable. His thin face was bloated and tinged a reddish blue. "Cyanotic," he observed.

"Carbon monoxide from the exhaust," Ansted told him. "A neighbor from across the street, Cornelius Perette, noticed the fumes coming out from under the door. He called the fire department. Then he banged on the door of the house. Mr. and Mrs. Rahr responded. When they went to the boy's room, he wasn't there. They couldn't find him. The parents were frantic. They threw open the garage door, not caring that the flames might spread. That was when they discovered it wasn't a fire. The boy was in the Volvo slumped against the wheel with the motor running. They couldn't rouse him, but the three of them managed to get him out to the fresh air. Too late."

"Accident?"

"Or suicide. No way to tell." Ansted sighed. "A lot of teenage suicide lately, particularly in the suburbs. A kid of fourteen shouldn't have had access to the car."

"Like I said, I talked to Billy on Saturday in connection with the Hanriot case. The kid was morose, defensive, but not suicidal. At least not then. I got the feeling that he had an expensive habit."

Ansted raised his eyebrows. "Let's take a look at his room."

They entered the house by way of the garage, passing through the kitchen, pantry, dining room, and then the central hall. They could see into the living room where Billy Rahr's parents, an elderly couple, sat on the sofa side by side, hands clasped and staring straight ahead, numbed by shock and pain.

Not by a flicker of an eye or a twitch of muscle did either indicate any awareness of the detectives' presence. So, quietly, almost surreptitiously, Reissig and Ansted continued upstairs.

The boy's bedroom was on the second floor and they only had to try a couple of doors before finding it. It was a typical decorator's version of a teenager's room, Gary thought. Maybe the Bruce Springsteen posters were Billy's but the rest was bought and paid for by the foot. It was neat and orderly, the bed made up.

"Didn't want to encourage anybody to come in and clean up after him," Ansted remarked.

Gary nodded and the two of them got to work. Quickly, efficiently, they went through bureau, desk, bedside table, and closet—taking down boxes, rifling through books. Nothing. The bed was last. Together they pulled off the coverlet and stripped away blankets and sheets. They turned over the mattress. A flap had been cut in the covering of the box spring. Ansted lifted it and reached in. He brought out plastic bags of pills, beige in color: crack—in its latest, most marketable version.

"Shame," Ansted murmured. "Damn shame. I don't understand these kids. They have everything."

"Quite a stash," Gary remarked.

"You're right. Think he was dealing?"

"No. I don't think he had anything like this supply on Saturday. I think he was hurting. He tried to sell me information. I wouldn't pay him, but I managed to get some of it out of him. Apparently, not all."

The two went downstairs to the living room where Mr. and Mrs. Rahr still sat exactly as before. Ansted stepped directly in front of them. "This is Detective Reissig," he told them. "Both Detective Reissig and I want to express our sympathy for the death of your boy." They didn't answer. "I regret to have to trouble you at this time, but there are certain questions we must ask."

They kept staring sightlessly ahead.

Victor Ansted bent slightly to make sure he came into their field of vision. "Mr. Rahr? Mrs. Rahr?"

William Rahr came out of the trance first. "Yes, Detective, I hear you."

They both looked old to be parents of a teenager, Gary thought. That the son had come to them late in life must have made him all the more dear. At the same time it made the gap between them wider and more difficult to bridge.

"Ask your questions. We'll do our best to answer." William Rahr seemed very old indeed. His voice quavered. "I don't know if we can."

"Was Billy allowed to use the car?" Sergeant Ansted asked.

"No, certainly not. He's . . . he was only fourteen." The tears welled up in the stricken father's eyes. His wife's hand tightened in his. "We had promised to buy him a car as soon as he was old enough to qualify for a license."

Apparently he hadn't waited, Ansted thought but kept silent. "How did he get hold of the keys?"

Rahr groaned, his haggard face twitched. "I suppose he got them out of his mother's purse and had copies made."

So they had been aware, Gary thought, both of them, but had said nothing to their son. That's the way it was with parents nowadays; they were afraid to exercise discipline; they were wary of antagonizing their own children, of driving them out of the house. Better to pretend not to see, not to know, than to drive them out and lose them completely.

"He didn't take the car last night. He didn't go out," Rahr said. At the look of open disbelief on Ansted's face he went on to explain, almost pleading. "He had dinner with us. He was cheerful, like his old self. We were so happy. After dinner, he said he was going up to his room to do homework. He put out his light at around ten. We went to bed early too. We went to bed and had the best night's sleep we've had in weeks."

Suddenly the woman beside him began to shake. She broke out into gulping, gasping sobs.

"Don't, sweetheart, don't." Rahr put his arm around her.

"He was so sly," Geraldine Rahr moaned. "He lied to us. He put on a show for our benefit so we would turn in early and he could sneak out and . . . make his buy." Geraldine Rahr had learned the jargon the hard way.

Reissig and Ansted exchanged glances. They had learned what they wanted, why put these people through any more pain?

But William Rahr volunteered the rest. "Billy came close to OD'ing once before. A year ago. We sent him away to a . . . camp. He was there three months and came back clean. Everything was wonderful. For a while. I don't know what happened, but we began to see the signs—subtle at first, then more blatant. We were afraid to admit what was happening. We rationalized that we had become supersensitive, we were seeing trouble where there was none. We watched Billy closely, maybe too closely. Oh, God, I don't know. He sensed our suspicions and accused us of not having faith in him. We tried to soothe him. We bought him things . . ." A bitter smile came and went. "He sold them to pay for what he really wanted. We might as well have handed over the cash."

"Do you know where Billy was getting the stuff?"

Rahr shook his head. "Around the school, probably," he groaned.

"Why didn't you go to the police? To Family Court?"

"What would they have done? Put him on probation, and when he broke that sent him to a correctional facility. We didn't want our son in jail." He took a deep, deep breath and let it all out again. He turned to his wife and kissed her withered cheek. "We did our best," he said to her and to himself; the detectives didn't matter. Then he got up, went over to the bar, and poured out a couple of sherries.

"We did our best," Geraldine Rahr repeated, her voice heavy with weariness and regret. "We cut off his allowance. We locked up all the valuables. My jewelry went into the vault. We thought he had no money."

Rahr brought the drinks over.

"Where did he get the money?" Geraldine Rahr cried out in a raw, open appeal to Reissig and Ansted. "Where could he possibly have got so much money?"

Gary waited till he and Vic were outside. "It looks like Billy found a buyer for his information."

"And if that stash upstairs is an indication, he didn't sell cheap," Ansted commented. Then he frowned. "So, if he already had the junk, what was he doing in the car? Where was he going? Why?"

"He was high," Gary replied. "He'd given himself a fix. He was going for a joyride in the forbidden car. He didn't care whether his mother and father upstairs heard the start of the engine. He was going to fly."

"So he turned on the engine and the drug got him."

"The extent of the cyanosis suggests he ingested a large amount of carbon monoxide. He was alive and breathing for a considerable time."

Ansted sighed.

Either way it was murder, Gary Reissig thought. It was murder as surely as if the weapon had been a knife or a gun. But who was the perpetrator? The dealer who had sold Billy Rahr the crack or the person who had paid him for his information? Had he known what Billy would do with the money? Once traced, the dealer could be prosecuted. They couldn't touch the other one.

CHAPTER TWELVE

Would Billy Rahr's friends give up his connection? Gary wondered. In the slums he would have little hope of turning the dealer. In the slums he had seen needle-pocked bodies carried out under the watchful eyes of other addicts. They knew how death had come; still they remained silent. The protective delusion remained: *It can't happen to me.* We all feel it in one form or another, Gary thought. But here, in the midst of privilege—he looked around once more at the imposing houses, the well-maintained grounds—the kids were less hardened. Here, maybe the death of one of their own might frighten them into talking, might even scare a couple of them into picking up the phone and dialing the drug hot line to get help. Gary wanted this particular dealer. Whether or not the dealer led him to the person who had paid Billy Rahr, and whether or not he in turn led to Alyssa Hanriot's killer, Gary wanted him.

The school buses would be coming soon, stopping at the corner to let the boys and girls off. Gary decided to wait. But when they came, carrying their books, laughing, running through the light mist, they hadn't yet learned about Billy. Once inside their houses, they would be told. He couldn't see into the parlors and kitchens, but he could almost feel the change. The mist itself seemed to thicken and close around the enclave. He started then, from house to house, one by one.

It was too soon. The shock was too fresh. The instinct was to deny knowledge, to hide. Later maybe, Gary decided. He'd be back.

When he walked into the squad room the next morning Marc was waiting for him. "The captain wants us. The autopsy report on Billy Rahr is in."

Gary raised his eyebrows. So soon? Must have been a lot of pressure from the parents and the community.

They went in together.

"According to the ME, it was the exhaust fumes that killed him," Boykin told them.

"But the drug caused him to pass out."

"Sure, but it was not the direct cause of death."

"If he hadn't turned on the engine, if he had sat in his room, would he have OD'd?"

"That's a hypothetical question." Boykin's annoyance flared. "They don't answer those."

"Sometimes they give opinions."

Dogali winced at his partner's temerity.

But Boykin was too disturbed to be angry. "Okay. The opinion is—he might have. It's not a scientific certainty. You can't go to court with it. You can't hold anybody responsible on that basis. If he had driven out of the garage, would he have smashed up?"

But Gary stuck to his argument. "If the kid hadn't smoked, he wouldn't have passed out and he'd be alive."

"All right, I'll buy that. Where does it get us?"

"We go after the pusher."

That meant a roundup of the known dealers, particularly the ones who worked the schools. It was done periodically and after a couple of weeks the pushers were back—either the same ones or their replacements. It didn't matter to the bosses as long as the junk was moving again. So the police got discouraged. It was futile. A waste of manpower.

Gary knew all that was going through the captain's mind. "A boy is dead."

And Boykin knew the community would not only support a

roundup, they'd be clamoring for it. Part of the pusher's job was to create new demand. That was why they circled the schools like birds of prey, to get the young ones. Destroy the demand, kill the market, and you put an end to the trade. How did you do that? By arresting the users?

"We'll set it up," Boykin said. That was the end of the discussion.

Dogali started for the door. Reissig stayed where he was.

"What about Easlick? If Billy got the money for the fix from blackmail, who else could he have hit? Billy saw Alyssa Hanriot sitting on the wall at the edge of the Easlick property. He saw Easlick drive up and drive into the garage. Moments later, Alyssa followed him in using the side door. Shortly after that, he saw her come out again."

"That's what he told us," Dogali put in, sensing that the captain's patience was wearing out.

"Why should he lie?" Gary retorted. "Billy also said no lights came on in the house. What reason could he have to lie about that?"

"What's your point?" Boykin asked.

"Maybe the lights didn't come on because Easlick didn't go into the house."

"Maybe." Boykin underscored with finality.

That was dismissal, unequivocal, and even Gary had to accept it. He returned to his desk to sit and stare. Dogali hovered over him.

"You think Easlick went out after Hanriot left? And the kid saw him?"

"It's one possibility."

"That would have blown a hole in Easlick's alibi for sure."

The phone on Gary's desk rang.

"Hundred-and-first Precinct, Detective Reissig." In seconds he was sitting up straight and alert. "Sure I'm interested. What've you got?"

"I'm not giving it for free."

The voice was hoarse, breathy. Disguised? Probably. It didn't matter. "How can I make you an offer if I don't know what you're offering?"

"Not on the phone."

"Where?"

"Under the boardwalk at Beach and Twenty-sixth. At eight."

"Why so late? Why not—"

But the informant had hung up.

The rain that had lingered over two days was blown away at last by a blustery mass of Canadian air. The stars were brilliant in their cold whiteness. The dark ocean reflected a path of the moon's platinum rays. Reissig and Dogali came together and parked on the far side of Seagirt. Dogali stayed in the car and Reissig crossed over.

The underside of the boardwalk was in deep shadow, dank as always even in the hottest summer, with the ever-present odor of brine and fish. Gary didn't find it offensive; in fact, he liked it; it was natural. Seeing nobody right or left, he ducked under and passed through to the other side directly on the beach. The sea was still agitated from the storm, breaking into white froth at the shore. He strolled down to the water till he could feel the spray on his face. He liked that too. Right after they were married, Lurene had sounded him out on the possibility of moving into New York, but Gary couldn't imagine living anywhere but right here. She'd get used to it, he thought. She'd get used to it and love it as much as he did.

Strolling along the water's edge, Gary breathed deeply, relaxed, and for a few moments was at one with the elements, almost forgetting why he had come.

The minutes passed quickly at first, then they dragged: fifteen, twenty, half an hour. What had happened? What had gone wrong? He waited another ten minutes. The tranquility was gone. You could never tell about these meets—whether the offer to sell was genuine or whether you were being set up. So far he had neglected the most elementary precautions.

Before he could do anything about it, a hoarse voice called to him from behind the dunes.

"Reissig?"

In the moonlight, silhouetted against the glistening sea, he made a perfect target. There was no place to hide. To run would be useless. He could only try to tough it out.

"You're late," he shouted. "I'm fed up standing out here in the cold. You'd better not waste any more of my time." He started back to the boardwalk and the concealing shadows.

"Hold it. Not so fast. Put your hands up where I can see them. Okay. Now, slowly, walk to the first pillar on your right and stop."

"This better be good," Gary warned, but he did as he was told.

The informant waited till Gary had reached the indicated place. "I can tell you where to find the murder weapon. I want a hundred dollars."

Gary placed the voice as coming from inside one of a row of abandoned cabanas built just at the edge of the boardwalk. "What murder weapon?"

"The gun. The gun that killed Alyssa Hanriot. Don't play games with me, Reissig. Either you want the information or you don't."

"I have to know where you got it."

"I overheard it. I overheard a drunk in a bar bragging."

Reissig sighed. "What bar?"

"Forget it."

"Okay, okay. I'll give you fifty." He counted out two twenties and a ten and extended them. The cabana door creaked open and the money was snatched out of his hand.

"Easlick. Easlick has the gun."

The door banged shut. Footsteps pounded on the wooden platform upon which the row of cabanas was built. Stepping up from the sand, Gary yanked at the nearest of the cabana doors. Locked. He didn't try any of the others, didn't try to give chase. He had expected the snitch would have made provision for a getaway and he could only hope Dogali as he sat in the car had observed him. Unfortunately, he had not.

"Damn," Reissig said.

"Did he show?" Dogali wanted to know.

"Oh, he showed all right." Gary indicated the boarded-up beach club. "He was in there ahead of us, waiting."

"Could be he's still in there," Dogali suggested. He liked physical action; he found the chase exhilarating. Big as he was and despite the weight he'd put on, he could still cover ground. Reissig, though smaller and more compact, packed power too but not like Marc. When Marconi Dogali tackled you, you stayed down.

Gary shook his head. "He's long gone. He probably passed through the far end into the housing complex." The complex overlooked the beach. Guards patrolled the grounds, but they were too few to adequately cover and protect an area comprising five twenty-story buildings and consisting of 565 apartments with an average of three and a half persons per unit. Once within the perimeter, the suspect could mix with the residents indistinguishably.

"So?" Dogali asked. "What did he have to say?"

"We should search Easlick's house for the gun."

"That's it? Terrific. We would never have thought of that." A glance at his partner told Dogali to drop it.

So, he shouldn't have forked over the fifty, Gary thought; he'd been had. Then he thought, maybe not. Since Easlick was the only suspect for the murder of Alyssa Hanriot, it didn't take a brain to figure that his place should be searched, as Marc had just intimated. It hadn't been done for the same simple reason Easlick hadn't been brought in for questioning —to avoid the slightest suggestion of harassment. In the civilian world people were judged by past record; only criminals were assumed to have no past. But now this information, though unsubstantiated, might, just might, serve as leverage in securing a warrant.

You don't disturb a judge after hours, whether at his home, on the golf course, at a banquet, or at the theater. Not if you want to ever apply to him again. Obviously, you can't reach him when court is in session. So you wait till court adjourns, then hope he'll see you in chambers. Gary was lucky. Judge Wattenburg's clerk was a woman who had taken a class with him at the John Jay College of Criminal Justice. They had never been lovers so they'd stayed friends. Also, she was ambitious and might need a favor from him sometime, so she fitted Gary in between the judge's scheduled appointments. She did more than that; she espoused his cause. By the end of the next day,

Gary Reissig had his warrant and that evening, along with Dogali and a second team, he rang Easlick's doorbell.

Freda Easlick stared at the men on her doorstep. She looked at them in a daze of confusion that slowly changed to indignation as she understood what they wanted to do. "You're like a bunch of Nazis," she told Reissig. "But this isn't Germany. You're not setting foot in my house." The words were hot and arrogant, but they lacked conviction.

"We have a warrant, Mrs. Easlick," Gary replied. "Everything's legal."

"They had pieces of paper too," she retorted.

"Please don't make me arrest you for obstruction, Mrs. Easlick."

Biting back a sudden surge of tears, she stepped aside.

Reissig expected continued diatribes, but she fell silent. He knew why and he felt sorry for her. Freda Easlick was a self-centered, arrogant woman, but she loved her son. In the face of the world she defended him, admitting no doubt, but deep down, Gary sensed, she wavered. And hated herself for it. Yes, he did feel sorry for her. That didn't change what he had to do.

Gary had already allotted the areas of search, so they got right to it. Every man was thoroughly experienced and went about the toss automatically, thoroughly, and neatly. They looked in closets, went through drawers, cabinets, files; examined the backs of pictures, took books down from their shelves, and replaced everything. If they came up empty there would be a second round, this time causing damage—the breaking of walls, ripping up floors. Digging in the garden. None of that was necessary. They found what they were looking for at the back of Roy Easlick's closet in a box of pornographic magazines.

Then they sat and waited for Easlick to get home from work. His mother waited with them. From the time they found the box and its contents, Freda Easlick did not utter a sound.

*   *   *

As soon as he turned into the dead end and spotted the cars in front of his house, Roy Easlick knew something was wrong. He hesitated, then turned into the driveway as usual to put his car in the garage. However, he entered the house by the front door.

"Mom?" He went up to her and kissed her on the cheek. "Are you okay?" Not till she nodded and gave a reassuring squeeze of her hand to his did he turn to Reissig.

"What's going on?"

Gary held out the Colt revolver. "Do you have a license for this?"

"Of course not. I'm on parole. We've been over this. Where did you get that thing?"

"We found it in your closet. In a box. Along with other stuff."

Easlick flushed.

"Oh, Junior," his mother moaned.

"I swear the gun isn't mine. I swear I don't know anything about it."

"We'll have to take you in, Mr. Easlick."

"Maybe I have no right to call on Him, but I swear to God that I had nothing to do with that woman!" he cried out, still red-faced in front of his mother. "I didn't assault her. I didn't harass her. I didn't kill her. I stayed strictly away from her." His voice was low, tense. He showed none of the superiority he had flaunted at their first meeting.

There was, of course, as yet no proof the revolver, a scratched and battered piece that must have been passed through many hands, was in fact the gun used to shoot Alyssa Hanriot. But Gary would have laid heavy odds on it.

"You'll be charged with unlawful possession of a lethal weapon," Gary told him.

They both knew that was a delaying action.

Franklin Rosenwall had his client out that same night.

The next day the lab went to work on the gun. Bullets were fired from the Colt, lined up with the bullet taken from Alyssa Hanriot's body, and studied under the comparison microscope. The comparison eyepiece fused the images of the fatal bullet and the test bullet into one; the marks caused by the rifling of the barrel matched. Identification: positive. A warrant was issued for the arrest of Roy Easlick. Two nights later he was back in a precinct holding cell. This time the charge was murder.

Getting him out took longer, but as Freda Easlick had indicated, Rosenwall was a smart lawyer. On Monday, the tenth of November, Roy Easlick went home to wait for arraignment before a grand jury.

A general sense of relief pervaded the 101, of a satisfactory conclusion to an ugly and troubling case. Ugly, because it was linked to the earlier child molestation, and troubling, because of the mistake in routing Alyssa Hanriot's original call on the night of the initial attack. But for the 911 dispatcher sending the RMP to the wrong address the officers might have arrived at the Senior Citizen's Center in time to apprehend the perpetrator. It was a mistake that could have happened to anyone, but it had triggered a series of events that ended in murder. Captain Boykin, following procedure, had made certain decisions. He could now put any sense of personal responsibility behind him. Gary could not.

He agonized. There were times when going by the book wasn't enough. Something extra had to be done. Sure, he had gone to Norah Mulcahaney for help in finding a policewoman to stay with Allie, but that was only for one night. Afterward, he should have stayed with her himself, or brought her home with him—regardless of Lurene's reaction.

As anticipated, the case captured the public's attention and was well covered by the media. The Long Island dailies and the city newspaper hied back to the original Easlick trial and the victim's appearance to give evidence against him. Everything was dredged up. The police work was actually commended and the 101 lauded. Some accounts even mentioned Reissig and Dogali by name. Friends came by the squad to slap the two detectives on the back, shake hands, offer to buy a drink. Dogali beamed. Reissig gritted his teeth and tried to show appreciation.

"What's eating you?" Dogali finally asked.

"Nothing."

"Don't give me that. You look like you're accepting condolences. What's the problem?"

Gary groaned. "Damned if I know. I don't usually go with hunches, but this time . . . It just doesn't feel right," he finished lamely. He expected his friend, a prosaic man who took everything at face value, to hoot. Instead, Marc nodded.

"Too pat, huh?"

Gary was not only surprised but encouraged. "That's it. It leaves too many holes. Like: Why didn't Easlick get rid of the gun?"

Dogali shrugged. "A lot of perps hang on to the weapon. Arrogance, I suppose. Figure they're so smart they're above suspicion."

"Or the gun was planted."

Dogali scowled. "Then all that business under the boardwalk. . . ."

"Was a come-on, to make sure we went after Easlick."

"Does that mean Easlick didn't do it?"

"I don't know," Gary admitted. "I don't see Alyssa Hanriot buzzing Easlick into the building at 3:00 A.M. and then admitting him into her apartment."

"Why did she go to see him in the first place?" Dogali asked, getting into the spirit of the exchange. "If she was so scared of him, why did she go to see him? Why did she follow him into the garage—and why did she come right out again?"

Norah's point, Gary thought, surprised that Marc had picked up on it whereas he hadn't. He was silent for a few moments. "How about the letters scrawled on the floor?"

"That's simple," Marc shrugged. "She was trying to tell us who the killer was."

"Then why did she write the initials in reverse?"

"We already covered that."

"Why in lower case?" Gary insisted. "Aren't initials usually written in capitals?" Pulling out the file, Gary found the closeup shot of the writing and placed it on the desk.

"Those aren't initials. Those letters are the beginning of a word."

Dogali scowled at it. "You're right." He was awed. "But

why didn't she write his initials? Or his name?"

"Maybe she couldn't. Maybe she didn't know his name."

It seemed to Gary Reissig, as he responded to the routine complaints, did the paperwork, and waited for Easlick's appearance before a grand jury, that the community was satisfied that Alyssa Hanriot's killer had been apprehended and relieved that the man they had uneasily tolerated in their midst was about to be arraigned. He sensed their real concern was the death of Billy Rahr. The cry for protection of the children rose and swelled. It was bad enough to live with the danger of personal attack on the streets, assault in one's own driveway, break-ins at midday—a housewife had been knifed by an intruder in her own kitchen while she was fixing lunch. But now the children were not safe—not even in the schools under the care of professionals.

Fear and anger in the Five Towns and the Rockaways intensified. As the parent's indignation grew, spilling out of PTA meetings and community action committees, so the importance and priority of the proposed raid grew. From a simple roundup of the dealers working in proximity to the school Billy had attended, it was now planned to cover all the elementary, junior high, and high schools along the border of Queens and Nassau counties. The top brass of both police departments would join in a combined operation pooling resources of precincts and narcotics squads. All very secret, of course. Later, when it was done, what the dragnet pulled in— regardless of how many of the arrested pushers would be convicted and actually serve time—would show the sincerity of the effort. That wasn't cynicism on the part of the police, but a recognition that there are only so many available beds in the jails. All the New York and Nassau police hoped was to show the communities they were being served and maybe throw a spanner into the machinery of the local drug trade. If they got lucky they might do both.

Under interrogation and privately with his lawyer, Roy Easlick continued adamantly to deny he had ever given Billy Rahr money for any reason. He only knew Billy as one of the kids on the block. He'd never said more than good morning to him. The lawyer held a press conference to reiterate his conviction that the grand jury would not return an indictment against his client. Privately, a possible link between Easlick and the teenager made Rosenwall uneasy. If it leaked, the outrage would be beyond control. The lawyer feared for his client's safety; so did the police.

CHAPTER
THIRTEEN

The combined task force consisted of sixty men plus detectives and narcotics agents. At 3:00 P.M. as students filed out of schools in the Five Towns and Far Rockaway areas, dealers waited at their customary posts. Some students boarded the orange school buses, others, carrying armloads of books strolled casually toward their drug connections. As the buses pulled out, the police moved in.

The children, particularly the young ones who had never been brought in before, were frightened. Some were veterans and they stonewalled with the same aplomb as the dealers. The paddy wagons rolled with mixed loads of pushers and their victims. Despite advance preparation, the scene at the precincts verged on hysteria. With the parents' arrival it approached pandemonium. The little ones, the nine- and ten-year-olds, were allowed to go home in the custody of a parent. The older ones, the veterans, would spend at least a night in a juvenile facility. Some of the parents were indignant, some tearfully grateful.

The pushers waited stoically to be sprung.

As the hours wore on into the night, it became evident the

wheels of justice were grinding a bit slower than usual. At least, the mouthpieces weren't turning up with the customary promptness to post bail. Not that the yellow sheets from Albany ever came down fast, but on this night it seemed they weren't coming at all. Cornered by a pusher, one of the detectives explained, with a gleam in his eye: *computer breakdown*. Thirty-five dealers had been rounded up and by the following morning only five had been processed. Those who remained, the little fish, became increasingly nervous. Were they being abandoned? Thrown to the heat as sacrificial offerings?

One who did not consider himself a little fish seethed. After a night in a crowded cell, rubbing against his sweat-encrusted companions, his pale silk suit was soiled and rumpled. He shouldn't have been left there overnight. Either somebody had goofed or the sweep had not been routine, Joe Vanilla thought. Convictions would stick and sentences be served, he decided. He wasn't going to wait around to be bailed out. He delved into his dwindling roll of bills to get a message to Detective Gary Reissig.

The guard passed the fifty on to Reissig, who held the crisp bill between thumb and forefinger.

"You didn't have to pay to see me, but thanks. This will go into the PBA fund," he told Vanilla. "Now, what can I do for you, Joe?"

"It's what I can do for you. You're carrying the Hanriot case, right?"

"So?"

"So I can tell you about the murder gun." Pause. "It was a Colt revolver. A .22."

No comment from Gary.

"She came to me looking to buy a gun."

Gary was very still, but inside everything was churning. "You're sure?"

"I saw her picture in the paper—before she came to me and after. She was scared. I told her I don't do guns. I thought she was going to bust out in tears. So I told her where maybe she could find somebody could help her. I was sorry for her."

"Sure."

"I read about her. She needed protection."

Blood rushed to Gary Reissig's face. He was being told by a drug dealer, the lowest of vermin, that Alyssa Hanriot had gone to the street to buy a gun because the police, in his person, couldn't or wouldn't protect her. And it was true. His stomach heaved. "What do you want from me?"

"I want to get out of here. Pronto."

"Give me a name."

They both knew Vanilla had sought the interview prepared to give a name, further fencing was a waste of time for both of them.

"The Weeper."

Gary knew exactly where to find him.

The Weeper was an emaciated youth of twenty-three who could pass for forty and who derived the nickname from red-rimmed, constantly tearing eyes—a condition perhaps caused but certainly aggravated by the cigarette permanently dangling out of the corner of his mouth. Gary easily convinced the Weeper it was in his interest to do him, Reissig, a favor.

"I'll owe you one. You never know when that could come in handy."

"Yeah, okay. I remember her. She was referred." He preened himself on the word, then reverted. "She didn't know nothing. I could have sold her any damn shit, but I was straight with her. I sold her a nice piece. Colt .22 good as new."

As he inhaled more smoke, more tears brimmed over in his reddened eyes, a sharp contrast to the snort of laughter. "I had to show her how to fire the thing. You believe that?"

Yes, he did, Gary thought with a sharp stab of sorrow. "When did she make the buy?"

"Ah hell, man, who can remember dates? It was like a couple of weeks ago."

"What day? A weekday? Friday? Two weeks ago Friday was Halloween."

"Yeah, yeah, you got it. Halloween. That afternoon, say maybe three or four o'clock."

Gary nodded. She bought the gun in the afternoon and at night, the same night, she went to visit Roy Easlick. A few hours after that she was dead—shot with her own gun.

Gary headed back for the squad, but on the way he changed his mind. He swung the wheel of the station wagon toward the Atlantic Beach Bridge, then turned off into a dirt track that led to an area of dunes and inlets much favored by fishermen. Though just off the main road near a couple of boat yards and a row of newly constructed two-family houses, it was well hidden and one could maintain illusions of real solitude; one could imagine being miles from civilization. On this cool November afternoon there was no one there. Gary looked out toward the horizon at the flaming line of the sun already low in the autumn sky while over his shoulder the moon was palely visible. He let the gentle lap of wavelets on the tiny crescent beach calm him and open his mind.

The fact that Alyssa Hanriot had gone out on the street to buy a gun had shaken him. On two counts. One, that she had been so desperately afraid and alone; two, that the weapon had been turned against her. That suggested a struggle. It also suggested that the murder had been unpremeditated. He frowned and nudged a horseshoe crab with his toe, turned it right side up, and watched it crawl back into the sea.

If the murder was unpremeditated and the gun belonged to the victim, wouldn't it have been natural to leave it behind? Wouldn't it have been instinctive?

Obviously, he was a long way from having all the facts, Gary thought, and until he had them he shouldn't try to formulate a theory. According to Norah, he had taken the easy way and simply accepted Easlick, the obvious suspect, as the perpetrator. He hadn't bothered to look for anyone else; just going through the motions. He had resented the inference that he was lazy or without imagination. But Norah was right, he hadn't really committed himself to the tedious routine that might uncover the lives of victim and suspect. He hadn't done the legwork or the research. Turning his back on the tranquility of the small cove, Gary climbed out of the dunes, back up to the road and his car. He drove to the nearest telephone and called Lurene to say he'd be late for dinner.

He spent the next three hours in the Peninsula Public Library.

He consulted *The New York Times Index*. Having fixed the dates of the trial, he then began to work with the microfilm reader to follow up the stories covering it. He discovered one very interesting thing—it came almost as a shock: Alyssa Hanriot's testimony had not been acclaimed by all. There were others beside Stuart Chanin who had rallied to Roy Easlick's support. He had been a highly regarded teacher. Many of the parents, the mothers in particular, refused to believe the charge against him. They had come forward and testified as character witnesses. They had thronged the courtroom, openly antagonistic to Alyssa. It had not been all praise and honor for her. There had been vituperation that extended to hate mail and threatening phone calls. She hadn't mentioned any of that, Gary mused. Probably she'd considered it part of the trial and as such over and done with. Alyssa hadn't been the kind to hold a grudge.

Reissig made a list of witnesses for the defense.

Start with the trial, Norah had said. Gary decided to go farther back—to the original incident. It had taken place at the Daniel Webster School for Gifted Children. Lewis Taubman director and owner.

Taubman lived in Manhattan on Ninetieth, just off Third. It was a block rising out of squalor. A dreary row of brownstones leaned against one another to keep from falling while across the street similar buildings had been lovingly restored, their façades sandblasted, repaired, new windows shining. The building in which Taubman lived was yellow brick and belonged in neither category; it was merely dreary, inside and out. It was a walkup and Taubman's place was on the fifth floor.

Lewis Taubman answered the door promptly but kept the chain on.

Gary displayed his shield. "I'm Detective Reissig and this is my partner, Detective Dogali."

Taubman released the chain and let them in.

He was short and overweight; about thirty, give or take, and already balding. The thin strands of his hair were dark, his skin olive. He could have tanned easily, Gary thought, but Taubman was sallow, obviously not an outdoor person. The room he led them into was long, narrow, freshly painted in flat white and freshly furnished in plastic: plastic table, plastic stacking boxes for bookcases and files, plastic upholstery in an assortment of vivid colors that assaulted the eye. You could walk into any of the Third Avenue Bazaars, Workbenches, or Pottery Barns, buy the whole room on your lunch hour, and have it delivered that night.

The trestle-style desk was littered with papers; the daybed covered by stacks of pamphlets. Neither office nor home, Gary thought. "Sorry to disturb you, Mr. Taubman."

Lewis Taubman shrugged. He was in shirtsleeves, but the shirt was white and fresh, the tie in place. "I can use a break." he waved them to the modular chairs. "What can I do for you, Detectives?"

"As I told you on the phone, Mr. Taubman, we're investigating the murder of Alyssa Hanriot. Roy Easlick has been charged. Since both Miss Hanriot and Mr. Easlick worked for you and the incident involving the Sagarman children occurred in your school, we thought you could help us."

He nodded. "You want something—coffee, a Coke?" At their demurrals, he reached for a cigarette from a box at the desk, lit up, and resumed his seat. "Shoot."

"I'd like to take you back to Easlick's trial," Gary began. "You testified on his behalf."

Taubman worked his lips in and out several times. "Not exactly. I testified that insofar as I knew he was a man of good character and a qualified instructor. He came to me with an unblemished reputation. I also testified that I never had occasion to doubt his moral rectitude."

"In other words, you were defending your own judgment in hiring Easlick."

"Okay," Taubman admitted. "Nothing wrong with that."

"Do you personally believe he was guilty?"

Taubman heaved a heavy sigh. "I can only say to you that

he didn't look the type. But then I don't know what that type looks like."

"How about Alyssa Hanriot?"

"If you ask me, she got carried away. Oh, I know there was a lot of pressure on her to testify. The DA told her it was her duty, civic and moral. She got very righteous. Hysterical almost. Without her the case wouldn't have gone to trial and it's no secret that I didn't want it to go to trial. I told her: Look, Easlick has agreed to resign. He also agreed to get out of the teaching business," Taubman added that almost as an afterthought. "Not that it meant much because I wasn't about to give him a reference and without it he wouldn't have been able to get a job. As for the two little girls, the victims, appearing in court wouldn't be easy for them, I reminded her. 'Consider all the consequences,' I said, and 'let it go.'"

"But she wouldn't."

"She was hung up on the moral obligation. She was determined. Stubborn. It put me out of business. I mean, the parents, even those who had stood up for Easlick, changed their minds once he was convicted. They took their children out of my school. I couldn't stop them. I couldn't reason with them. And I couldn't blame them. Look, tuition didn't run cheap. The school was for gifted children; that was no euphemism for handicapped. It meant exactly that—gifted, children above the ordinary. Our curriculum carried students through elementary, junior high, and high school. They all went on to top colleges and universities. That required a very skilled faculty. I didn't stint. Believe me, Detectives, there's a real need for this kind of school. Smart kids are much neglected, their potential unrealized in ordinary classes. Once the parents lost confidence in my school, there was nothing I could do to restore it. They removed their children and I was forced into bankruptcy. About eight months later, I tried again. I set up under a different name in a different area. I got a loan and leased a small townhouse here in the city. I rounded up good teachers and sent out brochures. I interviewed students and their parents. It looked like I was back in business." He paused, took a couple of long, slow drags on the cigarette. "Unfortunately, word got out about what had happened on the

Island and cancellations came in droves. Forget it. I am not primarily an educator; I'm a businessman. I buy into a good school and try to make it better. I ran a quality operation. But I know when to stop beating my head against the wall. So now I'm into real estate, though I have to tell you, I had no idea it would be so tough to get my license."

"You're taking it all very well," Reissig complimented.

Taubman shrugged. "What choice do I have?"

"You weren't angry at Alyssa Hanriot?" Dogali asked.

"Sure I was. I was mad as hell at her. But it wore off."

"What about Easlick? How do you feel about him?"

"I already told you."

"I mean, how do you feel about his getting out early, before serving his full time?"

Neither in appearance, in manner, nor in speech did Lewis Taubman fit the image of an educator, owner of a scholastically prestigious school. Reissig sensed he had the capability to adapt his style to those with whom he had to deal. At this moment, however, he sank to his natural level. "It stinks. The whole criminal justice system stinks."

Both detectives remained impassive.

"Do you believe Roy Easlick killed Alyssa Hanriot?" Reissig asked.

"Who else? I didn't." He started to chortle, but the impulse changed to dismay and then incredulity. "That's not why you came here, is it? You've got to be kidding."

"We're not kidding, Mr. Taubman."

"No, I didn't mean . . . Oh, God! I wasn't the only one who was against Hanriot's testifying, believe me. There was . . . what's his name—Chanin. His sister was engaged to Easlick. She was all cut up over the business. Naturally."

Naturally, Gary thought. Neither Easlick nor Chanin had mentioned the sister, nor her engagement to the accused teacher. Why not?

Taubman had no idea of the sister's whereabouts. Stuart Chanin was in Washington, D.C., for the day and his secretary could not give out the information. Mr. Chanin would be in his office in the morning. Actually, he would be returning late that afternoon, she admitted. If Detective Reissig cared to try to reach him at his home, that was, of course, up to him.

Gary and Marc drove the short distance from the station house to Lawrence heading along Central Avenue to Rockaway Turnpike at the point where it became Meadow Lane. At Kenridge Place they turned for the Hunt Club. Cutting through club property, they passed tennis courts—grass on one side of the road, clay on the other—then the golf course. Despite stopping at the main club-house for directions, they took several wrong turns before finding Chanin's house at the end of a single-lane road. It was built on the crest of a small hill, the front screened by trees, the back open and overlooking the Hewlett Inlet with the yacht club in the distance. Expensive, exclusive, very secluded.

A matronly woman in her fifties answered the door. For a moment, Reissig thought this might be the sister but it became immediately apparent she was a domestic. She asked them to wait in the hall, but returned quickly to usher them into a comfortable study where Chanin, in slacks, open-necked shirt, and backless leather slippers, sat working. He looked up pleasantly enough, but he didn't come around to receive the detectives. Reissig introduced his partner.

"What can I do for you, Detectives?" Chanin didn't even wave them to chairs.

Nevertheless, Gary sat down and Marc followed his lead. Gary casually crossed his legs and leaned back. Marc pulled out a pack of cigarettes.

"Mind if I smoke?"

Chanin started to protest, then raised both hands in resignation. "Please."

"The first time we spoke, I asked you why you hired Roy Easlick. Do you remember?" Gary asked.

"Certainly."

"Why did you lie?"

"I didn't. I told you his mother asked me to give him a job. Does she deny it?"

"What about your sister? How does she feel about your hiring her fiancé? Or is it ex-fiancé? You never mentioned your sister's connection with Easlick. Why is that, Mr. Chanin?"

"I saw no reason to bring her into it."

"It seems to me she's already in and has been for some time."

"I was trying to shield her," Chanin admitted and appealed at the same time. "She's been through a lot."

Reissig ignored both. "Did you instruct Easlick not to mention her? What else did you leave out? What other omissions were there in your story?"

"I didn't tell you any story, Detective Reissig. I answered your questions. Your direct questions."

"And I didn't ask the right ones?"

Chanin shrugged.

"All right. Let's go back and do it over. Aside from his mother's request and your childhood friendship, did you have any other reason for hiring Roy Easlick?"

"Yes. My sister intends to marry him."

CHAPTER
FOURTEEN

It was an answer neither Reissig nor Dogali expected. Chanin knew that. Yet he had not given it for shock value. He had given it reluctantly.

"She refused to believe the testimony against Roy. The two of them, Constance and Roy, were childhood sweethearts. Roy was very good-looking. From grade school on the girls were crazy about him. But he was shy. The only girl he felt comfortable with was Constance. And she was very proud of the friendship. She took for granted that it would evolve into something deeper. They went together all through high school. We thought, my parents and I, that college would put an end to it. Roy stayed close at Hofstra, but Constance went away to Vassar. That should have set them more than geographically apart. But in the summers when they came home, they were closer than ever. By then everybody expected they would marry. We accepted it. Without enthusiasm, but we accepted it. Only Roy never proposed. My parents became anxious; they urged Constance to break it off, to stop seeing him. She was wasting herself and her good years on a man who didn't want her. She was scaring off other possible suitors; my parents were very old-fashioned. But Constance was staunch. She made excuses for Roy: He wasn't settled; he wasn't in the right job; he wanted to make enough money for them to buy a house, and so on and so forth. Both my parents died within a year of each other and then Constance became my responsibility. I was deeply concerned by the situation, but there was nothing I could do about it." He sighed.

"Then this terrible charge was brought against Roy. Right away Constance announced they were engaged."

"What did Easlick say?"

"He didn't deny it."

"And you? What was your reaction?"

"Confused. Far from happy. I asked Constance when it had been decided and she was vague. I asked her why she hadn't told me earlier and she said it wasn't anybody's business but hers and Roy's. It began to look more and more like her way of showing support." He sighed again. "She wanted to get on the stand and proclaim her faith to the world. I talked her out of it."

"And when Easlick was convicted, how did she take that?"

"She refused to acknowledge it. I mean, she refused to . . . Perhaps it would be better if you spoke to her."

Gary had intended to ask for the interview and had expected resistance. "Yes, that would be good."

"I'll take you to her," Chanin said. "It's not far."

"She doesn't live here?"

"I told you I lived alone. Don't you remember?"

Stuart Chanin led the way in his silver-gray Cadillac; the detectives followed in Dogali's flashy blue Thunderbird. They headed out to Lido Beach following the bleak windswept shore. The sea was angry, covered with whitecaps to the horizon. Storm coming, Gary thought automatically. Shortly after passing the Jones Beach exit, they hit Meadowbrook Parkway and headed toward the center of the island. About thirty minutes later, they veered off onto a two-lane private road and followed it about a quarter of a mile to a fretted iron gate. Chanin spoke to the guard and they were waved on. They passed sloping lawns and a pitch and putt golf course, coming to a sprawling, Tudor-style mansion covered with ivy. Cut into the stone pediment of the façade were the words St. Anne's Retreat, barely legible in the deepening twilight.

The lobby could have been that of a good hotel: spacious, well-appointed, with fresh flowers tastefully arranged in vases on a pair of matching consoles and reflected in the mirror behind each. A long reception desk dominated the left side. On the right, double doors opened on a large dining room. The tables were covered with pink cloths and each had a small vase of fresh flowers. Waitresses in uniforms complementing the linens stood at their stations. A first-class hotel, Gary thought, as anyone would until he saw the guests making their way from the dining room to the lounge for the evening movie or concert. Some shuffled with the aid of a cane, but more used walkers, and most were in wheelchairs. All were old and few smiled.

Chanin went directly to the desk, signed them all in, and then strode to the elevators knowing without having to ask where his sister could be found. She was not interested in movies or concerts. She took no part in the planned activities —no exercise classes, not the cooking classes, or painting. In the daytime, weather permitting, she would sit in the garden. Otherwise, she'd be on the enclosed terrace. Chanin said nothing; he had offered neither comment nor explanation from the moment of arrival. He offered none as he slid open the plate-glass door and they stepped into the humid greenhouse atmosphere.

"Constance?"

She was the only one there, seated under a floor lamp, her head bent low over some sewing. The light gave a sheen to her silver-blonde hair but her face was hidden by its soft silken fall. She was slight in build, lost in an oversized beige and white Norwegian sweater and a long wool skirt that stopped just above her ankles revealing white lacy stockings and neat, doll-like black pumps with bows. Conservative, but not outdated, Gary reflected: a Vassar girl. Except for the bows. The bows were wrong.

Chanin forced a smile. "Hello, Constance."

She looked up. A smile illumined her face, lit up her gray

eyes. "Stuart." She raised her thin rosy lips for his kiss. Momentarily, her hands were still.

She was lovely, Gary thought, a few years younger than her brother but much younger than he'd expected having seen the other residents of this place. Also, she seemed to be healthy; she was sitting in a regular chair and there was no walker or even a cane at hand.

"I brought some friends to see you." Chanin indicated the detectives. "Gary Reissig and Marc Dogali."

She turned her head and included them in her smile. "Please sit down. It's so nice of you to come to see me. This is a nice place and they do take very good care of us all, but I do get lonely." Nevertheless, she did not set the embroidery frame and needle aside as they pulled up chairs, but rather bent her head and gave her full attention once again to the delicate tracery.

Chanin strove to divert it. "How are you, darling?"

"I'm fine, just fine." The smile remained fixed as she continued to push the needle in and out of the fine taut linen.

The smile was genuine, Gary thought. She was happy. In whatever delusion had caused her to be put here, she was happy.

"These are friends of Roy's," Chanin told her.

At that she paused momentarily to look on them, her countenance radiant. "And he sent you to me? How is Roy?"

"You haven't seen him?" Gary asked.

"Seen him? He's in Brazil, in the jungle. If you're his friends, you must know that." She frowned. "You're not going to tell me something's happened? Trouble on the job? He's going to be delayed? Oh, don't say he won't be back by March." She was becoming agitated.

"No, no, nothing like that," Gary assured her. March, not next year but three and a half years from now, he thought. Suddenly the significance was clear; March was the original date for Easlick's release. If he'd served his full sentence.

"He's not sick?" Constance Chanin persisted. "Tell me the truth."

"No, no, he's fine, really, believe me."

"We're being married in March, you know," the fragile

young woman confided, lapsing into that happy daze. "All the arrangements are made—for the ceremony, the reception, the honeymoon." She colored slightly. "Everything. Stuart's fixing up the west wing for us. Isn't that right, Stuart? We're going to move in with him, but only till we can find a place of our own, of course."

"I wish you much happiness, Miss Chanin."

"Me, too," Dogali added.

"Thank you." Her doubts appeared to have been swept away. "Now tell me about Roy."

Gary was at a loss. Certainly he couldn't attempt to tell her the truth; God only knew what kind of reaction that would trigger. He glared at Chanin. He understood why the banker hadn't prepared him and Marc for this—he'd wanted the greatest possible impact and he'd got it. Well, Gary decided, he couldn't put her any deeper into her fantasy than she already was. "He misses you."

"Oh, and I miss him! You have no idea how much! I hated for him to go so far, but it was a wonderful opportunity. I could have gone with him, but it's no place for a woman."

"No, it isn't."

"And, of course, I have a lot to keep me busy." She held up the embroidery hoop. "What do you think?"

Obediently, Gary leaned forward, as did Marc, for she indicated she wanted them both to see. It was a napkin on which she was embroidering an elaborate monogram: CCE. Constance Chanin Easlick.

"Beautiful," they murmured dutifully.

"I designed it myself and I'm embroidering it on all our linens—sheets, pillowcases, tablecloths, towels. There's so much to do. I hope I can finish in time." She bent her head and resumed the work, interminable, never-ending.

Stuart Chanin got up. "She's forgotten us," he murmured.

Quietly, they followed him out.

"Wouldn't it be better to get her to accept the truth?" Dogali asked.

"She won't. The psychiatrists have tried. She resists. She goes into a catatonic trance if the trial or anything connected with the charge is even mentioned."

"But you said she wanted to appear in Easlick's behalf," Gary reminded him.

"That's right, and I wouldn't let her. My parents left the balance of Constance's share of the inheritance in trust for her till she reached age thirty-five. She could get advances, but only with my permission. I told her if she took the stand I would withhold it. So then, when the verdict was handed down, she blamed me, said it was my fault, and wouldn't have anything to do with me. She became hysterical, violent. I couldn't handle her. I had to put her here; there was nothing else I could do. In the first weeks she was under heavy sedation, then gradually it was reduced. When she finally came off it, she was as you see her now."

"Whose idea was it to say Easlick's in Brazil?"

"Nobody's. She came out of shock with the story. The doctors say it's her subconscious providing a safe and acceptable explanation for Roy's absence. With each day details were added and the fantasy grew to become reality. Within the fantasy she was lucid and reasonable, able to care for herself, to function. I wanted to take her home; I would have taken her home, but I was afraid that outside she'd be exposed to the truth. Someone might blurt it out. She'd read about Roy, see him on TV. Here, she's insulated. Here, she's safe."

"So what happens in March?" Gary asked.

"They get married."

"Easlick has agreed?"

"Damn right. That's why I have him in the bank, on a short lead, where I can watch him."

The elevator came and Chanin rode down to the lobby with the detectives in silence. Passing the lounge, they could hear laughter from the amplified sound track of the movie being shown inside. It was not reinforced by laughter from the audience.

They went outside to their cars.

"What happens if, after they're married, someone tells your sister the truth?" Gary asked.

"Maybe being married and living with Roy will make a difference. I don't know." Chanin's shoulders sagged. There had been too much sorrow, worry, pain. The fight went out of him. "I have to do something, take a chance. I can't leave her like this, in here, for the rest of her life, can I?" It wasn't a question; it was a statement of his desperation, of a final gamble.

They got into their separate cars. Chanin drove off immediately; Gary and Marc sat awhile. Marc lit up; Gary wished he hadn't quit.

"It must cost plenty to keep somebody in a place like this," Marc commented.

"I don't think money is a problem for Chanin."

Marc took a long, slow drag.

"You know what?" he said. "It doesn't strike me that little lady upstairs has any screws loose. None at all. I think she knows exactly what she's doing."

"How do you mean?"

"Her brother was dead set against the marriage, as the parents evidently were before. He has control of the purse strings and it looks like he was using that to stop the marriage. Now he's not only agreed but he's making sure Easlick doesn't back out."

"So?"

"So, I don't see much security around here. It looks to me like inmates can pretty much come and go as they please."

"Residents," Gary corrected.

"Whatever. That soft little woman upstairs knows what she wants and she's going to get it. God help anybody that stands in her way."

Like Alyssa Hanriot, maybe, Gary thought.

Marc dropped him off at his house and Gary ran up the front walk, key in hand. The children were standing inside waiting for him.

"Daddy, Daddy!" Anna cried out in the loud, guttural tone of the deaf.

"Daddy, Daddy!" Robin's speech was slightly slurred but much clearer since he'd started attending the special classes.

Gary hugged them to him, then called out over their heads, "Lurene! Lurene? I'm home."

Peggy Inness, a teenager from next door who baby-sat for them, came out of the kitchen. "Mrs. Reissig said she'd be back around eleven."

He remembered. Damn. He'd been supposed to come home early and take her out to dinner and the movies. Letting the children go, he glanced down at his watch. Eight-thirty. He wanted to ask what time Lurene had gone but, instead, "Have Anna and Robin eaten?"

"I gave them their dinner. Could I fix you something?"

He hesitated. He really had nowhere to go and nothing urgent to do. He should stay home, give the children some attention. He had concerned himself almost entirely with Lurene's adjustment, but they also had an adjustment to make. The two seemed to be fine, but he should spend time with them. Not tonight, he decided. He was too disturbed that Lurene hadn't waited. She had gone off in pique, to teach him a lesson. He understood her restlessness; she was, after all, fifteen years younger. But she had to learn that he didn't punch a time clock, situations arose when it wasn't possible to call. Oh, hell, there were times when he just plain forgot. It was the Job.

"No, thanks, Peggy. I've got to go right out again."

He had no car, but it was a nice night for walking and Gary headed for the precinct, instinctively. Money, he thought. Love and money were the two principal motives for murder, always excluding assassination—another matter completely. Under love there were hate, passion, revenge, and that was what Gary had been principally concerned with. But Marc had mentioned the expense of keeping someone in a nursing home, so now he thought about that. Under money, there was greed and necessity. Was there anybody who might profit from Alyssa Hanriot's death? She had no money to leave and no family or close friends to leave it to. Except for Neil Jaros, her fiancé. Jaros had been three thousand miles away at the time of the murder, but he had intimate knowledge of Alyssa. Marc had talked with him at the morgue when he viewed the body. He had learned nothing of interest. At a loss for something to do, Gary decided he should talk to Jaros too.

He needed a car.

Marc was surprised to see him in the squad room. He started to ask what Gary was doing there, then thought better of it. Gary started to explain, instead asked if he could borrow Marc's car.

"Sure." Dogali tossed over the keys as though the blue Thunderbird weren't the dearest thing to his heart.

It was a short ride to Point Lookout. One section of the new luxury oceanfront condos was completed and the second under construction. Though the first block was already occupied, the landscaping done, lamps glowing mellow along the paths, it still had a bleak raw look about it, Gary thought. In that setting of sand and sea it always would. Living out here in the summer was one thing, but in the winter it called for a lot of inner resource. He wasn't surprised Neil Jaros didn't answer his bell, nor even particularly disappointed. He could wait. Out of habit, he turned on the car radio and let the police calls over a background of static serve as a lullaby of familiar sound to which he paid little attention. He slouched on the seat, head back, his mind blank.

In the summer there would have been all kinds of activity in the houses, on the beach, on the street. Now it was all but deserted. By half past eleven, half the houses in the development and almost all the private homes were dark. Lurene had told the baby-sitter she'd be home by eleven. Should he get out, find a phone, and call? While he debated, he saw a white Toyota hatchback turn the corner. It approached at slow speed, heading, as he had sensed it would, into the section where Jaros lived. A man got out, went around and opened the passenger door. A woman emerged. Gary couldn't get more than an impression as she passed under the street light. He could see she was young, blonde, dressed in yards of white gauze and a long white mink stole. Gold bracelets tinkled and glittered. Expensive. The man escorted her to the front door, for which he had a key. It had to be Jaros.

So soon, Gary thought. Jaros had found another woman so soon. He sighed as he watched them go inside. He started to follow, then didn't. He'd wait till they came out. He had a hunch it wouldn't be all that long.

He was right. A little after midnight, Jaros and the girl

came out again. Jaros put her back into the car with the same exaggerated care he had taken her out. It had to be his car, Gary thought, she didn't look the type who would drive anything less than a Jaguar; in fact, he was surprised she would ride in less. She must really be smitten with Jaros.

He let them pull out to the corner before following. They took the Loop Parkway and rode it out to Sunrise Highway, where they made a left turn toward the city. The Loop section was always sparsely traveled, on this particular night there were no other cars at all. Gary had to hang well back to avoid being spotted. But once on Sunrise, though the traffic was light there was enough to make the tail relatively safe. Besides, the way Neil Jaros was fawning over the woman, being tailed would never enter his mind.

The trip went quickly and uneventfully. As Gary had expected Jaros was taking the girl back to Manhattan. Coming off the Triborough they took the East River Drive, stopped for a light at Ninety-sixth, then turned and followed Park Avenue down to the Bellevue Plaza. The Bellevue was Trump Towers and Olympic Tower combined with a degree of true aristocracy each could only wish for. Gary watched as Jaros helped his passenger out and across the sidewalk. Under the bright marquee he got a better look and was surprised to discover the girl was actually plain. Her chin receded slightly, her eyes were pale and small and too close, her forehead narrow. The beige hair and the artistic makeup were only a superficial distraction.

Jaros escorted her to the front entrance and handed her over to the doorman like an expensive package. The doorman handled her the same way.

Then Jaros returned to his car. He opened the door on the driver's side and bent to get in.

"Have a nice evening?" Reissig asked from the back seat.

Startled, Jaros hit his head on the door frame as he drew back.

"Easy, Mr. Jaros. It's only me, Detective Reissig. We've spoken on the phone. Remember?" He held up his shield.

Jaros squinted. "God, you scared the life out of me, Detective Reissig. What are you doing here? What do you want?"

"Get in."

Jaros hesitated, then shrugged and sat behind the wheel.

"What's your girlfriend's name?"

"Marilyn Rand. And she's not my girlfriend."

"You could have fooled me."

"I mean, she's my fiancée."

"Is that so?"

Jaros had expected a different reaction. "Don't you know who the Rands are?"

The Rand Company was right up there with Ford, GM, Chrysler. If the young lady was the only daughter of Peter Alexander Rand, this was big stuff indeed. "You mean as in Rand cars?"

"Right. We're going to be married."

"Well. Congratulations." He was silent for a few moments before adding, "Quick work."

"No, it's not the way it looks. I've been seeing Marilyn for some time."

"At the same time you were dating Alyssa Hanriot?"

"It sounds worse than it is."

"Alyssa Hanriot considered herself engaged to you. She expected to marry you."

"You don't understand."

"Explain it to me."

"I was crazy about Allie. I wanted to marry her. Within weeks after we started going together I knew she was the one for me. I proposed. She held back. She wasn't ready for a permanent relationship, she said. She needed to find herself. She needed time. She had just come back from a stint with the Peace Corps, for God's sake! Okay, I was patient. A little over six months later she got involved with the Easlick business. Frankly, I didn't approve. I wanted her out of it. I mean, it's all well and good to be compassionate but you can't save the world single-handed. Also, I had my job to think about and being connected to the case wasn't doing me any good. But she wouldn't listen. She kept getting in deeper and deeper. Then I met Marilyn."

"Marilyn Rand."

"Right. I don't pretend that who she is doesn't matter or

that her money isn't a consideration. Of course it is. I'm only human. I loved Allie, but she didn't love me. Marilyn does. She'll do anything to marry me. She'll defy her family."

"I would think that's the last thing you'd want her to do." Jaros turned away to stare out at the street. "Does she know about Alyssa?"

"What's to know? I was engaged to another girl and it didn't work out."

"So you went on seeing the two of them."

"I meant to break it off."

"With which one?"

"I meant to tell Allie, but before I could Easlick got out and attacked her. She was cut, in the hospital. How could I put more trouble on her? When she was home, the harassment and the threats started. She was alone. I couldn't abandon her. I decided it was only decent to wait till she felt better. I hoped that by then you would have nailed Easlick and put him back in jail where he belongs."

"Where were you on the night Alyssa was murdered?"

"You can't suspect me! For God's sake, you know where I was. In LA. You talked to me on the telephone."

"Approximately forty-three hours later."

Jaros groaned. "I was there then, in LA. I can give you names, places. Check it out."

"Thanks. I will."

"Fine." Headlights from a passing car glinted on the windshield. Neil Jaros shielded his eyes with one hand, but not before Gary saw that he looked a lot more worried than he sounded.

"What the hell, okay, I wasn't in LA. I didn't go out there till late Sunday, just before you called. For most of the weekend I was right here. With Marilyn."

"Consolidating your position."

"Okay. Yes."

"There was no engagement."

"There is now."

"Ah . . . In other words, you do have an alibi."

"Why do I need an alibi? I didn't kill Allie. I had no reason to kill her."

"You had a classic reason. Have you ever read *An American Tragedy?*" Jaros looked blank. "Allie could have gone to your new girlfriend and told her you were cheating on her. Allie could have wrecked your chance at a fortune."

"Marilyn wouldn't have believed her."

"Maybe not, but her father would. Peter Alexander Rand would not allow his daughter to marry a two-timer. He'd make sure you never saw her again. He'd send her away, maybe marry her off to somebody else, somebody more suitable— from his point of view." There must be somebody other than Jaros available for the Rand heiress, Gary thought. It wasn't logical that such a girl, despite her lack of looks, shouldn't have a string of suitors.

"How did you meet Marilyn Rand?"

"Through Allie." A wry smile twisted Jaros' thin lips. "The Rand interests had just bought control of *Real People: The Human Side* magazine. Marilyn was hired as a reporter and was covering the Easlick case. She wanted an interview with Allie. It was her big chance to show she got the job on her own merit and not on her father's money. But Allie turned her down; she'd wasn't talking to reporters and that was it. Marilyn didn't give up; she'd seen me with Allie and came over. I felt sorry for her and answered her questions. I didn't know who she really was, of course."

I'll bet, Gary thought. "Marilyn was grateful for your help and you started seeing each other."

"Only because Allie wasn't around. She went away after the trial. It had been a strain; she needed the rest. I couldn't blame her, but I was lonely." He shrugged.

"You've been courting Marilyn Rand for nearly two years."

"Out of those two years we've seen each other less than a dozen times," he complained. "People like the Rands are never in New York. They're in Southampton and Saratoga; St. Martin's and Acapulco; Paris, London. When Marilyn is in New York she has a social calendar like you wouldn't believe."

"The longer you had to juggle the two girls, the riskier it got. Finally, it was too late to confess to either one. You were convinced that once Allie found out she would go directly to Marilyn. You couldn't let that happen. So you decided to get rid of her; only you didn't quite know how. Then, unexpectedly, Roy Easlick was released. His return provided the scenario for the murder and an obvious scapegoat."

"No."

Fitting together the pieces, Gary found he had a couple of extras.

His silence encouraged Jaros. "No, you've got it wrong. I would never hurt Allie. What happened in the basement of the Senior Citizens' Center—I couldn't do that—to anybody."

"So it was Easlick who assaulted her and by doing it he played right into your hands."

Jaros covered his face with his hands. "All right," he said. "All right. I didn't tell Allie about Marilyn because I didn't want to let her go. I still cared about her. I didn't want to give her up because . . . Well, you saw Marilyn."

"You intended to continue seeing Allie after your marriage to Marilyn."

Jaros was silent.

"You suggested it. You told her you were going to marry another woman and then you actually suggested the two of you should continue the relationship."

"No, no, of course I didn't. I had too much respect for Allie."

"You suggested it," Gary grimly insisted. "She was shocked and insulted and ordered you out of her apartment. Maybe she was yelling and you tried to shut her up. You tried to subdue her physically, to force yourself on her. She pulled the gun. There was a struggle. The gun went off."

He let Jaros think about it. Neil Jaros now had a choice. He could accept the version Gary had presented and go for accidental murder, get off with a real short sentence, if any—and lose his heiress. Or he could deny everything, cross his fingers and pray that he wouldn't have to call Marilyn Rand for an alibi: in other words, go for broke.

Jaros struggled with it before finally deciding to take the gamble.

"I didn't do it."

Neil Jaros had just bet his life.

When Gary got home at last the porch light was on but the rest of the house was as dark as all the other houses on the street. He put his key into the front lock and stepped inside as quietly as he could. He didn't turn on any lights; he had grown up in this house and knew every floorboard and stair tread. Softly he walked upstairs, turned left to Robin's room and, opening the door quietly, looked in. His son was sleeping soundly. Tiptoeing to the bed, he planted a light kiss on Robin's forehead. The child didn't stir. Next, Gary looked in on Anna. She was lying on her back snoring gently, a frown on her unlined forehead. A bad dream? At his kiss, the frown eased. Then she smiled and turned over on her side.

Gary was smiling too when he closed his daughter's door and continued to the far end of the corridor to Lurene. She would be sleeping too, he thought, and he had no intention of waking her. As soon as he stepped inside, though he didn't turn on a light here either, he sensed an alertness. In the light from the street he could see her lying with her back to him.

"Lurene," he whispered. "Lurene?"

No answer. He was mistaken.

He undressed in the dark, then slid into bed beside her.

Her body was rigid.

Without a word, he moved close and put his lips to her bare shoulder.

She shrugged him away.

"Ah, sweetheart . . ."

"Don't touch me."

"Darling . . ." He reached for her.

"No. Leave me alone. I'm trying to get some sleep."

"I'm sorry about tonight. I came home and you were gone."

"Will you please let me get some sleep? Or do I have to move to another room?"

"No, no, stay. We'll talk in the morning."

It wasn't long before she dropped off. Gary could feel her body relax beside him, but he lay stiff and unmoving till dawn.

CHAPTER FIFTEEN

Gary woke with a heavy feeling, mouth dry as though he'd had too much to drink. Instinctively, he put out a hand for Lurene, and finding her place empty, he opened his eyes with real anxiety. She wasn't in the room. Flinging off the covers, he sat up and swiveled his legs over the side.

"Good morning."

She came out of the bathroom fresh and rosy from the shower, wrapped only in a bath towel.

His heart dropped, then at her smile rose again.

"I'm sorry," he said.

"So am I. I was disappointed because we couldn't have our evening out. I was hurt. I thought you cared more about the job than me."

"One has nothing to do with the other."

"I know. I know. It's just that . . . I was lonely . . ."

Tears brimmed in her big dark eyes. Her full lips quivered. He got up and went to her. He took her in his arms, loosed the bath towel. Excitement, tension, then a vast release. They looked into each other's eyes and laughed.

"I'm going to have to take the car today," he told her as they were dressing.

She scowled. "I was planning . . . that's all right. It doesn't matter. You go ahead."

"So I'll drop you off at the dealer's and we'll sign the papers for the BMW."

"Oh, Gary! Oh, darling! Thank you." She flung herself on him.

He tried to disengage her. "Don't thank me now or we'll never get out of here."

"I don't care. I don't care." Laughing, she tussled him down on the bed.

The offices of *Real People: The Human Side* occupied six floors of a new black glass and steel high rise on Park Avenue. Marilyn Rand, heiress to the Rand empire of which the publication was a minuscule part, occupied a nine-by-twelve windowless office. It contained a standard metal desk and swivel chair, a set of steel filing cabinets, and a clothes rack. She wore her champagne-colored hair tied back with a black shoestring ribbon. Steel-rimmed glasses replaced the contact lenses of the night before, a neat gray business suit the glamorous gauze and mink. There were no gold bangles on her arms, but a plain, black-strapped digital watch. At the knock, she looked up from the word processor, concentration only partially broken.

"Detective Reissig." She half stood to extend her hand across the desk.

"Thank you for seeing me, Miss Rand. As I told you over the phone, I'm investigating the murder of Alyssa Hanriot."

"I thought the case was closed. Roy Easlick has been arrested, hasn't he?"

"There are a few loose ends."

"I don't know how I can help. I only spoke briefly with Miss Hanriot at the Easlick trial. There was no interview."

"But you did write a piece."

"It didn't carry a by-line." She let him see she was both surprised and impressed at his knowing it.

"It was based on information provided by Neil Jaros."

Again, her nod indicated appreciation for the ground-work he'd done. "Neil was kind enough to step forward and offer to help me out. He had background knowledge about Alyssa Hanriot that was useful. He had insights on her feelings and reactions."

That wasn't the way Jaros had presented it. "So you knew they were going together."

"It was very casual."

Yet he could offer insights? Gary thought, but didn't comment. "Can you remember Friday, the thirty-first of October? Do you recall what you were doing that night?"

Flushing slightly, she punched a couple of keys on her word processor and squinted at the screen. "That was Halloween. I had a date with Neil. In the early hours of Saturday morning, Alyssa Hanriot was murdered."

No dummy, Gary thought. Marilyn Rand knew when to acknowledge a fact and she seemed prepared to face the situation. She also seemed to have a blind spot when it came to Jaros. "Do you know that Neil Jaros had told Alyssa he was going to be out of town that night?"

"No." She waited warily.

"But he did keep his date with you? You were together Friday night and into Saturday morning?"

"Yes."

"I won't ask where you were or what you were doing, only what time he left you."

She flushed again. "It was well after four when he brought me home." She picked up a pencil and began to twirl it nervously.

"Neil Jaros lied to Alyssa Hanriot when he told her he would be out of town that weekend. He told us the same thing initially. Miss Hanriot was killed on Saturday morning, as you know. So your statement gives Jaros an alibi. You understand that I have to check it out—with the doorman of your building, with your parents."

"My parents were in Bermuda. The doorman was a substitute; he won't remember."

"You never know," Gary said. "Also, I don't imagine you were alone in your apartment. There must have been servants, a housekeeper probably, who would be listening for you to come in. That would be one of her responsibilities, I imagine."

Marilyn's face reddened and puckered. She looked like a little girl caught in a misdeed and struggling not to cry. "Why are you doing this? Everybody knows Roy Easlick is guilty. Neil had nothing to do with it. He had no motive. He had broken off with Alyssa long ago. Right after the trial."

"Is that what he told you?"

"Yes." She raised her underslung chin. It was a sad attempt at defiance.

"He visited her in the hospital. He took her home when she was released."

"I know that. He told me. She had nobody else. He couldn't just abandon her."

Gary thought of Constance Chanin. They were superficially alike, these two. Both had money and social position. Constance, frail and disoriented in a nursing home working on her trousseau, was strong at the core. She had created a world to suit her needs. She controlled it. Marilyn, in her daytime uniform and her nighttime glamour, seemed self-reliant and secure. Inside, she was completely dependent. She needed to lean on somebody. Jaros had recognized the need and managed to fill it. Although her dependency on him had not been complete till recently. He had let that slip. He had indicated there had not been sex between them till two nights ago.

"Did Neil tell you to say you'd been together on Friday until 4:00 A.M.?"

The sobs broke harsh and convulsive. The tears coursed down her sallow face.

Jaros' second line of defense had been breached, Gary thought as he started back to Queens and the squad. He still needed to place the sports promoter at the scene. Gary's own reconstruction of the argument between Neil and Alyssa was logical. It could have resulted in a struggle and it would explain Alyssa's being killed with her own gun. What still didn't fit was the removal of the weapon, now less than ever. Once the gun went off and Alyssa was dead, Jaros should have got out. It didn't make sense to take the gun, not for him any more than for Easlick.

Gary had just turned onto the Van Wyck Expressway when the news came over the car radio. Franklin Rosenwall had held a news conference at his Rockefeller Plaza office. Shrewdly timing it so that it would make the late editions and the six o'clock TV show, he announced that fresh evidence had been uncovered in the Hanriot case pointing to a new suspect. He declined to say what the evidence was, saying only that it would favor his client. He predicted charges against Roy Easlick would be dropped and that he would never come to trial.

Gary went straight to Captain Boykin. "What has he got?" he demanded. "Is he talking about Jaros? How did he find out?"

"Take it easy," Boykin stayed calm himself. "Rosenwall has his own investigators and they're pretty good. On this one though, my guess is that he had one of them tailing you and he doesn't know any more than we do."

"He's certainly getting mileage out of it," Reissig grumbled.

"He'll get more in court. He'll play up Jaros' motive for all it's worth. He'll reenact the whole Dreiser melodrama. He'll have the jury crying for the dead girl and for Marilyn too. He'll have them pitying Easlick and make him look so innocent they'll even begin to question the verdict of the first jury that convicted him of child-molesting."

"When his turn comes, Jaros can do the same."

"Jaros isn't going to be charged. All we've got against him is a possible motive. Nothing to support it."

"He hasn't any alibi. He wasn't where he said he was. He expects Marilyn Rand to cover for him, but she's already broken down."

Momentarily, Captain Boykin wavered. He was interested, but he set it aside. "Not good enough," he decided. "I'll point something out to you, Reissig: If it had been Jaros who attacked Hanriot and then conducted that campaign of harassment over the phone and in person, how come she didn't know it? Hell, they were engaged. Maybe in the pitch dark of the basement she couldn't make him out, but there was physical contact and it's hard to believe she wouldn't have sensed a familiarity. I'll pass that. I'll accept that he could disguise his voice and fool her over the telephone, but he let her see him. According to Hanriot, he just about presented himself to her. I'm surprised you missed that."

"No sir, I didn't miss it." It was what had stopped Gary from leaning hard on Jaros, that and those damned initials on the floor or whatever they were. As for Allie's earlier visit to Easlick, Gary had a hunch about that.

"If you're going to suggest two perpetrators—one who assaulted and then harassed Hanriot and another who killed her, forget it," Boykin concluded. "It's Easlick. He fits. He's been charged and indicted and as far as we're concerned the case is closed. Got it?"

"Got it, Captain."

CHAPTER SIXTEEN

On the advice of his lawyer, Roy Easlick was following a normal routine. On the morning of the thirteenth, he arrived at his office at five minutes to nine as usual. As soon as he walked in, Roy spotted the plain white envelope. The mail had not yet been sorted and distributed, but the letter lay on his desk in the exact center of the blotter. Cheap and ordinary; he recognized it. Only the night before he had been on the phone with Rosenwall, who had assured him his troubles were over. He had come in feeling good. At the sight of that envelope, the bottom dropped out of his newfound security. He felt the throbbing heat of fear. Roy Easlick didn't want to touch the thing, yet he was also irresistibly drawn to pick it up and open it.

He fumbled nervously with the sealed flap, finally tore it open and drew out the familiar folded sheet of thin, scratch pad paper. As he did so, two gelatin capsules fell out. This was something new. He unfolded the sheet. Capital letters printed with a black felt-tip pen jumped out.

"SCUM," the message began. Sometimes it was CREEP or PERVERT. "SCUM: YOU'RE NOT GOING TO GET AWAY WITH IT. WHY DON'T YOU TAKE THESE AND DO EVERYBODY A FAVOR?"

It was several minutes before Easlick felt calm enough to open his office door and speak to his secretary.

"Ina, did you put a letter on my desk this morning?"

"No, sir."

"Has anyone been in my office?"

"Not since I came in."

So the letter had been placed on his desk either very early this morning or very late the night before. Whoever delivered this one and the others seemed to have no trouble gaining access. Roy had found the first message in his mailbox, properly and formally addressed, but not stamped. *By Hand* had been neatly printed in the lower lefthand corner of the envelope. Afterward, they came with only his name and appeared on the bureau in his room at home, on the dashboard inside his locked car. Once the headwaiter at one of his favorite restaurants delivered it to his table with a bow. The mere sight of it was enough to bring on a burning fever and chills. The letters were all in the same vein:

PERVERT: THEY SAY YOU'RE CURED, BUT YOU'RE NOT. YOU NEVER WILL BE. YOU KNOW IT AND SO DO I. YOU'RE SICK, SICK, SICK. THE NEED IS EATING INTO YOU. THE DESIRE IS CONSUMING YOU.

CREEP: YOU DON'T DESERVE TO LIVE AMONG DECENT PEOPLE. GET OUT. DEBAUCHER OF CHILDREN. GET OUT. GET OUT BEFORE IT'S TOO LATE.

Roy Easlick now understood what Alyssa Hanriot had suffered. He had resented her and her righteousness, but he was not responsible for the harassment she had undergone. Secretly, he had thought she deserved it, but now he was sorry for her. He had told no one about the hate mail he was receiving. Who would care? Most would have thought, as he had in Alyssa's case, that he had it coming. That would have been the police attitude. Particularly Detective Reissig's. He might even have thought Roy was writing the letters to himself.

The two capsules with the tiny, varicolored grains visible through the gelatin lay on the desk where they had fallen. This was the first time the writer had suggested Easlick take his own life. Staring at the pills Easlick felt an overwhelming urge to pick them up and pop them into his mouth. Swallow them and it would all be over. The stress, the anxiety, his mother's pain and his own would be ended. Because the writer was correct on one count—Roy Easlick was sick and not getting any better. The prison psychiatrist had pronounced him cured, but the desire was growing inside him again and it would not be quelled. One of these days, despite his best efforts, he would give in to it. The demon would possess him again.

With his free hand, Roy opened the drawer, dumped the pills and slammed it shut. He was about to crumple the letter and toss it into the wastebasket, but someone might find it and read it. So he folded the paper and put it into his breast pocket. Then he flung open the door.

"I'm going home," he announced. "I'm not feeling well."

"Oh. I'm sorry, Mr. Easlick. Can I get you anything? Do you think you should drive?"

But Roy Easlick was already out and heading for the elevators.

Freda Easlick was just about to start dinner when she heard the car turn into the driveway. She looked out the kitchen window. Roy was home early; it wasn't even five. The tentacles of dread gripped and tightened. She saw the garage door go up and the car pass inside. She waited till she heard him enter the house.

"Roy!" she called and went through the pantry to the front hall.

He had reached the stairs and was clinging to the banister.

She said nothing. It would be useless; she had learned that much. There was nothing to do but stand and watch him stumble up the stairs and then lurch along the hall to his room. She waited till the door slammed shut behind him. Then she let the tears come.

She cried, but that was no use either. Doggedly, she prepared their meal. Then she went up to get him.

He was lying on top of the bed snoring—jacket off, tie

loose, but otherwise fully dressed. The sour stench of liquor came from his open mouth and exuded from every pore. No use trying to rouse him. She went away, managed to eat, to watch television. Before going to bed herself, she looked in on him once again. He hadn't moved. She dreaded that he would get up in the night for another drink. But tonight he was under too deep, she thought, and bad as that was, it also provided a measure of relief. Nevertheless, Freda Easlick stayed awake to listen long after she'd turned out the light. The house was silent. Finally, out of sheer nervous exhaustion, she drifted into uneasy slumber.

At 4:00 A.M., the night still black around her, Freda Easlick wakened possessed by a sudden, unexplained dread. She jumped out of bed, snatched her robe and padded barefoot down the hall to her son's room. The coverlet had been pulled off his bed to a chair nearby. His clothes were scattered. He was in pajamas and under the covers.

Thank God.

She started to pick up after him. No, let him see it when he awoke in the morning. She went back to her bed and slept heavily till nine.

She woke with the sense of having survived a crisis but with the full knowledge that it would not be the last. She was a determined woman, however, and she had no doubt she would prevail in the end. Her son would stop drinking, marry Constance Chanin, and everything that had happened to him because of that terrible Hanriot woman would be forgotten. She dressed quickly and went down to the kitchen half expecting Roy would be there already, red-eyed and repentant, drinking coffee.

But he was not there.

By then it was nine-thirty. After a bout of heavy drinking Roy usually got up early. Could he have left for work? No, she looked and the car was still in the garage. He must be really hung over, she thought, and the fear took hold again. The more she tried to quell it, the more it possessed her. Real terror threatened to overwhelm her. She ran from the kitchen to the main hall and up to her son's room as she had the night before. She didn't tiptoe this morning; she flung the door open and stopped. She caught her breath. He was still in bed, lying on his side. She went around, bent down, and peered into his face.

She screamed. She screamed again.

By the time the neighbor who kept a spare set of keys for Freda Easlick got them and let herself in, the screaming had stopped. She found Mrs. Easlick trying to do CPR on her son. She called the police. The EMS van came in record time, but it was too late. Roy Easlick was dead.

CHAPTER
SEVENTEEN

Freda Easlick would not leave her son's body. She demanded the paramedics continue the CPR. When they convinced her it was useless, she insisted they use electric shock. They explained they didn't carry the equipment, so she personally called the police a second time. She wouldn't give up. She tried to reach her own doctor and railed at the answering service. She would not accept the fact of her son's death.

Even Gary Reissig wasn't able to convince her, much less calm her. His arrival, however, did divert her fire—onto him.

"I'm going to sue you, Detective Reissig. I'm going to bring you up on charges of negligence, incompetence, dereliction of duty. You hounded my son. You drove him to drink. This is all your fault."

Deputy Chief Medical Examiner Benjamin Kuser immediately understood the bereaved woman's condition. For her sake, he went through the motions of determining the victim's state. He felt for the carotid pulse just under the jaw line, then he listened for the heartbeat—totally unnecessary and outmoded. Then he straightened up and told her.

"I'm very sorry. He's gone."

At last, Freda Easlick was defeated. She whimpered rather than cried and allowed herself to be led downstairs and turned over to the care of the neighbor from across the street, who had come to her aid when she started screaming. With Mrs. Easlick safely out of the way, Reissig and his people could get to work.

The room was large, comfortably old-fashioned, and dominated by a fine fourposter on which Roy Easlick lay sprawled in his pajamas. It had not been a particularly warm night, yet the bed clothes were tumbled in a heap at the foot of the bed. Along with his scattered clothes, it was indication of his condition.

"Sure looks like he tied one on," Gary observed.

"When we got here his mother told us he was passed out. She kept insisting we should somehow revive him." The younger of the two paramedics, overweight, intense, and shaken, volunteered.

"You get the impression that wasn't anything new?" Gary asked.

The young medic nodded vehemently. "He had a real alcohol problem."

The answer confirmed Gary's theory.

"I felt bad about not doing more for his mother's sake and . . . just in case . . ." The medic looked sheepishly to his partner.

He wasn't much older in years but he certainly was older in experience, and he flaunted that. "I didn't have to put a hand on him to know he was gone." Suddenly he realized he was in the presence of the ME. "Sorry, Doctor, but you do get an instinct . . ."

"Instinct is fine as long as you don't rely on it exclusively." The medic colored.

Gary intervened. "So how does it look, Doc?"

"Excuse me." The older medic was anxious to make up for his indiscretion. "According to what his mother told us, the victim did indulge in heavy drinking sporadically. On those occasions, he sometimes woke in the middle of the night and couldn't get back to sleep again. When that happened he was in the habit of taking a sedative."

Ben Kuser grimaced. "We all know the combination is unpredictable. The subject can go into coma and remain unconscious for days, or longer. The coma can be irreversible. The combination can also be immediately lethal."

"You think that's what happened? You think it was an accident?" Gary asked.

"Possibly. On the other hand, he was under indictment for murder."

"You think he took his own life?"

"I'm not going to guess. I have to know exactly what's in his system before I can even form an opinion."

Gary nodded. "It wouldn't hurt to take a look through his medicine cabinet."

"Go ahead. In fact, collect all the medicines, prescription and nonprescription, just in case."

The EMS team left and the morgue wagon arrived.

While Ben Kuser continued his examination of the victim, Gary Reissig searched the scene. He started with the suit the victim had been wearing. In the breast pocket of the jacket he found the note that had been on Easlick's desk. He read it and held it out for Kuser.

"Somebody was eager to help Easlick on his way."

Swiftly but methodically, missing no possible hiding place, Gary went through both bedroom and bath. In the medicine cabinet he found only what might be expected. In the bureau shirt drawer, however, tucked under the lining paper, he found a collection of letters similar to the one in the victim's pocket. None were dated, but they were arranged in order of ascending virulence, probably as they had been received. Why had he kept them? Usually the recipient of this kind of venom felt both frightened and contaminated and got rid of it right away, as though by destroying the message he could deny the reality of the hate.

Had Easlick kept the letters with the intention of showing them to the police? Then why hadn't he done it? Had he shown them to his mother? Gary didn't think so. Freda Easlick would never have kept silent; she would have called him, the captain, or the commissioner, if she could get to him. She would certainly put Franklin Rosenwall on it right away.

* * *

"Actually, now that I think of it, he seemed okay when he came in," Ina Weitz told Gary. Though it was Sunday, she had come in at Stuart Chanin's request so that Gary could both talk to her and get a look at Easlick's office. Matronly, in her late forties, with crimped graying hair and pince-nez glasses on a black ribbon, she seemed eager to help.

"I didn't pay particular attention, you know, just looked up to say good morning as he passed through. A few minutes later, he stuck his head out and wanted to know if I'd let anybody into his office. Naturally I hadn't. He looked black, but didn't say any more about it. A few minutes after that he came out and said he was going home. He did look sick, I must say. Shaky. I asked him if he was all right to drive, but . . ." She shrugged. "Mr. Easlick didn't take suggestions easily."

She was too mature and had been around too long to be a young executive's secretary, Gary thought. She had a tendency to patronize her boss and apparently Easlick had not appreciated it.

"This was a little after nine?"

"About twenty after, yes."

His mother had stated that Junior hadn't got home till nearly five in the afternoon. Where had he been in between?

"I'd like to take a look around. Will you come in with me, please?"

The routine precaution turned out to be worthwhile. In the top drawer of Easlick's desk, Reissig found the two capsules referred to in the final note. He was willing to bet that's what they were. Which meant the note had been delivered here to the office. No wonder Easlick had looked black and then sick. Placing the capsules in a glassine evidence envelope, Gary sealed it in Ina Weitz's presence and had her sign her name along with his across the flap.

It was clear that this last of the poison pen letters had hit Easlick hard. Maybe not enough to drive him to suicide, but it had certainly triggered a drinking spree. Canvassing the bars in the neighborhood, Reissig traced Easlick's route from the office to the garage where he kept his car. Considering the amount of liquor consumed, he was amazed Easlick had been able to make it home in one piece.

Either the medical examiner's office wasn't busy or Ben Kuser was intrigued enough to give the Easlick case high priority, but the autopsy was concluded over the weekend and by Monday the report was ready: death by cyanide poisoning. The time estimated was approximately sixty seconds after ingestion between 2:00 and 4:00 A.M. on the Friday—almost two weeks exactly after Alyssa Hanriot's death. The agent for the cyanide had been the capsule of a nonprescription headache remedy that had nationwide distribution. The same brand, moreover, that had been tampered with in a recent series of random poisonings. Easlick had had a bottle of it in his medicine cabinet, as did millions of others.

Coincidence or murder?

Gary Reissig did not believe Easlick's death was an accident. The capsules were easy to tamper with. The method had been used several times without a specific target and was well publicized. It was inevitable that it would be used against a particular person by a perpetrator with a specific motive.

Nevertheless, the alarm had to be sounded and the public warned just in case it was another of those atrocities committed by an unknown psycho indulging his lust for power by killing strangers. The product was pulled from the shelves and consumers who still had a supply were urged to return the unused portion for a refund. Of course, the makers stressed the suicide aspect. It was their out. It could save them millions. Freda Easlick in the midst of her grief battled the allegation with energy and determination. She talked to any and all. She appeared on radio and television talk shows. She bombarded the interviewer with her opinions nonstop so he had little chance of eliciting anything other than what she wanted him and the public to hear. Over and over she insisted:

"I'm his mother and I know. My son did not kill himself. He had no reason."

Taking his own life would have been an admission of guilt, Freda Easlick reiterated. He had not killed Alyssa Hanriot, therefore he had no reason to kill himself.

It was a good point, Gary thought as he watched her on a

local news show. He was at home alone. Robin and Anna were in bed and Lurene was at a meeting of the town council. He missed her, but he was glad she was making an effort to be a part of the community. It augered well.

Meantime he watched and admired Mrs. Easlick's tenacity. She was abrasive but loyal. She might even be right. He didn't buy the suicide theory either, but the reason had nothing to do with Easlick's guilt or innocence in the Hanriot homicide. Rather it had to do with his lawyer's news conference on Thursday afternoon. At that time Rosenwall had announced to the press and the public that there was new evidence in the Hanriot case and a new suspect, and given it as his opinion that his client was off the hook and would not even come to trial. That was big news for Easlick. He should have been up, more optimistic than at any time since the charge and indictment. Hardly a moment for him to go out and kill himself.

In addition, the logistics of the poisoning didn't support suicide. The capsules in the desk drawer at the office were analyzed and found to contain cyanide, but Easlick had left them there and gone off on a drinking spree—ending up in his own bed to sleep it off. It was not likely he woke and decided to kill himself. Even less likely that he kept a hidden supply of cyanide just in case. No, as his mother insisted, Roy Easlick probably had wakened with a pounding head and went to look for relief. The contaminated pills were there, but not by accident. They were there by design, put there for just such an eventuality.

And if Easlick was murdered, that blew the whole Hanriot case wide open.

Gary needed to talk. Shouldn't Lurene be home by now? he wondered and looked at his watch. If she were here, it wouldn't help, he thought. It wasn't that Lurene didn't know anything about the case, but that she really wasn't interested. It would be nice to be able to discuss it with Norah. Should he call? If all he wanted was someone to listen, then why not Marc? Marc was turning out to be considerably shrewder than expected.

Slumping in his chair, Gary reached for one of Lurene's cigarettes. It was four years since he'd stopped smoking, but the urge still came over him. One, he thought, just one. He picked it up, put it in his mouth, opened the match folder, already tasting the smoke in his nose and lungs. The deaths *had* to be linked, he reasoned, match unstruck, but how? Did Easlick kill Alyssa and was he in turn killed to avenge her? Who cared enough about Alyssa Hanriot to do that, Gary asked himself with a pang of pity. Not the two-timing fiancé —and Jaros was all she'd had.

He twirled the unlit cigarette between thumb and forefinger.

The killer had gone to great lengths to terrorize Alyssa Hanriot before killing her. She had been so frightened that she'd gone out into the street and bought a gun. Right after acquiring the weapon she'd gone to see Easlick. She waited hours for him. When he finally arrived, she followed him into the garage. For what purpose? To warn him she had a gun? Or to use it? Was Alyssa so desperate that she went there with the intent to kill? If so, then what changed her mind? Easlick's condition, of course. He'd been out drinking. With the uncanny instinct for self-preservation God gave drunks, he'd managed to get himself home and into his own garage and then passed out. The sight of Easlick helpless in an alcoholic stupor had been too much for Alyssa. She couldn't kill him when he was like that. She simply walked out and went home.

It felt right because it was right, Gary thought. Once more he reviewed Billy Rahr's statement regarding the lights. The garage lights had come on and then gone off, presumably automatically, whereas the house had remained dark—because Roy had not gone into the house. Not then. Later, upon waking, he was not likely to have been sober enough to go to Alyssa's place, gain entry, wrestle her gun away from her and kill her with it. No, Gary thought, on his past record, admitted relunctantly by his mother, the best Roy Easlick could have done was to make it upstairs to his own room and bed for what was left of the night—or morning.

Gary jumped to his feet. It was beginning to come together. He paced up and down, thinking furiously.

Assume Easlick was innocent. Norah had suggested that way back, but he had not examined the next logical premise

—if Easlick was innocent—someone had set him up to look guilty. The phone calls, the threats, the execution of Allie's poor little cat, had all been done by someone else and all with the intent of pointing to the child molester. If you accepted that, then it was clear why the murder weapon had been taken from the scene—to plant it on Easlick later, of course. Certainly getting into the Easlick house would have presented no real problem to someone with that kind of ingenuity—not when it would be the final piece of evidence that should have convicted Easlick.

Gary stopped in front of the telephone. He itched to call Norah, to share with her the excitement of the unraveling of a case that he knew, though they hadn't spoken again, she would be following closely.

Thoughts tumbled in his head one on top of the other. At last, with the discovery of the murder weapon by the police Easlick was arrested and indicted. The real killer had succeeded. Then, suddenly, Easlick was out again. Only on bail, but his lawyer announced with fanfare that his client would never come to trial. The real killer panicked. He was afraid Easlick would slip through the cracks. He decided not to wait for the system to put Easlick away once and for all but to do it himself. The poison pen letters served a double purpose—to drive Easlick to suicide, or failing that, to make it look as though he'd killed himself.

Only the timing was wrong.

Gary picked up the telephone and without looking it up, dialed Norah's number. If Roy Easlick didn't kill Alyssa, he thought as he listened to the ringing, then who did? Jaros had a strong motive. So did Marilyn Rand. And Constance Chanin. Constance might want to punish Allie for her testimony against Easlick, but would she kill the girl and then make it look like Easlick was the one who did it? It was never easy to follow the reasoning of a disturbed mind, but Gary couldn't see Constance destroying the man she loved. And she did love Roy, had loved him most of her life. Of that, Gary had no doubt.

"Hello?"

At Norah's voice Gary froze.

No, he thought, no. There were still too many unanswered

questions. This was not the time to talk to Norah. He didn't want
to ask for her help, not again. What he wanted was to present her
with a finished case, a solution. All the loose ends tied.

"Hello?" Norah said. "Who is this?"

It was his case, Gary thought. He would solve it. He'd
applied to Norah at the start for Allie's sake. He couldn't deny
that their brief discussion had pointed him in the right direction. Now, he was on the verge of breaking the case. He had
got this far on his own dogged hard work—and Marc's too, of
course. The sound of a car turning into the driveway decided
him. He hung up. Putting down the unlit match, Gary ground
out the cigarette and hurried out to the front door to meet his
wife. She was glowing.

"Long session," he remarked feeling suddenly left out.

"We went for something to eat afterward. I didn't think
you'd mind."

"No, no, of course not." But he did mind; he had expected
she would come directly home. It occurred to him that he went
out with the guys for a couple of beers after the shift, but that was
to gear down from the pressure; that was another thing.

"I thought you'd be asleep by now anyway," she said, the
evening's pleasure still enveloping her.

"Without you in my arms?"

The next morning Gary Reissig outlined his thoughts to Dogali.
They got out the Hanriot file and reviewed the stumbling blocks.
One, it had never been proved that Easlick was in fact the perp of
the initial attack on Alyssa or that he was the one who had
conducted the ensuing campaign of threats and harassment.
Alyssa had not been able to identify him or anybody else. She
had not actually recognized the voice on the phone, nor the man
following her. They had all accepted it to be Easlick. At the time
there had been no reason to assume otherwise.

But if you granted that Easlick was not the killer, then the
things that had bothered him, that seemed not to fit, made
very good sense. For instance, the gun.

"She was shot with her own gun. Yet the killer took it
away," he said to Dogali, but really thinking aloud. "He took
it away so he could plant it later on Easlick."

Could the letters too have been a plant? Gary wondered. Easlick's actions prior to his death indicated he was deeply disturbed and suggested he had received them. "But only after," he said aloud.

"After what?" Dogali asked.

"The letters didn't start till after Easlick's indictment and subsequent release. The real killer used them to set the stage." Rifling through the folder, he came on the photostats of the letters and slowly reread each one feeling the hate as a palpable force and feeling too the terrible pain and despair that nourished it. The writer was as sick as the man he accused. The writer was in the grip of a terrible obsession and the message was essentially always the same. Next Gary reviewed the notes Alyssa Hanriot had received. The evil was the same; the hate and intent to destroy.

Gary had always considered himself a stolid man, his feet planted in reality. He worked from tangible evidence; he eschewed hunches. But this case had entangled his emotions from the start and at a time when his own emotional balance was unstable. Now out of that combination, as out of swirling mists, a picture was taking shape. A perception of the truth.

He had to know more, but he couldn't afford the time for lengthy interviews and research. To act precipitously, however, could be risky. He must at least talk to Frances Sagarman privately. Should he take Dogali with him? He hesitated. He decided Marc's presence might be intimidating and he needed to inspire confidence. Also, Marc's forthrightness could sometimes be more liability than asset. His partner was totally supportive and absolutely dependable, but if it required guile—forget about it.

The Sagarman place was not so impressive in the daytime; the grass needed raking, the shrubbery should be trimmed. Gary got no answer at the front door. There was a car in the garage, though, so he decided to try the side. As soon as he turned the corner he heard a radio playing. He rang the bell at the kitchen door and Frances Sagarman peered at him through the screen.

"Yes?"

"I'm Detective Reissig from the One-Oh-One, Mrs. Sagarman. Remember me?"

"Oh yes, of course." She just stood there.

"I'd like to speak with you. May I come in?"

She hesitated. "I'm just getting ready to leave."

"It won't take but a few minutes."

"Well . . . I have to pick up the girls from school," she explained even as she opened the door for him.

"I understand." He sniffed. "Something smells delicious."

"Date and nut bread. My specialty."

She smiled and it made a difference. It eased the lines in her tanned, leathery skin. She not only looked less tense, but a lot younger.

"What do you want, Detective Reissig?"

The smile disappeared; the deep frown between the eyes returned. Soon it would be permanent. He knew she was under strain and had anticipated it would grow yet he hadn't expected her to be this tight.

"I'm investigating the death of Roy Easlick."

"When is it going to be over?" she cried out. "When is it all going to end?"

"When we know what happened."

"He committed suicide. That's what the papers said. I heard it on the radio."

"And you believe it?"

"He had every reason. Didn't he?"

"We don't think so."

"Oh, my God." She sank into the nearest chair.

Reissig pulled out the one opposite. There was no use asking her whereabouts on the night Easlick died—the tainted capsule could have been planted anytime, minutes or days or weeks before the victim ingested it. An alibi wouldn't apply here.

"When was the last time you had any contact with Roy Easlick?"

She sighed heavily. "The day of his sentencing."

"Not since?"

"No."

"Not since he was released?"

"I told you—no."

"He didn't approach you?"

"How many times do I have to say it?"

"But your husband went to the police and asked for protection."

"We were frightened."

He nodded. "The girls especially, I suppose."

She licked her lips. The frown deepened.

"The experience must have been terrible for them." Gary was completely sincere. "According to the court transcript and everything I've been told, the children were deeply disturbed and unwilling to identify their assailant. I suppose they were given psychiatric counseling."

"Yes."

"And the treatment was successful."

"Yes. The doctor said they were fine."

"That's good to hear. Under the circumstances I suppose having Easlick back in the neighborhood threatened a relapse? So you and Mr. Sagarman were afraid of the psychological effect on the girls as much as any overt act by Easlick."

Frances Sagarman looked more than worried; she looked frightened, frightened and uncertain.

She wanted to confide; Gary could sense it and he tried to help her along. "I have children of about the same age as your girls, Mrs. Sagarman. I would be just as concerned." He pitied her, but he couldn't spare her.

"Our local police weren't so sympathetic."

He heard the frustration in that cry. He yearned with her. And went on.

"I suppose you had to tell the girls Easlick was back?"

"We were afraid not to. We talked about it. Agonized over it and decided we had no choice. So that they'd be extra careful, you know."

"How did they take it?"

"In stride. I think . . . I think they'd almost forgotten."

For a moment, in recollection of that bit of normalcy there was a trace of the earlier smile. "Ed and I talked to them and assured them there was nothing to worry about, that we would be with them all the time. We tried not to overemphasize or characterize the threat. Everything goes on as usual. I mean, they're going to school and participating in all their regular activities, except that one of us is always with them."

"And they've been all right? Not frightened or anxious?"

"Naturally, they're not crazy about the supervision. But they understand it's only for a little while."

"Now it's over," Reissig said.

There was a short pause as though she was thinking about it. "Yes. So if that's all, Detective Reissig, I really do have to go. The girls will be getting out and I have to be there. If you don't mind . . ."

"But it's all over," he objected. "You *have* told them it's over, haven't you?"

"In a way," she temporized. "Not that the man who . . . bothered them is dead. That seemed too awful. We just said he'd gone away and wouldn't be back, ever."

"Then what's the urgency?"

"I don't want to be late. Please, you don't understand and I haven't time to explain. I have to go. Would you please move your car? You're blocking the driveway."

"Just one more question: Where were you on Halloween?"

"What?" She looked at Reissig as though he had suddenly lost his mind.

"Did you or your husband take the children trick or treating?"

"Are you crazy? Do you think we would let them out at night?"

"Accompanied. You said yourself you let them do the normal things as long as one of you was with them."

"You haven't understood at all, have you?" she cried out, annoyed, disappointed, and distressed.

Gary tried once more. "On that night you were both home?"

"Yes, yes, yes. Now please, get your car out of my way."

CHAPTER EIGHTEEN

Gary backed out of the driveway and waited while Frances Sagarman—in a car nearly as old and in very much the same condition as his—roared down the street racing the light at the corner. She made it and, tires squealing, turned. He already had the station wagon in gear and followed. She was driving well above the local speed limit, but he had no trouble keeping her in sight. Mrs. Sagarman proceeded on Broadway following the perimeter of the golf course. On Woodmere Boulevard, she turned right and stopped in front of a large, rambling, Victorian-style house. It had a wide porch, cupolas, and gingerbread trim, and squatted at the center of a half acre of lawn dotted with oaks and elms. The whole was enclosed by chain-link fencing. A discreet sign at the edge of the drive proclaimed it to be the Haynes Academy, and in smaller letters specified: For Young Ladies.

A private school, of course. Gary knew it. It accommodated perhaps a hundred pupils, no more. He looked at his watch: ten after three and the last of the standard school buses was pulling out. Frances Sagarman had pulled-up, was out of her car and running up the front steps across the porch to a door with a colored fanlight. She went in. Gary parked and waited.

Would a useful purpose be served by questioning the girls? he wondered. Would he be permitted? Not if the Sagarmans could stop it, he thought, and he wouldn't do it without their agreement. No tricks on that. No subterfuge.

Moments later Frances Sagarman came out, an arm around each one of her girls. The worried frown was still in place as she guided them to the car, two little towheads in green plaid skirts and solid green blazers with some sort of insignia on the pocket—the school uniform. To Gary they seemed pale and small for their ages, but that could be their coloring—and some children developed late. Nancy, the elder, chattered at her mother full speed; the little one tagged slightly behind trying vainly to get a word in. Frances Sagarman bundled them both into the front and went around to her place behind the wheel.

Gary waited till they were out of sight, then he got out of his car and walked up the path to the front door. There was an old-fashioned bell pull. He drew it out and released it to hear a pleasant tinkling somewhere inside at the back. After a few moments, the door was opened by a rosy-faced, middle-aged woman with an apron over a plain, dark dress. He identified himself and asked to see the principal.

"Mrs. Hartness isn't in today. Would you like to speak to Miss Lemke? Miss Lemke is Mrs. Hartness' assistant."

Very polite, Gary thought, and said yes, he would like to speak with Miss Lemke. She was even more courteous. She asked if he would like to speak to the Sagarman girls' home room teacher, who was surely still in the school.

"Room 207," she told him and accompanied him over to the stairs to point out the way.

Miss Winifred Duneen sat at her desk at the front of a small, bright school room. She'd been correcting papers when Gary knocked and entered. Petite, her brown hair cropped close in the latest style, she wore an elegant mantailored pants suit of dark brown tweed with a white silk shirt. She looked up over the top of her half glasses and her brown eyes were bright. Would she be as forthcoming as the other two, Gary wondered as he held out his ID. "I'm investigating . . ."

"The death of Roy Easlick and the murder of Alyssa Hanriot." She shrugged in a self-deprecating way. "We don't talk about much else these days. In fact, we were miffed here at the school that nobody came around to interview any of us." Her brown eyes were mischievous and the corner of her small pouty mouth went up into a smile.

"That oversight is now rectified," Gary reported, smiling too.

"Oh, we're not supposed to talk to anybody. It's just that we don't like being ignored."

"Then how do you suggest we handle this?"

"It depends on what you want to know. If Easlick killed Alyssa Hanriot and then himself, it would be all over, wouldn't it? The case would be closed." A twinge of doubt took hold but was dismissed. "But then you wouldn't be here, would you?"

"No," he agreed. He couldn't bring himself to mislead her. "I don't want to hurt the children, not in any possible way. On the contrary, I want to safeguard them."

Winifred Duneen sighed. "I believe you, but I still have to get permission from my principal, Mrs. Hartness."

"How about a deal? I'll ask what I have to ask and you answer what you can. I won't press. That's a promise."

Their eyes met and held, each judging the other. Finally, the diminutive teacher smiled, though tentatively this time. "Okay. Ask away."

But Gary took his time. He wanted to be thorough, but he didn't want to give her cause to refuse to answer and perhaps end the interview.

"I understand the incident involving the Sagarman girls did not take place here, that is, not in this school."

"No, no indeed. That school closed down as a result of it. The girls were enrolled here after the trial was over."

"Nancy is twelve and Beth ten," Gary said. "Isn't it unusual for both girls to be in the same home room?"

"This is an unusual school and those were the arrangements Mr. Sagarman made for the girls. They do separate and go to different classes during the course of the school day."

"Have you been their home room teacher since their enrollment?" She nodded. "Has there been a change in their attitude, their temperament?"

"I'm not a psychiatrist."

"You are a teacher and you do understand children. I'm interested in the girls' attitude when they first came here."

Winifred Duneen considered. "They were, as you might expect, quiet, somewhat withdrawn. Maybe I shouldn't say this, but it seemed to be no more than the shyness of new girls in a strange school. It passed."

"And how have the girls been recently, since Easlick's release? I'm told they did know he was out and I assume the staff here was also aware of it."

"We most certainly were."

"How did it affect the girls?"

"It's hard to say. The parents fuss over them so much. Too much, in my opinion. They're overly protective. For instance —the girls don't use the school bus. Their mother delivers them in the morning and picks them up at the day's end. If she's as much as fifteen minutes late, we have instructions to notify Mr. Sagarman. He rushes right over. On no account are we to permit them to take the bus or to be driven home by anybody else, not even a teacher." She caught herself. "Particularly not a teacher, I suppose."

Sagarman's office was close enough so it wasn't too great a hardship, Gary thought. He didn't blame the man for being super-cautious.

"It only happened a couple of times," Winifred Duneen continued. "Once, Mrs. Sagarman's car broke down. The other time, her watch stopped and she got here just as her husband was about to leave with the girls. She was reduced to tears."

"Are the girls good students?"

Thinking it signaled the end of the formal interrogation, the teacher allowed herself a small sigh. "Average."

"How about sports and extracurricular activities? Are they active? Do they have any special interests?"

She seemed surprised at the question. "They don't participate. They don't take part in anything that isn't rigidly supervised. They're not even allowed in the school yard during the lunch break."

"Pretty hard on them."

"Yes. Yes, it is."

"You mean it's still going on?"

"Oh yes."

"When did these restrictions begin?"

"The moment they were enrolled."

Gary frowned. "And they were in force during the period Roy Easlick, the man who had molested them, was locked up?"

"That's right."

"When he got out, I assume the precautions were intensified."

"There wasn't much more that could be done. Certainly, the parents became more nervous. Jittery. Some of it was rubbing off on the girls. Inevitably."

"Are they still in therapy?"

Winifred Duneen shook her head. "I don't think so. As far as I know, they haven't been seeing the psychiatrist since . . . well over a year."

Dr. Simon Waterford was reticent, as was both his professional duty and his personal inclination.

"The fact of a psychotherapist relationship is not confidential, Doctor," Gary reminded him. "And it's not the emotional health of the girls that I'm primarily interested in, but that of their parents."

"Which I know nothing about."

"Surely the emotional health of the parents is a factor in the emotional state of the children."

"Mr. and Mrs. Sagarman were not my patients."

"So you wouldn't be giving me a professional opinion."

Waterford threw his head back and laughed. "I've never had it put to me like that before."

Simon Waterford specialized in the treatment of disturbed children. He was short and sturdy with a massive chest and strong legs. He looked like a soccer player and in fact played for the Eastern Stars, a top local amateur team. Added to his evident physical prowess, the bushy black hair and handlebar mustache would have made him totally intimidating but for the twinkle in his hazel eyes. His office presented a similarly reassuring dichotomy: it was elegant enough to impress the parents and bright and colorful enough to ease the anxiety of his young patients.

"Have you ever been involved in a murder investigation before?" Gary asked.

"No. And I don't believe I am now."

"That's what I'm here to determine, Doctor. The answers to a few nonmedical questions should be helpful for both of us." Then he added—it had worked with Winifred Duneen—"If I get out of line, just say so and I'll leave quietly."

Waterford was more wary than the teacher. "It's to be your decision?"

"No, Doctor, yours. And I will try not to breach the doctor-patient relationship." Waterford's gaze remained fixed and skeptical. "First, I'll tell you what I already know," Gary offered. "I know that the Sagarman children, Nancy and Beth, did testify at the Easlick trial. They managed very well till the moment came to identify their attacker. Then each one broke down."

Waterford didn't comment.

"Prior to their taking the stand there was a great deal of controversy regarding their giving evidence. The defense tried to stop it, naturally. Arguments raged back and forth. The uncertainty must have had its effect on the girls. In spite of it, they acquitted themselves well until they were asked to point a finger directly at Easlick. I suppose there was a natural fear of retaliation."

Waterford nodded. "Absolutely. I'm convinced the jury saw it that way."

The doctor had committed himself: Gary had broken through the barrier.

"I assume the attitude of the parents also affected them."

"Certainly. The mother was unstable. She blamed herself for having arrived late at the school to pick them up on the day of the incident. She resisted every kind of public attention. She didn't want Easlick prosecuted, even if it only involved the girls telling their story to the police or a judge."

"And the father, Ed Sagarman?" The question was automatic. In his interview with Gary, Sagarman had indicated complete cooperation with the DA's office.

"He didn't know about it till it was all over," Waterford replied. "I think that's another reason Frances Sagarman was so determined to contain the publicity."

"What do you mean, Sagarman didn't know? I don't understand."

"He wasn't there. He was overseas."

Stunned, Gary struggled to fit in this new information. "You mean, he wasn't here when the attack on the girls took place?"

"That's right. He was in London."

"He wasn't here for the trial? For any of the trial?"

Waterford shook his head.

"What was he doing in London?" Gary was completely nonplussed and too disturbed to pretend otherwise.

"Working. He was working for *Time* magazine and was over there on some kind of assignment."

"I'm sorry to belabor this, Dr. Waterford, but I can't believe Ed Sagarman didn't come home as soon as he heard. He doesn't strike me as the kind of man who would put his job ahead of his family," Gary said. "I would have thought no matter how important the assignment he would have dropped everything and come home. Even if it meant getting fired."

"He didn't know. His wife didn't tell him. She was afraid. She was terrified he would hold her responsible for what had happened. It added to her own innate sense of guilt."

"So how did Sagarman find out?"

"By chance. Over the wire. He was a reporter and he was in London covering one of those big spy scandals that seem to break out periodically over there. And he saw his own name on the ticker."

God!

"The release covered only the end of the trial and the verdict. By the time Sagarman got back, Easlick had been sentenced and put away. It was finished."

"What would you say if I told you the Sagarmans are

watching the girls with the same nervous intensity now as when Easlick was at large? In fact, they guarded them almost as strictly during the time he was in jail?"

Waterford sighed. "I'd say they were severely traumatized by the entire sequence of events. It isn't the kind of thing a parent can be expected to get over easily."

Certainly Frances Sagarman still showed signs of shock. She was nervous and insecure, Gary thought. He now understood her anxiety about getting to the school, but it bordered on the neurotic. Her diffidence in the initial interview, the way she had taken a back seat and let her husband do the talking —effacing herself as much as possible—could now be seen as more than mere shyness. Whether or not her husband blamed her for what had happened to the girls, obviously she blamed herself. Could she have transferred some of that guilt to Alyssa Hanriot? She hadn't wanted a trial and but for Allie's determination there wouldn't have been one. Then Easlick's unexpected release revived it all. The responsibility for the safety of her children had become a burden beyond her capability to bear.

"I'd say the Sagarmans are behaving much as any parents would under the circumstances." Waterford got up and held out his hand. "And that's as far as I'm going."

CHAPTER
NINETEEN

Gary didn't agree with Waterford's conclusion and he didn't think the doctor believed it himself. Nevertheless, Waterford had revealed a fact unknown to Gary before and it presented a new angle to the case. It changed the sequence of events. It intensified the emotional impact of what had happened to the girls. At this point, Gary was making an assumption based on Waterford's information. He was willing to bet a month's pay that he was right. But since it would be the linchpin of the case, the single fact on which he would base the solution, he should make absolutely sure. God knew he had little other real evidence to go on.

He made his call from the squad. After a considerable wait, the number answered. Gary asked to be put through to Personnel. He identified himself, made his query, and waited while it was punched into their computer. The answer came quickly:

No, Edwin Sagarman had not been fired from Time. *He had resigned in order to take a job nearer his home and family.*

His deduction confirmed, Gary could proceed. Edwin Sagarman had come home to a tragedy that caused him to reorder his life. Maybe he blamed himself for having been away at a time he was so desperately needed. Maybe he blamed his wife for not notifying him immediately; obviously he no longer trusted the girls to her care. He loved them enough to put the glamorous world of international journalism behind him and take a drone's job on a small local weekly so he could be near them and look after them.

At last it all fitted. Every event had its own logic and led inevitably to the next. He understood the killer and the motivation. For the first time in his life and career as a cop, Gary Reissig could empathize with a perpetrator.

He laid it out for Dogali and as usual his friend and partner took it on faith. "So what do we do now?"

"Since we know the answers, we should at least be able to ask the right questions," Gary replied.

They were out the door and heading for the stairs when Gary recognized the ring of his own phone. Ordinarily, he would have kept on going and let one of the other detectives pick it up. Something told him to get it himself. He sprinted to his desk.

"Hello? Hundred-and-First Precinct. Detective Reissig."

"Thank God. Oh, thank God. Can you come over right away? Please, can you come over right away?" Her voice was low, just above a whisper.

"Mrs. Sagarman? What's happened? Are you all right?"

"No, no, I've been shot. Please come."

"Shot?" He motioned Dogali over. "Have you called 911?"

"No. I don't need 911. I'm all right."

"Who shot you?"

"Nobody. It was an accident. Please come over."

"I will, but you've got to have medical assistance."

"I tell you I don't need it. I'm all right. I don't want anybody but you. Please, Detective Reissig, I want you to come alone. I don't want you to call anybody or bring anybody. Promise me."

"Mrs. Sagarman, if you'll just calm down and give me some idea . . ."

"There's no time. He'll hear me. Just come. Alone. Quietly. No sirens or anything like that."

"Mrs. Sagarman . . . Frances . . . Where are the girls?"

But she had hung up. For a long moment Gary stood with the receiver still in his hand.

"What's going on?" Marc asked.

"I should have seen this coming. I did see it coming, but I thought there was more time."

"What did you see coming?"

"She wants me right away and she wants me to come alone. So you contact the captain at his home or wherever. Get hold of ES and tell them to stand by. You stick by the phone. I'll be in touch as soon as possible."

"Domestic Dispute?" Marc asked.

"Worse," Gary sighed.

It was just after seven, but at this time of year and with the return of Standard Time, it was already night. The quiet, tree-lined streets were normal. The street lanterns glowed reassuringly and the well-lit houses sat snug and safe—the Sagarman place no different from the rest. For the moment, Gary was reassured. The situation couldn't be so bad; Frances Sagarman probably overreacted. She had told him to come quietly and that was always a wise precaution, so he parked a block off and walked the rest of the way. At the front door he paused before knocking.

Domestic Dispute, Marc had deduced. It was the most common of complaints. A patrol officer could get as many as five or six of them a night, but it remained the most frightening of calls. The thirty seconds between knock and entry were the worst in a cop's life. He never knew what waited for him on the other side of the door: a rolling pin or a pot of boiling lye; a husband beating up on his wife and both ready to turn their rage on the cop; a psycho armed and holding hostages. As Gary squared his shoulders and prepared to knock, the door opened. Frances Sagarman had been watching for him.

She looked terrible. Only a few hours had passed since he'd seen her and she'd turned from a tired woman careless of her appearance into a crone. Her face had literally fallen, skin sagging from its frame; her shoulders were stooped; panic glittered in her eyes. It only needed for her hair to have turned white, Gary thought. She was wearing a man's blue shirt over dark pants. The left sleeve was rolled up to reveal a clumsy bandage wrapped above the elbow and stained with blood.

"Thank God you're here." She reached for him and pulled him inside.

"Did your husband do that to you, Mrs. Sagarman?"

She nodded, but was quick to defend him. "He didn't mean to. Honestly. The gun just went off."

"Where is he now?"

"Upstairs." She paused. Desperate as she was, though she had called for Reissig, she still couldn't bring herself to admit the truth.

"Where are the girls?" he asked gently.

Her eyes filled. "With him. Locked up with Ed. Oh, please, can you get them out?"

"Has he still got the gun?"

"I—I can't say."

"If you want my help, you have to be honest with me, Mrs. Sagarman," Gary pleaded. "Frances, I have to know if he's armed. It's not that I'm afraid for myself but for Nancy and Beth." He expected she might come to Sagarman's defense once more, to insist he would never hurt his children. She remained silent.

He listened for indications of what might be happening upstairs. But there was no sound. A pall seemed to have fallen over the entire house. Small noises outside unnoticed in the usual course—a cricket's chirp, the rustle of dry leaves, voices of passersby, a wheel rattling over a manhole cover— underscored the unnatural, expectant silence.

"Frances, I'm going to call for backup. There are people specially trained to handle situations like this." He expected a violent protest, but again she surprised him: She merely dropped her head. Quickly, before she could change her mind, Gary picked up the phone on the hall table and dialed. He spoke softly and urgently to Dogali and was careful to hang up quietly. "Now tell me exactly what happened," he said in the same low tone they had both used since his arrival.

Frances Sagarman sighed. "I was fixing dinner. Ed was home early and the girls were upstairs doing their homework. There's a party at the school the day after Thanksgiving and the girls were very anxious to go. I promised to ask their father for permission." She licked dry, cracked lips. "He said no: arbitrarily, without considering. I tried to reason with him. I reminded him that there was no threat anymore, not with Easlick dead. I said the girls should be allowed some latitude. They should be allowed, in fact encouraged, to lead normal lives, to be like other children. They should have friends, go out and play, have fun. I told him it was important for them to go to this party.

"He turned red with rage. He said the girls could never lead normal lives, not after what happened, and I was a fool if I thought otherwise.

"Of course, he meant because they can't have children of their own," their mother explained. "But lots of women who can't have children lead normal, happy, otherwise productive lives."

The full impact of what Easlick had done hit Gary. It went beyond the actual violation. It changed lives.

"He told me I didn't know what I was talking about," Frances Sagarman continued. "Couldn't I see the girls are terrified of contact with strangers, men or women? He shouted at me. Couldn't I see, or didn't I care?"

"Is that true? Are the girls afraid of strangers?" Gary asked.

"They're shy, but they take their cue from us. I told Ed it was our fault because we're overprotective. We're forcing them into an unnatural solitude. They can't play with their friends unless one of us is along to supervise. They can't go to anybody's house, much less stay over. It should make them nervous and introverted, but in spite of it they're cheerful and good-natured. How much longer can they stay that way?" she appealed.

"Go on, Frances."

"The next thing, Ed was accusing me of having put them up to asking to go to the party. He said I was putting ideas into their heads. He said he was going upstairs and would straighten it out once and for all." A nerve in her right cheek began to throb uncontrollably. "I thought he was going up to tell the girls they couldn't go to the party. That's all I thought he meant.

"After a few minutes, I could hear them crying. Ed came down, went to the kitchen and heated up some milk. He was muttering to himself. It was all about how things couldn't go on as they are. How it wasn't fair to the girls. At one point, he turned to me and said I was right, the girls were not leading normal lives. I was relieved. He added that it would be kind to spare them the years of loneliness and sadness and ostracism; that it was best for them to end it now. Still I didn't understand." Her face puckered into bitter self-accusation. "I guess I didn't want to. As he walked past me, I saw the gun stuck in his belt."

She paused, lingering over the horror.

"I didn't even know he owned a gun. I screamed and threw myself on him. I grabbed him by the belt and tried to take the gun away, but he was too quick. Holding the thermos of milk in one hand, he pulled out the gun with the other and fired."

"Then it wasn't an accident."

Frances Sagarman shook her head. "He said he would kill me if he had to," she blurted.

Gary sighed.

Upstairs it continued quiet. Where was Dogali? And the ES? They should be here by now, he thought. He looked out the front window and saw no signs of their presence.

"I wish I'd forced him to kill me, it might have shocked him back to sanity," Frances Sagarman wailed.

Gary didn't answer; he was assessing the situation. He had reminded Marc that both he and ES should avoid showing themselves. It was their job to blend into the shadows and his to know they were there. And they were not.

"All right, Frances, let's go up. I want you to stay calm and let me do the talking."

She led him to the closed door. Reissig waved her to one side and knocked.

"Mr. Sagarman, this is Detective Reissig. I was over here a few days ago?" He waited. No reply, no sound at all, no indication there was anybody inside. "Mr. Sagarman, could we talk? It's important. Could you step out for a few moments? Just a few moments. There's a new development in the case I'd like to discuss with you."

"She called you, didn't she? My wife went ahead and called the cops on me!"

"Your wife is worried about you and about the children, Mr. Sagarman."

"I'm all right and so are they. Or will be. As soon as they finish their milk they'll fall asleep and it will be over."

A spasm of horror passed through Gary Reissig. Paralyzing. For several seconds he couldn't move or speak. Finally, he looked to Frances Sagarman. "Did he put something in the milk?" he whispered.

Her fears had not included this. "I don't know. Oh, my God, I don't know."

"Sh," Gary put his fingers gently over her lips. When he addressed Sagarman again it was as calmly and evenly as before. "I don't understand. What do you mean—it will all be over?"

"I'm giving them the ultimate gift—peace. They are emotionally crippled. They can't ever lead normal lives. It's my duty as their father to spare them the fear, sorrow, and emptiness that lie ahead."

Were the children hearing all this? Did they understand what it meant? Gary wondered. "I have two children of about the same age as Nancy and Beth," he said. "The boy is retarded and the girl is deaf. At first I grieved, like you. I blamed myself for passing on defective genes. Then I realized I was centering on myself, on my own feelings instead of on them and theirs. I began to see they have resources so-called normal kids don't have. They get things out of life the rest of us miss. They are happy."

"You want to think so," Sagarman retorted. "If you really loved them you'd know it was impossible. If you loved your children you'd understand how I feel about mine."

"I do love them." At least he had Sagarman engaged in a dialogue, Gary thought. And suddenly he knew what he must say to reach the man and touch him. "I love my children more than you love Nancy and Beth."

The silence was so long Gary feared the challenge would not be accepted.

"Would you kill for them?" Sagarman asked.

Reissig broke out into a cold sweat.

"Would you?" Sagarman repeated. "Would you have the courage?"

That repetition, the admission and justification implied in it, convinced Gary the threat against the children had already been implemented. The action had been taken and the drug placed in the milk. What it was, how potent, and how much the children had ingested, he had no idea. He only knew he had to get Nancy and Beth out of there and to a hospital. Sagarman finally seemed disposed to talk. Ordinarily that would be a good thing; time cooled passion and was in favor of the negotiators. But if the girls were drugged and sinking into unconsciousness, time was the one thing he could not afford.

Gary tried to think. He sensed Sagarman wanted to unburden himself. Here was a good opportunity to get a full confession and also free the children. But suppose he botched it? A mistake could taint the confession and worse, get the little girls killed.

"Well, would you have the courage?" Sagarman demanded.

"I don't know."

What would happen if he broke down the door? Did Sagarman have the gun with him? It seemed reasonable to assume he did. The question was, what would he do with it? What would his reaction be? Gary was willing to risk getting shot, but suppose Sagarman turned the gun on the girls?

He sighed and repeated, "I don't know. I don't think so."

"I did."

Gary heaved a silent sigh. "I can understand your wanting to avenge yourself on Easlick, but why Alyssa Hanriot? Why would you want to hurt her? She was on your side."

"That's how much you know."

God, he was ripe. Gary groaned inwardly. The suspect was

aching to spill it and he had no witness—Mrs. Sagarman didn't count—and no wire. "You told me yourself you admired Alyssa Hanriot's courage."

"What did you expect me to say?" Sagarman snapped back. "She wanted everybody to think she was a crusader, that she cared about the children—my children, all children. If she'd really cared she wouldn't have testified. No, she was out to make a name for herself. My wife begged her to be silent. Pleaded with her. Ms. Hanriot wanted her name in the papers; she wanted the interviews, the talk shows. That's the road to fame and fortune these days."

"It didn't turn out like that," Gary reminded him. "She was branded a troublemaker by the owner of the school. It was nearly two years before she was able to reestablish her credentials and get regular work."

"She brought it on herself. If that woman hadn't insisted on testifying, there would have been no trial, no publicity, no fanfare. That's what engraved the experience on my girls' minds. Indelibly. If it weren't for Ms. Hanriot, the incident would have been forgotten, erased by time."

"So you decided to punish her." Gary paused. "Why did you wait so long?"

"I had to wait for Easlick to get out, didn't I?"

Of course, Gary thought. "You didn't intend to kill her, not at the start. Just scare her to death."

"That's right. I wanted her to jump at every sound, to scream at every shadow. Like my girls did, like they have been doing all this time. And my wife too."

Off to the side, Frances Sagarman began to cry softly.

"So that attack in the basement conditioned Alyssa Hanriot for the harassment to come," Gary said. "The next phase began when you called her on the telephone and let her think you were Easlick. Then you rented a car, same make and model as his, and showed yourself to her. You and Easlick have the same build and with a dark wig you could pass, certainly from a distance. She believed it was Easlick hounding her; why shouldn't she? As she got more frightened, you got bolder. Even if anything should go wrong and she found out it wasn't Easlick after all, you were safe. She couldn't identify you because she'd never seen you; you were abroad at the time of the trial and when you came back, she was away."

"Right. I had it all figured. She accepted it, why couldn't you?"

"I did."

"Then why didn't you arrest Easlick and send him back to jail?"

"Would that have been enough for you?" Gary asked.

"If you'd locked Easlick up, Hanriot wouldn't have had to get a gun and go after him herself," Sagarman retorted.

True, Gary thought bitterly, true. Then he snapped to attention. "How did you know that?"

"I was there. I saw her go into the garage with the gun in her hand. I waited for the shot, but nothing happened. Minutes later she came out. I went in to see for myself. Easlick was passed out at the wheel. Dead drunk." Sagarman's voice trembled with anger and frustration.

What Gary felt was not satisfaction at having figured that much out, but regret that he had not perceived Alyssa was being manipulated toward committing murder. "You could have killed him yourself, right then and there."

"Then I couldn't have put the blame on her."

Gary sighed. "So you reversed the plan. You decided to kill her and frame him."

"You ignored every clue," Sagarman accused. "I never dreamed you'd even consider anybody but Easlick had a motive to kill that woman."

Norah considered it, Gary thought. As always, Norah'd had an instinctive feel for the situation and its emotional components.

"What about the boy? The boy across the street?" Gary prodded. Billy had seen Alyssa go into the garage, so it was logical he had also seen Sagarman. "The kid saw you, didn't he? So you bought him off. You paid that boy a lot of money. You must have had some idea what he would do with it. As a parent, didn't you have any feeling about that?"

"Not one bit," Sagarman measured out the words with bitterness. "And you shouldn't either. He was no innocent child, that one. He didn't want the money; he wanted the crack. He wanted the junk. I had to go out and get it for him."

"Who cares?"

Frances Sagarman cried out from behind Reissig. "Who cares about him?" She tugged at Gary's arm. "Please, you're wasting time. I want my girls. Ed!" she called in desperation. "Ed, open the door. Please, darling. If you won't let them out, then let me in. Let me be with them, hold them in my arms. Ed, please, please listen to me. Please, don't do this." Frantic, she pounded on the door with her fists.

"Stop it, Fran, stop it. You're frightening them," Sagarman told her in a tone that was surprisingly reasonable. "Haven't they been frightened enough? It's all right, Beth, honey. Daddy's here with you. Nancy, sweetheart, it's all right."

He spoke to them, but they didn't answer. In fact, there was no sound of crying or any indication they were still conscious.

"Oh, God, can't you do something?" Frances Sagarman appealed to Gary.

He looked at his watch. Only eighteen minutes since he'd come up the stairs and knocked on the door, but it seemed like an hour. Where was everybody? Where was Marc? If only he had some idea of the children's condition. "Mr. Sagarman, the girls should have medical attention. Let me take them to the hospital."

But Sagarman ignored the plea. He resumed his account with the earlier, embittered, self-justifying whine. "That boy, Billy Rahr, not only saw me go into Easlick's garage, he followed me when I left. He saw me climb the fire escape of Hanriot's building and go in through her bedroom window. When he told me that, of course I had no choice but to give him what he wanted."

Concerned as he was, Gary took note that the window had been the means of entry and that Sagarman had been thinking clearly enough to lock it behind him when he left by the front door.

"She was in the kitchen, but she heard me," Sagarman continued. "She called out. I really didn't have any plan. I wasn't carrying any weapon. I had no idea what I would do, how I would kill her. Maybe strangle her."

He was babbling, Gary thought, piling detail on detail almost at random, as though compulsively trying to recreate the moment.

"I hid behind the bedroom door and she came and stood on the threshold. When she put on the light and moved a few feet inside, I could see she had a gun. It was providential. I jumped her. We struggled. We went down on the floor. I was on top of her holding one hand over her mouth so she couldn't scream and squeezing her wrist with the other. Squeezing, squeezing till she dropped the gun."

"Did she know who you were? Did you tell her why she was going to die?"

For an instant the intensity was broken, then Sagarman seized on the question.

"I meant to. Oh, I meant to. Yes. I certainly wanted her to realize what she had done to me and to my family. But she wouldn't be still. She was squirming, thrashing under me . . . Fighting me."

He was so eager to explain. So unnaturally eager, Gary thought, dragging it out . . . dragging it out. Suddenly, Gary gasped. Sagarman was not talking compulsively, but deliberately. He was stretching out the account. Wasting time.

The confession was intended to distract him so he wouldn't take action till it was too late to save the girls, Gary realized in a wave of horror. And he had fallen for it!

Dismay and humiliation coursed through him. The classic hostage situation was reversed here; time was working for the captor. While Sagarman talked, his children fell into a fatal and final slumber.

"I intended to wipe the gun off and leave it, then I thought that would point to suicide and I didn't want that."

Nor did Allie, Gary thought. She didn't know who her killer was, only that it wasn't Easlick. And that's what she was trying to tell him with the enigmatic scrawl: *e-r*—error. She was trying to tell them they were making an error.

"So you took the gun away and later planted it on Easlick." Now Gary too was talking with the purpose of distraction as he tried to work out a way to get into the room and to the girls. "You went to a lot of trouble to tip us off that we'd find the gun in his house."

"Would you have acted on an anonymous call? Even after you found the weapon, you still turned him loose. Damn you, you turned him loose!"

"So you put cyanide in his headache capsules," Gary accused.

"You forced me to take matters into my own hands," Sagarman countered.

"So now it's done. Roy Easlick and Alyssa Hanriot have paid and your girls are safe. It was a terrible experience for them. But they'll forget. Their teacher tells me they're cheerful by nature and—"

"What does she know? She doesn't see them here at home. She doesn't see them crying whenever the doorbell rings. She doesn't see them run upstairs to hide when a stranger comes to the house."

"Your wife says you don't allow anyone in the house. You don't have guests. No friends. Not for them or yourselves. You've cut yourself and them off from outside contact. Maybe all of you need to be with other people again."

"It's too late."

"Give them a chance, Mr. Sagarman. Ask them if they're afraid. Have you ever asked them how they feel? Why don't you ask them now? Nancy?" Gary raised his voice. "Beth?"

"Be quiet," Sagarman ordered, his voice harsh. "They're almost asleep."

"Nancy? Beth?" Gary called again more loudly and the reply was a whimper.

"Mamma? Mamma . . ."

"Now you've wakened Nancy. Go away. Go away."

Gary put his ear to the door. He heard steps, the creaking of bedsprings, then Sagarman again—placating, soothing. "There's nothing to be scared of, sweetheart. Daddy's here. Daddy will look after you and make sure nothing harms you. Daddy will keep you safe. You don't ever have to be frightened again. I promise."

At that the other child began to cry.

"Now, now, be good girls. Finish your milk, both of you, and go to sleep."

Gary's heart jumped. Relief flooded over him: not only were they both alive, but they hadn't drunk all the milk. They couldn't have ingested the full dose of whatever drug he had put into it.

"Mr. Sagarman, please, I know you don't mean to harm your children and that you believe you're doing the right thing for them. But suppose they could be made to forget all the bad things of the past? Suppose it could be erased from their minds, maybe by hypnosis? Wouldn't you want to give them that chance?"

"Well . . ."

"Think about it, Mr. Sagarman."

"I don't know. Would it work?"

Outside in the street a car door closed. Quietly, but Gary heard it and so did the troubled man.

"What was that?"

"Nothing. A neighbor."

"It better be. Because if you've sent for backup, if anybody tries to get in here, into this room, I'll kill them. I'll kill the girls, I swear I will. I've got a gun. Ask Frances. If anybody tries to get in here, I'll shoot the girls."

"Nobody is going to do anything without your permission, sir." Gary raised his voice to cover the sound of the front door opening and the steps on the stairs. Dogali, finally, he thought, and backed toward the landing to meet him.

"What took you so long?" he whispered. "Where is everybody?"

"Who's there?" Sagarman demanded. "Who are you talking to? Whoever it is, I want him out. Out. I want everybody out; that means you, Reissig, and you, Fran, you too. Get out. You're frightening the girls. You're making them cry."

Pale, his mouth dry, cold sweat on his brow, Gary murmured to his partner. "Where's ES? What's holding them up?"

"There's a hijacking situation at Kennedy. Special Operations has every available unit tied up," Dogali explained. "They're going to release some men to us, but ETA is at least another forty minutes."

Gary's stomach dropped. "We can't wait that long."

"I won't have this turned into a three-ring circus; I'm warning you," Ed Sagarman called out. "I told you already— no sirens, no spotlights, no SWAT teams with rifles on rooftops. None of that." His anger was betrayed by a tremor in his voice.

Gary caught it immediately and he saw Dogali had too. "Yes, sir."

"Let the girls sleep. They'll be asleep soon." The quaver was unmistakable.

Gary put his lips to Dogali's ear. "I think he's put a heavy sedative in their milk. I don't know exactly what and I don't know how much of it they've ingested. They're still awake, but for how long?"

"Are you sure he's armed?"

"He shot his wife. Whether or not he took the gun in there with him . . ."

"Who's out there? Who are you talking to?"

"Only my partner, Mr. Sagarman."

"Send him away."

"Okay, whatever you want."

"Send him away and anybody else you've got out there. I'm warning you. I'm not opening this door till the girls are asleep. Safely asleep. If any attempt is made to break in here, I'll shoot them first and then whoever else I can get. Believe it. I'm begging you to let them go quietly in their sleep."

The two detectives looked at each other. "I've got to go in," Gary said.

"Stall."

"That's what he wants. Don't you get it? While we stall, the children are dying."

"Damn."

"Look, I figure like this: He may have a gun; we've got to assume he does. But he's not sitting with it in his lap because he doesn't want the children to see. So he's got it hidden. Handy, but not that handy. The shades are drawn and anyway his attention is focused on the door. There's a ladder in the garage. You keep him talking while I get it and climb up. I don't know how fast he is on the draw, but I'm going to be faster."

"Orders are to wait for ES."

The men of the Emergency Service were considered the heroes of the department. They were the ones called to scale a bridge and save a would-be jumper; they rescued victims trapped in cars and elevators. They moved to the forefront in confrontations with armed men and in the handling of EDPs, Emotionally Disturbed Persons. Like Sagarman. They were specially trained in the rescuing of hostages. Their equipment consisted of gas masks and bulletproof vests. They used plastic shields, six-foot T bars, and pump-action shotguns. Reissig and Dogali had neither the equipment nor the expertise.

Gary sighed. "We can't wait forty minutes."

"Captain Boykin is on his way."

According to the latest directive from the PC's office, in direct response to the tragedy of the Bumpurs case, a ranking supervisory officer should be at the scene. "When is he going to get here?" Gary demanded. "If those children slip into a coma while we wait and then can't be roused . . ."

Dogali groaned. "Suppose we break in and he carries out his threat and shoots them?"

Gary looked to Frances Sagarman. He had already asked her if she thought her husband was armed and she had said yes. Now he asked, "Will he use the gun? Will he use it on the girls?"

"I don't know. God help me, I'm afraid he might."

Gary looked to his partner. Dogali nodded. "He knows you; you keep on talking to him. I'll go around to the window. Give me five minutes."

"Mr. Sagarman?" Gary raised his voice. "You said you waited till Easlick was released before acting against Alyssa Hanriot so you could put the blame on him. When that didn't work, you tried to drive him to take his own life. Finally you had no choice but to kill him yourself. All right, but the truth is we can't prove that. We can't prove you were responsible for his death, nor for Miss Hanriot's, nor that you gave Billy Rahr the dope."

Sagarman was silent.

"Are you listening, Mr. Sagarman?"

Gary knew he was, and intently. Gary knew he had the man's full attention. He went on slowly, choosing his words, spacing them so the full import would reach the agitated man —and also give Marc Dogali plenty of time to get into position outside the window. "The truth is, sir, we can't prove a damn thing. But if your children die, there'll be nobody to blame for that but you. Nobody else. On the other hand, if you bring them out now, if you open the door and turn them over right now, you'll have a chance to make a case for yourself. You'll have a chance."

And he would, Gary thought. He could offer a plea of insanity and make it stick. Why not, it was true. "Open the door, Ed. Please. Open the door."

Glancing at his watch Gary noted the five minutes had passed and decided Marc should be on the ladder outside the window. "Think about it, Ed. It doesn't all have to end here."

"Listen to him, darling. Oh, listen to him, please." His wife added her entreaties.

They waited for his answer. Time seemed suspended. The click of the furnace in the basement was clearly audible. The roar of a passing motorcycle shook the house. Moments passed and silence closed in again. Then in a voice surprisingly plaintive, Sagarman asked, "What do you want me to do?"

"Unlock the door. Come out."

"What will happen to Nancy and Beth?"

"They'll be taken to the hospital for a checkup. As soon as we're sure they're all right, they'll come home again."

"Can my wife go with them?"

The sound of a siren and a screech of tires at the corner cut off Gary's reply. The car stopped, the motor was turned off, doors slammed. Then the sequence was repeated in quick succession—once, twice, three times. Gary winced. There were no further identifiable sounds, but the atmosphere was charged. Gary visualized the men in camouflage hugging their rifles as they leaped out the back of the van and ran to take positions around the house. The ES unit had arrived—early. Sagarman, his senses rubbed raw, knew it instantly.

"They're here!" he accused. "They're here. I can feel them, the sharpshooters. You promised you wouldn't send for them. You lied to me. You lied!" His voice rose stridently. "You tricked me. Well, I warned you what the consequences would be."

What the hell was the matter with them? Gary fumed. They should have left the sirens off and cut the motors two blocks away. "Nobody's going to hurt you, Ed, I swear. Nothing's going to happen to you."

"Save it. It's too late."

No, Gary thought, not yet. Rearing back, he raised his foot and aimed it at the door. Outside the bedroom window on the ladder, Marc Dogali clutched the tire iron in both hands like a baseball bat and swung.

They came through at almost the same moment.

Sagarman stood bewildered at the foot of the twin beds between the two cops. The girls were huddled together on the right bed, their arms around each other, eyes closed. Neither moved. The smashing of the door and the shattering of the glass hadn't reached them. On the bedside table two glasses filmed with white stood empty.

Sagarman pulled the gun from his waistband.

"Drop it," Gary ordered.

The father looked from one detective to the other, then to the drugged children. Slowly, he raised the gun.

"No!" Gary shouted and flung himself forward on top of the girls.

A shot rang out.

The explosion was so close it caused a ringing in his ears. The pain went through his head like a knife and he wasn't able to distinguish the second shot. He thought it was an echo of the first.

Then Sagarman went down.

CHAPTER TWENTY

Two shots, but not from the same gun.

Nancy and Beth remained unconscious and were not aware of what had happened.

Their father had turned the 7.63-millimeter Mauser on himself, put it in his mouth and fired, blowing out the back of his head. They were spared the sight of his brains and blood and slivers of bone spattered on the wall behind him. Not quite simultaneously, Detective Marconi Dogali fired his .38 Police Special and the bullet hit Sagarman in the heart. They were spared the sight of the blood frothing from his chest.

The bullets were easily identifiable. Either one could have proved fatal. The question: Which one had been fired first? Detectives Reissig and Dogali, their commander, Captain Boykin, the entire force, the media, and the public awaited the medical examiner's pronouncement.

Layman's reasoning that Sagarman could not have pulled the trigger if the policeman's bullet had already entered his heart was prevalent. Medical expertise, however, offered the possibility that Sagarman might have been fatally hit by Dogali but did not die instantly and in that millisecond of remaining life managed to squeeze off the shot into his own head. There was even the possibility that with his finger curled around the trigger a spasm after death might have resulted in the firing.

The waiting was agonized.

The decision, based on a combined forensic and legal rationale: Edwin Sagarman fired first. He had taken his own life. Detective Dogali was exonerated. He celebrated. Gary Reissig and the whole department breathed more easily.

Then Internal Affairs stepped in: routine in any shooting by a police officer, but not quite this time. This involved the death of an EDP, an emotionally disturbed person. It also involved two little girls held hostage by their father, the EDP. Moreover, the little girls had, two years before, been victims of a sexual assault. There was no question that the media would seize on the story and wring out of it every bit of shock, horror, pity, and outrage. Norah Mulcahaney, watching from the sidelines, knew it was inevitable that the actions of the detectives, Reissig and Dogali, would be called into question by the IAD.

Procedure when dealing with an EDP was strict. The officer should *a*, request an ambulance, which had been done; *b*, attempt to isolate and contain the deranged person till arrival of a patrol supervisor and an ES, Emergency Service, unit. That was where the trouble began. The commanding officer, in the person of Captain Boykin, was en route and the ES unit had actually arrived at the scene when the detectives, in direct contravention of the order, took matters into their own hands. Detective Reissig had been specifically warned to take no action. He had ignored the order and broken in on the subject. By so doing, Reissig had pushed the already unstable man to the edge and caused him to turn his weapon on himself. Marc Dogali was off the hook, but Gary was on it.

Marc supported his partner, but he'd arrived late on the scene. He had no direct, personal knowledge of the EDP's condition, what Mrs. Sagarman, the deranged man's wife, had told Reissig about his condition, nor what had transpired between Sagarman and Detective Reissig before he arrived.

Norah wanted to help. She had herself experienced investigation by IAD and understood what Gary was going through. She knew and respected his ethics and his professionalism.

From what she'd heard and read, Norah believed he had acted correctly; from her personal knowledge of him, she was sure of it. She considered calling and offering assistance, but decided it would not be proper. It was up to his commanding officer to support Reissig. Captain Harold Boykin was a good man, an efficient commander: He went by the book. The question: Was he willing to acknowledge there were situations the book didn't cover? Situations in which the officer in the field had to trust instinct? How far would Captain Boykin stick his neck out for one of his men?

As Norah had anticipated, the Hanriot murder and Sagarman's death became a prime topic within the department. It was argued in every precinct and squad room. From the civilian clerks to the brass in the Big Building, everybody had an opinion; everybody took sides. The balance shifted—for, then against Gary. Norah noticed that while it was in his favor, when it seemed he must be completely exonerated, justified, even commended, Lurene Benoit Reissig appeared to enjoy the publicity. She posed along with Gary proclaiming her faith and support. She basked in the spotlight.

Then, unexpectedly, Frances Sagarman changed her evidence. At the beginning, she championed Gary. Nancy and Beth had had their stomachs pumped and suffered no permanent damage from the Valium in the milk, nor from the brief period during which they were unconscious. Gratefully, she attested: "Detective Reissig saved the lives of my children!"

But upon close and repeated questioning by the board of inquiry, Frances Sagarman admitted she had not told Detective Reissig that she had actually seen her husband put anything into the children's milk.

"I thought . . . I was afraid . . . he might have done it."

"Had your husband ever done such a thing before?" James Bandler, in charge of the inquiry, pressed. "Had he ever threatened to do such a thing?"

"No, never. But at the hospital that night when their stomachs were pumped, they found . . ."

"That is not the question, Mrs. Sagarman." Inspector Bandler was a thin, dry, stern man, who in six years with Internal Affairs had forgotten that he should be not a prosecutor but a devil's advocate. "What we need to know is precisely what you told Detective Reissig."

Tears spilled down Frances Sagarman's gaunt cheeks. "I explained to him how it was with Ed, how over the years his obsession about the children's safety grew. How I begged him to get medical attention, but he refused. Roy Easlick's release pushed Ed to the edge. He was out of control. In that context . . ."

"We have a psychiatrist's report on all that, Mrs. Sagarman," Bandler cut in. "Did you tell Detective Reissig that you knew, of your own knowledge and observation, your husband had put drugs into the children's milk? Yes or no, ma'am?"

Frances Sagarman was distraught. The turmoil of the last two years of fear and uncertainty culminated in this moment in which she must decide for or against a man who had answered her call for help. "No," she admitted and burst into tears.

It was a severe blow to Detective Reissig's case. The word got out and spread fast. Someone was kind enough to inform Lurene Reissig.

"What will they do to you?"

Gary shrugged. "They could suspend me, but I doubt they will. They could flop me back into uniform."

"Demote you? Oh, no! They won't, will they?"

She became reticent, avoiding reporters and photographers. When the hate calls started, Lurene took the receiver off the hook. If Gary was at home and insisted on answering, she ran into another room.

The men and women who worked with Gary Reissig appeared as character witnesses at the formal hearing.

His partner, Marc Dogali, reiterated that Reissig had made every effort to talk Sagarman out. He testified that Sagarman had pleaded with them through the closed door to let the girls pass away quietly in their sleep.

His commander, Captain Boykin, lauded Detective Reissig, called him one of his best men, a good officer who followed regulations. He believed that Detective Reissig had responded to what he perceived to be the situation. That by breaking down the door he had acted in the best interest of the hostages.

Norah seethed. Not good enough!

Forget protocol, Norah thought, and called Captain Boykin. She informed him of her intention and asked to see all the
available reports including the DD5s filed by Gary Reissig and
Marc Dogali as well as by the sergeant heading the ES unit.
Next, she contacted Inspector Bandler. Since she couldn't
claim to have new evidence, she merely asked to appear as
one more character witness. She was told they had enough.
Norah insisted. Bandler couldn't deny her.

Lieutenant Norah Mulcahaney reported in full uniform and
displaying her commendations. She sat straight in the witness
chair, feet firmly planted, chin high.

"Detective Reissig and I are assigned to different precincts,
but about a year and a half ago we had occasion to work
together on a case involving a serial killer. I found Detective
Reissig to be dedicated, respectful of procedure, totally reli-
able."

She was, in essence, repeating those who had sat in that
chair before her. The panel was bored.

"About a month ago, Detective Reissig called me. He was
working on an assault and attempted rape. The Hanriot case.
It appeared that the perpetrator was continuing to terrorize his
victim and she was in mortal terror of being attacked again.
Unfortunately, manpower being low, it was not possible to
assign her protection. Detective Reissig asked me if I knew of
someone who could stay with her and I was able to send
Officer Cowan for one night. I mention this to show that Detective Reissig has a sense of responsibility to the victim, that
he's not a cop who locks his cases away in a drawer at night
along with his service revolver."

That fell flat. The panel was neither amused nor impressed.

"Shortly after that, Detective Reissig stopped by my office
to report he would be conducting interviews in the precinct
and we discussed the case. It had turned into a homicide and
was linked to an incident of child molestation involving the
Sagarman children. As a father of two, Gary Reissig was
deeply concerned with what effect reopening the affair would
have on them."

The panel knew all this and were openly impatient. She'd

better make her point fast. Norah squared her shoulders.

"When he was called to the Sagarman house, therefore, Gary's main concern was saving those two little girls. He took a calculated risk; he did what I believe I would have done and most of you would have too. It's true Sagarman had been threatening to shoot the girls if anybody attempted to break in, so now I ask you—when the father raised his weapon, which one of us would not have responded by pulling his own gun and shooting the deranged man? Gary didn't. Instead he threw himself on top of the children into what he expected would be the path of Sagarman's bullet. He shielded Nancy and Beth with his body. Which one of us would have done that?"

Her dark blue eyes gleaming with intensity, Lieutenant Mulcahaney swept the panel, man by man.

"I have studied the reports from the various units at the scene. ES had been delayed, and Edwin Sagarman was on the verge of releasing his daughters and giving himself up when they finally arrived—sirens full blast. It's my opinion that the sirens, the lights, and the noise were what panicked the subject and brought the situation to crisis point."

Bandler started to interrupt, but Norah continued.

"Detective Reissig had specifically requested a silent approach. He warned of the subject's precarious emotional balance. The warning was ignored. Why? I think that should be our very grave concern."

Shock tremors went through the entire room. No one, not even Gary Reissig himself, had raised the subject, much less had the temerity to turn it into a charge. James Bandler scowled. Norah's chin remained firm and her blue eyes steady.

"Your comment and suggestions are noted, Lieutenant Mulcahaney," Bandler said. "Thank you."

"Thank you, sir."

Gary was sitting in the hall outside the hearing room when Norah Mulcahaney came out. He rose and went to her.

"Norah. I can't thank you enough for coming forward like this."

She shook her head. "It was my duty."

It wasn't the answer he'd wanted, or even expected.

Sensing that, she added, "I have confidence in you, Gary. I've always had. I didn't say a thing in there that I don't believe with all my heart."

He swallowed. "I wish . . . I'm sorry things went the way they did for us. I shouldn't have tried to dictate the terms of our relationship. I had no right."

"It turned out for the best. Let's forget about it."

"It's just . . . I wondered . . . could we be friends again?"

She met his look. "We never stopped."

At the end of the hall the elevator door opened and Lurene Reissig came out. Catching sight of Gary, she hurried over.

"Marc called. He said there would probably be a decision soon. I thought I should be here with you."

He reached for her hand. "Darling, I want you to meet Lieutenant Mulcahaney. Norah, this is my wife, Lurene."

The two women looked each other over. Each saw something she had not expected.

Norah held out her hand. "You must be very proud of Gary."

"Proud?"

"Breaking into that room was a tough decision. He put his life and his future on the line. Not many have that kind of courage."

Her look melted. Her voice softened into the old, all-but-discarded Southern drawl. "I never thought of it like that."

"Well," Norah took a step back. "Good luck to both of you." She turned and started down the hall.

"Lieutenant?" Lurene Reissig called out and went after her. "Will they fire him, do you think?"

Norah looked hard at her. "He's a good cop and a good man. They know that."

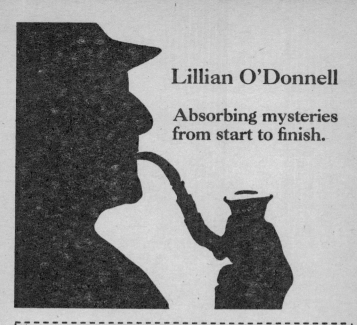

Lillian O'Donnell

Absorbing mysteries from start to finish.